WINGS
OF
FIRE

WINGS OF FIRE

OF

FIRE

THE LOST HEIR

by
TUI T. SUTHERLAND

SCHOLASTIC INC.

No part of this publication may be reproduced, stored in a retrieval system, or transmitted in any form or by any means, electronic, mechanical, photocopying, recording, or otherwise, without written permission of the publisher. For information regarding permission, write to Scholastic Inc., Attention: Permissions Department, 557 Broadway, New York, NY 10012.

This book was originally published in hardcover by Scholastic Press in 2013.

ISBN 978-93-5275-086-3

Text copyright © 2012 by Tui T. Sutherland
Map and Border design © 2012 by Mike Schley
Dragon illustrations © 2012 by Joy Ang

First printing, October 2013
Book design by Phil Falco

This reprint edition : January 2023

Printed in India

For Jonathan and his
magnificent SeaWing costume

Queen Glacier's
Palace

Ice Kingdom

Sky Kingdom

Under the Mountain

Burn's
Stronghold

Kingdom of
Sand

Scorpion Den

Jade Mountain

Ice Kingdom

Kingdom

A NIGHTWING GUIDE TO THE
DRAGONS

Sand

Scorpion Den

Jade Mountain

Queen Scarlet's
Palace

Dia

m of
a

W

OF PYRRHIA

Scavenger
Den

Scavenger

Rainforest Kingdom

SANDWINGS

Description: pale gold or white scales the color of desert sand; poisonous barbed tail; forked black tongues

Abilities: can survive a long time without water, poison enemies with the tips of their tails like scorpions, bury themselves for camouflage in the desert sand, breathe fire

Queen: Since the death of Queen Oasis, the tribe is split between three rivals for the throne: sisters Burn, Blister, and Blaze.

Alliances: Burn fights alongside SkyWings and MudWings; Blister is allied with the SeaWings; and Blaze has the support of most SandWings as well as an alliance with the IceWings.

MUDWINGS

Description: thick, armored brown scales, sometimes with amber and gold underscales; large, flat heads with nostrils on top of the snout

Abilities: can breathe fire (if warm enough), hold their breath for up to an hour, blend into large mud puddles; usually very strong

Queen: Queen Moorhen

Alliances: currently allied with Burn and the SkyWings in the great war

SKYWINGS

Description: red-gold or orange scales; enormous wings

Abilities: powerful fighters and fliers, can breathe fire

Queen: Queen Scarlet

Alliances: currently allied with Burn and the MudWings in the great war

SEAWINGS

Description: blue or green or aquamarine scales; webs between their claws; gills on their necks; glow-in-the-dark stripes on their tails/snouts/underbellies

Abilities: can breathe underwater, see in the dark, create huge waves with one splash of their powerful tails; excellent swimmers

Queen: Queen Coral

Alliances: currently allied with Blister in the great war

ICEWINGS

Description: silvery scales like the moon or pale blue like ice; ridged claws to grip the ice; forked blue tongues; tails narrow to a whip-thin end

Abilities: can withstand subzero temperatures and bright light, exhale a deadly freezing breath

Queen: Queen Glacier

Alliances: currently allied with Blaze and most of the SandWings in the great war

RAINWINGS

Description: scales constantly shift colors, usually bright like birds of paradise; prehensile tails

Abilities: can camouflage their scales to blend into their surroundings, use their prehensile tails for climbing; no known natural weapons

Queen: Queen Dazzling

Alliances: not involved in the great war

── NIGHTWINGS ──

Description: purplish-black scales and scattered silver scales on the underside of their wings, like a night sky full of stars; forked black tongues

Abilities: can breathe fire, disappear into dark shadows, read minds, foretell the future

Queen: a closely guarded secret

Alliances: too mysterious and powerful to be part of the war

THE DRAGONET PROPHECY

When the war has lasted twenty years . . .
the dragonets will come.
When the land is soaked in blood and tears . . .
the dragonets will come.

Find the SeaWing egg of deepest blue.
Wings of night shall come to you.
The largest egg in mountain high
will give to you the wings of sky.
For wings of earth, search through the mud
for an egg the color of dragon blood.
And hidden alone from the rival queens,
the SandWing egg awaits unseen.

Of three queens who blister and blaze and burn,
two shall die and one shall learn
if she bows to a fate that is stronger and higher,
she'll have the power of wings of fire.

Five eggs to hatch on brightest night,
five dragons born to end the fight.
Darkness will rise to bring the light.
The dragonets are coming. . . .

PROLOGUE

Underwater, Webs couldn't hear the screams of dying dragons.

Underwater, the battle was as far away as the three moons. Fire couldn't touch him. Talons couldn't scar him. The blood washed away from his claws.

Underwater, he was safe.

Safe and a coward . . . still better than loyal, brave, and dead.

Webs shuddered awake.

A catfish was staring at him blankly. Its whiskery tendrils drifted in the current. The expression on its face said, "Why is there a dragon sleeping on my river stones?"

Webs ate it, and that made him feel a little better.

The Talons of Peace must know what's happened to the dragonets by now, he thought. *They have spies in the SkyWing palace. They don't need to hear it from me.*

The other Talons did not need him to stand up in front of them and say, "We failed."

But where could he go? He was already hiding from his own tribe, the SeaWings. Did he have to hide from the Talons of Peace for the rest of his life as well?

Webs paddled to the surface of the river and cautiously poked his head out. It was dark, with the

Claws of the Clouds Mountains blocking most of the moonlight like vast shadowy teeth. He'd been swimming downriver for days. The Sky Kingdom was far away now.

The Sky Kingdom, and the five dragonets he'd sworn to protect.

Webs dragged his long, aching body out of the water and took three steps into the forest before he noticed the dark shapes waiting for him.

He spun around, but a new dragon loomed out of the river to block his escape. Black spiral patterns marked his green scales, and his teeth gleamed in the moonlight.

"Webs," said the other SeaWing in a pleasant voice, "I thought you would never wake up."

Webs drew his talons through the riverbank mud. "Nautilus," he said. He hated the tremble of fear in his voice. "I have important news for the Talons."

"You don't say," said Nautilus. "I suppose you got lost on your way to the usual meeting place."

"So we thought we'd come find you," said one of the dark figures, in a voice like icicles dripping. *Cirrus,* Webs thought. It was never a good sign when Cirrus the IceWing appeared.

"The SkyWings found our cave," Webs said. *Just tell the truth. It's not your fault.* "And Queen Scarlet took the dragonets."

"Yes," said Nautilus drily. "We gathered that much from how she's practically been standing on the tallest mountain shouting, 'I have the dragonets of destiny! They're all mine!' "

"Tell us everything," Cirrus hissed. "How did they find you?"

"Well," Webs said slowly, "it started when two of the dragonets tried to run away." *Maybe three.* He wasn't sure where Glory had been on the night he could only find Starflight and Sunny. But he knew she couldn't have gone into the river with Tsunami and Clay.

"Why would they run away?" Nautilus asked sharply. "What did you do to them?"

Webs felt his gills flare. "We kept them alive," he snarled. *And trapped them underground. And chained Tsunami. And planned to kill Glory, because she wasn't part of the prophecy. But what choice did we have?*

"Surely you caught the runaways and brought them back," said a voice in the shadows. Webs recognized Crocodile, a MudWing new to the Talons of Peace. His hopes rose. In his few meetings with her, she'd been sympathetic. Perhaps he had one ally here.

"Er," Webs said, "no. Not exactly. They kind of . . . came back on their own. To get the others." He cleared his throat. "We weren't expecting that." *Kestrel thought they'd be long gone as soon as they hit the sky.*

"It sounds as if they felt like prisoners," Nautilus said in a soft hiss.

"*You* told us to keep them underground," Webs protested. "That was a decision made by all the Talons!"

"But we wanted them agreeable, not rebellious," said Nautilus. "That was the entire point, wasn't it?"

A murmur went around the circle of dragons. There were seven including Nautilus, as far as Webs could tell. He wondered if he could fight his way past seven dragons.

"It wasn't our fault," he muttered. "Maybe there's something wrong with them."

"What does this have to do with the SkyWings?" Cirrus hissed.

"The SkyWings followed Clay and Tsunami back to the cave," Webs explained. "That's how Queen Scarlet found us. We tried to fight back, but she killed Dune and took Kestrel along with the dragonets."

"Will she make them fight in her arena?" asked Crocodile. "Can they win?"

"They're only dragonets," Cirrus growled. "Of course they won't survive the arena."

"Surely she'll spare the SkyWing, at least," Crocodile said.

Webs flinched. He had never been brave enough to confess to the Talons of Peace that they'd lost their

SkyWing dragonet and replaced it with a RainWing. But now that the dragonets were out in the world, everyone would know soon.

"You know what Queen Scarlet did to all the SkyWing dragonets who hatched on the brightest night," Cirrus hissed. "Mercy is not exactly in her nature."

Webs raised his head and looked around at the eyes that glittered in the dark. "Can't we go get them?" he asked. "Maybe if all the Talons attacked at once . . ." His voice faltered. Who was he kidding? *He* wasn't about to go rushing into the SkyWing palace to die. And he was closer to the dragonets than any of the Talons, who hadn't even met them.

"All the Talons?" Cirrus hissed. "Forty dragons against the hundred SkyWing palace guards? A brilliant plan. No wonder we left the dragonets in your capable claws." His diamond-shaped head darted up and snapped a bat out of the air. Tiny bones crunched in his teeth.

"A suicide mission may not be necessary," Nautilus said. "Something happened in the SkyWing palace yesterday. We don't have any clear reports yet, but one spy said he thought Queen Scarlet was dead — killed by the dragonets."

Webs flared his wings in surprise. "By *my* dragonets?" he asked.

"Maybe they have a talent for escaping," Nautilus said. "Although another spy was sure they all died trying to fight their way out."

Webs's stomach felt as if it were full of poisonous jellyfish. The dragonets *couldn't* be dead. Not after all he'd given up for the sake of the prophecy. *And to save my own scales,* a small voice whispered inside him.

"If they are loose in Pyrrhia, how do you suggest we find them?" Nautilus asked. "Non-suicidal suggestions only, please. Well, for us. You may feel free to kill yourself whenever it's convenient."

"I don't know," Webs admitted. He had no idea where the dragonets might go. He didn't understand why they would *want* to be on their own, cut off from their protectors. The worst ten days of his life were the ones between the battle where he had abandoned his queen and the day the Talons had found him. Alone, with no tribe to support them and no Talons to protect them . . . how would the dragonets survive?

"If we can't get the dragonets back," Nautilus mused, "I suppose we'll have to consider our backup plan." He scratched his gills thoughtfully.

"What backup plan?" Webs asked.

"The one you don't get to know about," Cirrus said.

"But — but we have to get them back," Webs said. "They're *the* dragonets. They're the only ones who can stop the war."

"Have a little faith in the prophecy, Webs," Nautilus said.

"Yes, don't worry," Crocodile said reassuringly. "The Talons of Peace wouldn't put all their eggs in one nest. It's a good backup plan."

Webs looked from one shadowed face to the next. Apart from Crocodile, he saw nothing friendly in the eyes staring at him.

"I don't understand," he said. Was there another prophecy he didn't know about?

"Of course," Nautilus said, "that means you would be a problem."

Webs barely had time to say "What?" before Cirrus was suddenly on his back, pinning him to the ground. His wounds from the SkyWing soldiers flared up with bright new pain. One wing was twisted behind him, and he could feel the IceWing's serrated claws digging into his scales.

"What are you doing?" Webs yelped. "I'm one of you! I've been with the Talons of Peace for seven years!"

"And you failed us," Cirrus hissed.

"Now, now —" Nautilus said, then paused. "No, that's fair."

"I'm going to dig your heart out and feed it to the fish," Cirrus growled.

Won't that be ironic. Webs thought gloomily of the fish he'd just eaten. "But we're the dragons for peace," he said, his teeth gritted with pain. "If we kill each other, aren't we as bad as Burn and Blister and Blaze?"

"Sorry, Webs," Nautilus said. "Peace is more important than any one dragon. And you would disrupt our backup plan. We're doing this for your own good. For the prophecy. For peace."

Webs heard the horrible echo of his own words — the same thing he'd said to the dragonets whenever they complained about life under the mountain. *It's for your own good. Peace is the most important thing.* He'd believed it when he said it. No doubt Nautilus did, too.

Nautilus gestured with one talon. "Cirrus, rip out his heart."

The jaws of the IceWing sprang open, and Cirrus flung Webs down onto his back. His icicle-sharp claws flexed, ready to tear into Webs's underbelly.

Suddenly Crocodile cannoned into him, knocking Cirrus into the undergrowth.

Webs didn't hesitate. He flipped upright and shot into the sky as fast as his wings could carry him. He heard shouts as Crocodile struck out at the dragons around her, and he felt a stab of guilt. Should he stay to help her fight?

But why go back for death when he had a chance at life?

He heard wingbeats behind him and flew harder. He imagined Cirrus breathing down his tail, or Nautilus hissing closer and closer.

But it was Crocodile's voice who called to him.

"Fly, Webs!" she cried. "I've knocked them out — they didn't see that coming. Ha!"

"Thank you," Webs called back, twisting to see her heavy brown shape soaring behind him.

"Where will you hide?" she asked.

He shook his head. "I have no idea. I've heard there's a dragon in Jade Mountain who might —"

"You should go home," she said, tilting her wings to swoop under him. "From what I hear, Queen Coral is in a merciful mood these days."

The thrill that ran through Webs from horns to tail nearly took his breath away. *Home? Back to the sea, after all these years? Is it possible?*

"She'll never forgive me, not after everything I did," he said. "It's not just that I deserted her during a battle. She must know I was the one who stole her egg for the prophecy."

"You might be surprised," said Crocodile. "Isn't she supposed to be one of the greatest queens in history? That's what all the SeaWing scrolls say. Perhaps she'll forgive you. Why not take the chance, if it means you can go home again?"

Webs was silent. One of the moons was rising, shimmering off his blue-green scales. From up here he could see the ocean, far off in the distance, but it seemed as unreachable as the moon itself.

"Up to you," Crocodile said, banking away from him. "I'm just telling you what I've heard. Good luck, either way."

"Good luck to you, too," Webs called. She vanished into the trees, and he wondered where she would go now.

He missed the sea with every scale on his body. He missed the palaces, the currents, the whale songs, the feasts, the gardens . . . the other SeaWings.

If the Talons are done with me . . . if I promise her I'll be brave this time . . .

Maybe I can *go home again.*

Ice Kingdom

Sky Kingdom

Under the Mountain

Burn's Stronghold

Kingdom of Sand

Scorpion Den

Jade Mountain

PART ONE
THE EDGE OF THE OCEAN

CHAPTER 1

A wave roared onto the beach and crashed around Tsunami's talons. Her webbed claws sank into the wet sand. Her blue wings billowed in the wind.

She lifted her head, breathing in the wild sea air.

This was where she was supposed to be. This was her ocean.

"Let me guess," Glory said mockingly behind her. "You *guys*, that's the smell of *freedom*."

"Freedom smells a lot like fish," Starflight observed. "Which, to be clear, is kind of nose-curlingly awful."

"I love it," Tsunami said. This was what the Talons of Peace had stolen from her. They'd kept her trapped in the stale, dreary air under the mountain her whole life, when she was meant to be out here, flying and swimming and living like a real SeaWing.

Starflight glanced up at the sky and edged back toward the dark foliage that lined the beach. "Shouldn't we stay under the trees? What if a patrol spots us? I mean —" He stopped and took a deep breath. "We *must* stay under the trees. All right. Yes. Everyone back into the trees right now."

The others ignored him, although Sunny gave him a pitying glance.

Tsunami bent her head to study the waves washing over her talons. Small shapes, silver and green and yellow, darted through the shallows. The ocean smelled much more alive than the cave river.

Was it only a week since they'd run away from their guardians? It was hard to remember exactly how long they'd been trapped in the SkyWing prison.

But there was one thing Tsunami remembered clearly: the sound of bone snapping under her talons.

She poked a hole in the sand with her claw. *I had to kill that SeaWing. Queen Scarlet forced us to fight. There was no other way out of the arena. He was crazy. It was him or me.*

The same thoughts kept circling in her head like lame-winged dragons. She shook her head and flared her wings. This was ridiculous. Was she a dragon or a scavenger? Dragons were meant to be fierce warriors; one little death shouldn't rattle her so much.

Besides, Glory had done worse with her deadly venom, and she didn't seem bothered at all.

"You know what I love?" Clay said mournfully. "Fish. Lots of fish. Big fish I can eat, not these little wriggle-scraps."

The MudWing sat down on the sand beside Tsunami. His stomach growled loud enough for all of them to hear.

Sunny giggled. "Clay, it's only been a day since you caught that enormous pig for all of us."

"Wasn't enormous," Clay said. He sighed, his wings drooping. "That was the smallest pig in the *whole world*."

"You should have eaten my carrots." Sunny clambered up to sit on his back and peer out at the ocean. The sun was just rising in a peach-pale sky, casting broken paths of light across the water. Two of the moons, barely slivers like thin claws, were vanishing behind the mountains.

"I'm serious, everybody," Starflight said. "It's not safe out on the beach, not with all the MudWings and SkyWings looking for us." The NightWing was standing well out of reach of the waves, trying to shake sand off his talons.

As far as Tsunami was concerned, they'd already wasted a day flying south of the Diamond Spray Delta, basically because Starflight had worried and complained until everyone agreed. Yes, the SkyWings were after them. Yes, they were probably mad about the dragonets' escape from SkyWing prison. And they were pretty definitely mad about the part where Glory maybe killed their queen on the way out.

But Tsunami didn't want to keep running. She wanted to find her family. Once they knew who she was, she was sure the SeaWings would protect her and her friends.

Most of all, she really wanted Starflight to stop fretting, complaining, and bossing. It made the others nervous and harder to organize. She almost wished the NightWings hadn't given him back.

"Why are *you* so worried?" Tsunami asked him. "If they do recapture us, won't your NightWing friends come swooping in to rescue you again?"

Starflight fluttered his wings indignantly. "I'm not worried for *me*," he said. "I'm trying to keep all of us safe." He glanced at Sunny and ducked his head.

"I'm keeping us safe just fine!" Tsunami protested. "When have I ever led us wrong?"

"Well," Glory pointed out, "there was that one time we got captured by SkyWings and their queen nearly killed us all. . . ."

Tsunami smacked her tail into the water to send a cold wave over Glory. The RainWing hissed and jumped away from the sea.

"Stop it!" Sunny said. "Stop fighting, all of you. Clay, stop them." She patted the top of his head to pull his attention back from the tiny fish swimming around his feet.

"Oh, yes, let's hear from our bigwings," Glory teased. Her scales this morning were gold like Sunny's, but with drifting splashes of ocean blue. She sat down and yawned at Tsunami, displaying her venom-spitting teeth.

"Hey," Clay said, nudging Tsunami's wing with his own.

"It's all right for Starflight to worry. We don't even know if Queen Scarlet is alive or dead. But," he added quickly, "I know you want to find the SeaWings as fast as possible. So let's find them instead of fighting about it, and then we can get to safety sooner."

Tsunami shot one more narrow-eyed look at Starflight, then turned back to the ocean. Clay was right; the important thing was to find her family and a safe place for them all to hide.

"Aww," Glory said. "So wise and big."

"I think he is," Sunny said, wrapping her forearms around Clay's neck. Starflight sat down, flipping his tail around his talons unhappily.

Glory settled her sun-colored wings. "So now what? Should we shout 'Hey, SeaWings, we've got your missing princess!' and wait for dragons to bound joyfully out of the ocean?"

"With a feast!" Clay cried, startling a seagull into the air. "There was a feast at the end of the story! When the missing SeaWing princess got home, her parents were so happy they made a feast. I remember the feast. They ate a whole whale. That was a good feast. I bet *I* could eat a whale. Do you think we'll get a feast?"

"*The Missing Princess* was just a story in a scroll," Starflight said. "We have no idea what we'll actually find in the Kingdom of the Sea."

"That's true." Clay's wings drooped. "It might not be what you're hoping for, Tsunami. Like finding out my mother sold me for a cow."

"Hey," said Glory. "It was at least *two* cows."

"Hmmm. Comforting," said Clay.

It wouldn't be like that for Tsunami. She was sure of it. Maybe Clay's dreams of his family had turned out all wrong, but hers would be perfect. Especially now that she knew her egg had been stolen from the Royal Hatchery.

She was the daughter of the SeaWing queen.

Not only that, but according to Starflight, none of the queen's other female dragonets had survived to adulthood. Tsunami was the only living heir to the SeaWing kingdom. One day, she would be queen of the SeaWings.

True, that meant one day she'd have to fight her own mother to the death to become queen. But that day could be as far off as she wanted it to be. Not something she had to think about now.

She spread her wings and breathed in the salt-spray air again. Out of the corner of her eyes she kept seeing tiny creatures pop out of the speckled sand and then vanish again.

"I could just dive in and look for the SeaWing palace," Tsunami suggested.

"Out there?" Starflight sounded alarmed. He spread his wings and shook sand off them, blinking anxiously.

"Where else do you suggest I find the SeaWings?" she asked.

"Swimming in the ocean is not like swimming in an underground cave river," Starflight lectured. "There are strong currents and unpredictable waves and, and big things with teeth —"

"I'm a big thing with teeth." Tsunami grinned at him.

He didn't laugh. "It's not safe," he said. "What if we lose you?" Tsunami wanted to poke his wrinkled-up worried snout with her sharpest claw.

"Starflight, cheer up," Sunny interjected. "Tsunami can do anything. And how is she supposed to get home to her family if she can't go into the sea?"

"Oh, no!" Clay heaved himself to his feet, scattering sand and nearly dislodging Sunny, who grabbed his neck with a yelp. Sand and seashells and tiny, astonished crabs flew through the air as he lashed his tail.

"Ow! Stop that!" Glory commanded, covering her eyes.

"What about us?" Clay's big brown wings flapped. "I didn't think of that! Tsunami, we can't go with you to the SeaWing palace. We can't breathe down there! How can we stick together if you're underwater?" He clawed at the water, leaving deep gouges in the wet sand. "What are we going to do?"

Tsunami kind of adored Clay when he was in a tizzy. She also adored that it had taken an entire day for it to occur to him that the Kingdom of the Sea was underwater.

"Seriously?" Glory said to Clay. "All of those geography lessons, and not a single one sunk in?"

Clay turned in a confused circle. Crabs scurried out of the way of his giant talons. "What?"

"The SeaWings have an above-water palace, too," Starflight said in his "see, you should have studied more" voice. "So they can receive guests, like their SandWing ally Blister. It's on an island somewhere in the Bay of a Thousand Scales."

"Oh." Clay sat down with a whooshing sigh.

Sunny patted his shoulder. "I didn't remember that either," she offered. "So we go there, right?"

"Not easily," Starflight said. "Both SeaWing palaces — underwater and on land — are well hidden. That's how they've lasted so long in this war, even though they don't have fire like the other tribes. Nobody can find them to attack their homes."

"Sounds like the NightWings," Glory sniped.

"It's nothing like the NightWings!" Tsunami cried. "SeaWings aren't trying to act all mysterious and pretentious. They're just being sensible about guarding their home."

"There are over a thousand islands to search, but it's still probably —" Starflight stopped midsentence and glanced at the sky again. "Does anyone else smell fire?"

"Three moons, Starflight. I'm not hiding in the trees every time some little thing spooks you," Tsunami said.

"Wait, I think he's right," Sunny said, lifting her head. "I hear wingbeats."

"I do, too," Starflight said. The spiny ridge along his back stood up in alarm, and he bolted for the trees, running as fast as he could.

"From this far away?" Tsunami said skeptically. "I don't see anything up there." But just as she said it, she spotted a cluster of red specks like spattered blood in the sky, winging down from the mountains in the northwest.

A SkyWing patrol was coming their way.

CHAPTER 2

"Quick, into the water," Tsunami ordered. It was closer than the trees, and would hide them just as well.

"No way," said Glory. She sank to the ground, spreading her wings, and shifted color. Her scales flowed into the rocky, sandy pattern below her until she was impossible to see, especially from the air. It happened so fast, Tsunami nearly lost track of where she was. Glory was getting better at that trick.

"Fine. Come on, Sunny." Tsunami reached for the little SandWing.

"I'd rather not," Sunny squeaked. "I can make it to the trees. I'll fly really fast." She jumped off Clay's back and flapped after Starflight.

Tsunami stamped her foot, spraying ocean water across the sand. Glory made a muffled, grumpy noise.

"It'll be safer in the sea," Tsunami huffed. She cast a worried look at the sky. The specks were getting closer fast — maybe faster than Sunny could hide. But it was too late to catch her now. Tsunami turned and dove into the ocean.

Clay was already burrowing into the shallow mud shelf, displacing startled flatfish and sending up clouds of minnows. The MudWing didn't have a problem with water like the others did, since he could hold his breath for up to an hour.

Tsunami breathed in and salt water rushed into her gills. It surprised her how sharp it felt, like inhaling smoke. It was nothing like the crystal clear water of the underground cave. What's more, the current kept trying to shove her back to the beach, then yank her out again.

But she plowed forward and down, past Clay, beating her wings as the water got deeper. Schools of tiny purple fish whirled away from her like stars exploding. Over the edge of the sand shelf, the deeper ocean floor was covered in bundles of eel grass. Waving dark green tendrils reached up to brush Tsunami's underbelly.

She glanced up at the sky above her — still empty — and decided to risk surfacing. She had to be sure Sunny was safely hidden.

The thunder of wingbeats echoed in her ears as she poked her head out and turned toward the beach. The little SandWing was almost to safety. Tsunami could see Starflight standing under the trees, reaching his front claws out to pull Sunny in.

Overhead, an orange shape shot past, flying at full SkyWing speed — faster than any other tribe could fly. A red dragon flew close behind the first, followed by three more. Their enormous wings nearly blotted out the sun as they whooshed over the dragonets' heads.

Tsunami sank a bit lower in the water, but it seemed like the patrol was going too fast to notice a lone SeaWing in the ocean. Maybe these soldiers weren't hunting for the escaped prisoners.

Then she saw the last dragon — sunset orange, flames flickering from his nose, with a jagged tear on the tip of his left wing. He flew slower than the others, bringing up the rear, and his head swung back and forth, dark eyes searching the ground below them.

Tsunami found herself holding her breath. The SkyWing's snout swung toward the trees just as Sunny's tail whisked out of sight.

He paused, beating his wings back to hover in the air for a moment.

Was he staring at the trees?

Had he seen Sunny?

What if he called the others back? The patrol dragons were several wingbeats away already — but one shout could bring them hurtling around at lightning speed. Sunny and Starflight were no match for six full-grown SkyWing soldiers.

Actually they were no match for *one* SkyWing soldier. The two of them together would probably have trouble fighting a sleepy bat.

A curl of smoke rose from the SkyWing's nose, and he opened his mouth. If there was any chance of saving her friends, Tsunami had to shut him up.

She burst out of the water in a great leap, smashing her tail behind her for momentum. Her wings powered her up to ram right into the SkyWing's underbelly.

He coughed out a puff of fiery smoke and clutched his midsection, the breath knocked out of him. Tsunami had a few moments before he could recover enough to call for help. She ducked around him, slammed her tail into his head, and landed on his back as hard as she could.

The SkyWing nearly fell into the water, but he fought back up into the air. Tsunami kicked at his wings with her claws and slid back toward his tail, trying to drag him down with her weight. He was too big and too strong for her up here; only taking him by surprise had given her a temporary advantage. She needed to get him in the ocean to even out the fight.

The orange dragon snarled and twisted, shooting a blast of flames out of his snout, which barely missed her. Tsunami yanked him down toward the water, but his massive wings beat harder and harder. It felt like a hurricane whistling around her ears. She could tell that he was gaining height, and in a moment he'd be strong enough to call the other soldiers back.

You're not getting my friends! Tsunami thought fiercely. She found the vulnerable spot on his tail and sank her teeth in. He convulsed with pain, nearly throwing her off, and shot another blast of fire under his wing at her.

At first Tsunami thought he had missed. Then she felt a searing trail of agony spreading along her neck. It felt as if someone were trying to saw through her scales with a scalding-hot wire.

She closed her eyes and clamped her jaw harder, determined to hang on although spots were starting to dance in her vision.

Suddenly the dragon lurched toward the sea. Tsunami's eyes flew open.

Clay had flung himself between her and the dragon's snout, spreading his fireproof wings. His claws clamped on to the SkyWing's back, and the extra weight drove the soldier down and down, toward the sea.

Together, Clay and Tsunami dragged the SkyWing into the ocean. He fought wildly the whole way, but his flames couldn't hurt Clay's fire-resistant scales, and his giant wings couldn't help him once he was underwater and cut off from breathing.

As soon as they hit the water, Tsunami swam to the SkyWing's head and held it below the surface until he stopped thrashing.

She let go and so did Clay. The dragon's body began to drift slowly toward the seafloor.

A shudder rippled through Tsunami's scales. *Him or me.*

This didn't feel right.

Why couldn't she be ferocious and not *care*?

She swam after the dragon and grabbed one of his wings, then looked back up at Clay. He met her eyes, and to her relief, didn't even hesitate before swimming to the other wing.

They dragged the SkyWing up onto the beach. The current had carried them farther away than Tsunami had guessed, and it was painfully hard to swim back to shore, especially with a full-grown dragon weighing them down.

She gritted her teeth, ignoring her exhaustion and the pain from the burn on her neck. She was a SeaWing. This was supposed to be her element. She was the boss of the ocean, not the other way around.

By the time they reached the beach, the rest of the patrol had vanished from sight. She wondered how long it would be before they noticed this one missing and came back to look for him.

Tsunami collapsed onto the sand beside the SkyWing. Clay peered into the dragon's snout, then started thumping his chest.

"What is *wrong* with you?" Glory's voice snapped. The RainWing materialized from the sandy background, turning her scales a darker shade of brown so they could see her. She glared at Tsunami. "Why did you do that?"

"Oh, you're welcome," Tsunami said. "Just saving your life, as usual."

"By attacking random dragons?" Glory cried. "In another moment they would have been gone! And what are *you* doing?" She jabbed Clay in the side with one of her wings.

"Uh," Clay mumbled. "Fixing him." He kept thumping the SkyWing's chest.

"What?" Glory yelped. "You can't let him *live*!" She tried to grab one of Clay's forearms, but Tsunami shoved her away.

"We don't have to kill him," Tsunami said. "We'll tie him up and leave him here."

"Great," Glory said. "How about a trail of cow parts, too? And a map of where we're going? Or perhaps we could set this part of the forest on fire, just to make *sure* everyone knows how to find us. Would you like me to spell out 'DRAGONETS WUZ HERE' in giant rocks?"

"Fine!" Tsunami said. "Here he is. *You* kill him."

Glory looked down at the unconscious dragon and hesitated. "I don't kill dragons who can't fight back," she said finally.

"Why not?" Tsunami said. "Just splat some venom on his face and melt him, if it's that easy for you."

Glory sank her claws into the sand, scowling. Bubbles of dark purple began spreading across her scales.

Sunny and Starflight landed on the beach beside them. Sunny gave the SkyWing a horrified look, and Tsunami remembered that she'd been trapped in another part of the palace during the arena fights. She'd never seen her friends battle another dragon.

"Is he all right?" Sunny asked Clay.

"Try this," Starflight offered, coming over to help. Clay shifted aside, and they rolled the dragon onto his stomach.

"Why did you attack him?" Sunny blurted at Tsunami. The little SandWing's harmless tail flicked back and forth anxiously.

"To save you!" Tsunami said, stung.

"But he wasn't even doing anything," Sunny protested. "He was just flying by."

All four of them were looking at Tsunami like she was the kind of dragon who hid under rocks and bit innocent passersby for fun. She arched her neck indignantly.

"I thought he saw you," she growled. "He was about to call out to the others. I saw him open his mouth!"

"So did I," said Glory. "I'm pretty sure he was yawning."

"*Pretty* sure?" Tsunami said. "Would you risk our lives on 'pretty sure'?"

Was he yawning? Did I attack him for nothing? That can't be right. I saw danger and reacted appropriately. Didn't I?

"Maybe if you'd just stopped to *think* for a second —" Starflight said.

"Or forever? Like you? Think think think, worry worry, never do anything?" Tsunami cried.

The SkyWing suddenly coughed, and seawater flooded out of his snout. Clay ruffled his wings with a pleased expression.

"Oh, wonderful. Our enemy will survive. Well done. We have to get out of here," Glory said. She took a step back and glanced at the sky where the other soldiers had disappeared. "So what do we do with him now, O Great Leader?"

Tsunami had no idea. She glanced around frantically. Maybe if they could find some vines to tie him up with . . .

"There's a tree," Starflight said, jumping to his feet. "In the forest."

"No *way*," Glory said. "A *tree* in the *forest*?"

"Being sarcastic is not helping!" Tsunami snapped at her.

"I mean, a fallen tree," Starflight said. "We can use it. Glory, stay and guard him; Clay and Tsunami, come on, quick."

Clay charged up the beach behind him. Tsunami paused for a moment — she didn't like leaving the soldier, even if he wasn't fully awake yet. She also didn't particularly like taking orders from Starflight.

"Go on, hurry," Sunny said, nudging her with one wing.

Not far into the forest, a large tree had fallen, with the top of its branches brushing the sand. Clay and Tsunami shoved and rolled it onto the beach and dragged it back to the SkyWing while Starflight flapped around squawking instructions. *As if we need to be told how to move a tree,* Tsunami thought grumpily.

The soldier's eyes were blinking awake as they reached him. He coughed and coughed again, lifting his head to peer groggily at the dragonets.

"So how does the tree help?" Tsunami asked.

"We put it on top of him," Starflight said. "So he'll be trapped in place, at least long enough for us to get away."

Tsunami hated to admit it, but it was a good idea. She helped Clay wrestle the tree over until it lay heavily across the orange dragon's back and wings. The SkyWing tried to push himself up, but the tree kept him pinned to the sand.

"What if he's stuck here forever?" Sunny worried. She reached over and brushed some sand off the SkyWing's snout. He snorted a puff of smoke, and Clay pulled her back. "Maybe we should just let him go."

"We can't do that," Tsunami said.

"I wish you hadn't attacked him," Sunny said, ducking her head.

"Me too," said Glory.

"It wasn't the smartest move," Starflight agreed.

Tsunami's gills flared, and she spread her wings. "You don't know that!" she said. "Maybe I saved us! Again!" She looked at Clay, but he only shrugged as if he wasn't sure. *Thanks for the support, guys,* Tsunami thought angrily. *When all I'm trying to do is keep everyone safe.*

"Don't worry, Sunny," Clay said, patting the little SandWing's head. "His friends will come looking for him eventually."

"Eventually or soon," Glory said. "So like I said, let's seriously get out of here."

"Wait," the SkyWing rasped. His voice was hoarse and deep. He wriggled, lashing his tail across the sand. "Don't leave me like this."

Starflight stepped into his line of sight and gazed down at him. "Remember we could have killed you," he said. "Remember that the dragonets of destiny were merciful. We want peace, not more death. We have come to save Pyrrhia."

"Oh, good grief," Tsunami said as Glory rolled her eyes. "No more hanging out with NightWings for you."

"I thought it sounded nice," Sunny said. Starflight shot her a grateful look.

"Sunny, don't encourage him," said Glory.

Carefully Starflight draped a few large leaves over the dragon's head, so he couldn't see where they went. He pointed toward the forest and mouthed, "Just to be safe."

Tsunami sighed. More flying in the wrong direction. She wanted to go *home* already. Home to the ocean and the SeaWings and her royal parents.

But she couldn't argue about it with the SkyWing listening, and the others were already nodding. All of them were ready to follow anxious, overly cautious Starflight yet again. And none of them thought she'd done the right thing by attacking this SkyWing, even though it was to save their stupid scales.

As they lifted into the sky, she cast a longing look over her shoulder at the ocean.

Soon, she thought. *Soon I'll be with my own dragons.*

— CHAPTER 3 —

The Bay of a Thousand Scales was farther away than Tsunami had realized. She'd been studying the map of Pyrrhia since she was tiny, but it was hard to fit that picture over the enormous world below her. She kept expecting to find neat little spirals of islands that would fit in the palm of her talons. Instead, she found herself flying over vast expanses of empty ocean, dotted here and there with a solitary outcropping of rock.

After they took a long detour inland to convince the SkyWing they'd gone in the opposite direction, they circled around south and flew out to sea. They managed to make it to a small rocky island shortly after night fell, but according to Starflight they were still a long way from the Bay of a Thousand Scales. He'd calculated the distance and their speed and had a long boring lecture ready to explain it all. The rest of them fell asleep halfway into it, and he spent the next day sulking about that.

Still, Tsunami had to admit — if only to herself — that it was useful having someone with all the geography and flight plans in his head. For a few days they stopped whenever they saw an island, ate a seagull or fish if they could catch any, and then flew on. Tsunami tried diving into the ocean several times and was disappointed to discover she couldn't swim as fast as she flew. The only good news was that the ocean water helped to heal the burn on her neck.

It was four mornings later when Tsunami finally woke up on an island that was officially part of the Thousand Scales.

She started awake from a dream in which their cave had collapsed and was slowly crushing her to death, and discovered that Clay had rolled over on top of her in the middle of the night. Grumbling, she wriggled out from under him and let his tail flop over onto Starflight's head.

The five dragonets were packed into a cavern halfway up a tall sea cliff. It was cramped and uncomfortable and smelled of seagull droppings. Clay had barely been able to scrunch his wings low enough to crawl inside.

And why were they sleeping in this horrible spot instead of on the nice white sandy beach below?

Tsunami sat down in the cave entrance and glared at Starflight, which wasn't very satisfying since everyone was still snoring away. Clay was stuffed against the back wall with Sunny between his front talons and Starflight curled up alongside. Even Glory had her tail draped over Clay's. Her scales glinted orange and gold in the light of the rising sun, with bursts of red when she shifted sleepily.

Starflight had been acting *so weird* since the NightWings gave him back. Suddenly it seemed like he wanted to argue with Tsunami about *everything*. If she said, "Let's sleep on the beach! It'll be fun!" he'd say, "No, no, we have to sleep in a hidden cave; that'll be much safer." Safer! As if there was anything to worry about all the way out here, in the middle of the night.

But everyone was still mad at her about attacking that soldier, so they all voted with Starflight.

She didn't like that development at all.

Tsunami watched them sleep for a moment. It was so hard to lead effectively when everyone kept *questioning* you and *complaining* about everything. She only wanted what was best for them. Didn't they know that? She'd always figured she would fight a hundred SkyWings to protect them.

But maybe I shouldn't. Maybe my friends don't want my protection after all.

Maybe they wanted Starflight to be their leader instead. Even though he'd never risked one scale on his body for them.

Tsunami glanced down at the sea, sparkling aquamarine below her. Somewhere in those blue-green depths was her family — her parents, her kingdom, everything that should have been hers, if the Talons of Peace hadn't stolen her away and ruined her life.

Perhaps the problem with her friends was that they were from different tribes, all stubborn and muddled up instead of sensible like SeaWings. Maybe her own kind would understand her better. They'd *appreciate* her instead of yelling at her.

Well, she didn't have to sit here waiting for everyone else to wake up. It wasn't like they'd be much help when it came to searching anyway.

Tsunami stretched her wings and then tipped forward out of the cave opening. Wind whistled past her snout, tugging at her tail as she plummeted down the cliff. At the last moment, she snapped her wings open and sailed across the top of the water, skimming it with her claws. Joy tingled through her scales. She spun and dove into the water.

The sea was warmer here and busy with underwater life. Her splash sent what seemed like thousands of fish scattering away, several of them disappearing into a pinkish-orange coral reef that curled out of the sand like a petrified forest. A blobby dark blue octopus goggled at her from the branches. Tsunami kept seeing flickers of bright yellow and silver at the edge of her vision as fish fled from her webbed claws.

No welcoming committee of delighted SeaWings, though.

No glowing jellyfish marking a path to Queen Coral's castle. No cavalcade of bowing seahorses and bejeweled lobsters to lead the way.

Not that she'd been picturing the homecoming scene from *The Missing Princess* or anything.

Tsunami swam along the coral reef, peering at the creatures hiding in the nooks and holes. A hideous thing she thought might be an eel stared back at her. Little orange-and-white fish nestled in the waving lavender anemones.

She still wasn't used to swimming in the sea, and that frustrated her. Unexpected currents kept knocking her off balance. The salt water felt like it was scraping roughly against her gills. Where were her natural SeaWing instincts? Her world was supposed to make her stronger, faster, tougher — not pathetic.

She swam all the way to the next island, fighting the currents. More of the pinkish coral reef stretched across the sand here as well, dotted with waving green fans and lacy dark purple ferns. Her wings felt sore and tired, so she spread them wide and floated near the surface, not far from the land.

Something flashed below her in the shadows of the coral reef.

Something very large.

Tsunami had a brief vision of all the large, toothy things that might live in the ocean, then dismissed it. If it was a shark, she would kill it and bring it back to the others to eat — mainly so she could see the look on Starflight's face.

She flicked her tail to swim closer.

It was another SeaWing.

A shiver rippled across her scales when she saw him, and part of her wanted to bolt right back to her friends.

Don't be a smoke-breather, she scolded herself. *This is what you were hoping for: a dragon from your own tribe.*

She took a deep breath. The strange SeaWing had dark blue horns and sky-blue scales several shades paler than hers. He was paddling by the reef, shifting his talons and wings slightly to change course. His head turned alertly from side to side.

Well, it wouldn't hurt to follow him for a while first, Tsunami told herself. She crept along the top of the reef, peering over the edge at him. Her claws caught on small gaps in the coral. She accidentally poked an indignant black lobster, which came bustling out with its long whiskers bristling and pincers snapping. It took one look at her and hustled right back into hiding.

Up here, the reef was covered in a layer of green mosslike algae. Tsunami passed a couple of large sea turtles slowly swimming nearby. An enormous, tentacled thing like a sea spider sat nibbling bits of algae. The tips of its eight dark purple legs glowed orange-yellow and so did its eyes.

The SeaWing down below stopped suddenly and glanced around. Tsunami flattened herself against the reef. Knobbly bits of limestone poked into her underbelly. She peered through one of the holes at the other dragon.

He spun slowly, staring into the ocean depths. Had he heard her?

But he didn't look up. The dragon checked around him one more time, then lit up the stripes along his wings.

Almost immediately another dragon swam out of a cave in the coral reef.

Hmmm, Tsunami thought, *much less handsome.* His green scales were perfectly nice, but she didn't care for the black spiral patterns on them. She'd never seen a pattern like that on a dragon before. And his face wasn't nearly as handsome or friendly-looking as the first dragon, although perhaps that had something to do with the giant bruise swollen over his left eye.

She wondered if they were guards switching patrol duty. If so, they were being quite strange about it.

The two dragons floated in place, staring at each other, for what seemed like an eternity. Occasionally the stripes on one SeaWing would light up, then on the other. They moved their talons about as if waving away fish, even though no fish went anywhere near them.

And then the spiral-marked dragon ducked back into the cave, and the blue dragon swam on.

Some kind of SeaWing patrol ritual? Tsunami wondered. *I guess I'll have to learn all that stuff in order to become queen.* She lifted her wings to swim after the first dragon, and a pair of yellow-striped fish wriggled out from under her and shot away.

The sky-blue dragon swam back the way he'd come, toward the stretch of open sea between this island and the one where Tsunami's friends were sleeping.

Now or never, Tsunami thought. She'd rather meet this dragon than the other one, and she'd rather do it while he was alone, if she could. That seemed easier than trying to explain herself to a whole bunch of dragons at once.

She beat her wings to catch up, dove over the edge of the reef, and swam around in front of him.

The SeaWing started back in an eddy of ripples. His eyes were a blue so dark they were almost black.

Tsunami pointed up at the surface. *Come on out of the water so we can talk,* she tried to signal. Hopefully he'd figure out what she meant.

To her surprise, he whipped around and fled. His tail smacked a wave of water in her face.

Well, that's *unfriendly,* she thought. She swam after him, swinging her tail to propel herself even faster. He glanced back over his shoulder, saw her chasing him, and put on a burst of speed.

Why was he running away? And how was he so *fast*?

"Stop!" she tried to yell through the water. "I just want to talk!"

Of course that didn't work. He didn't even slow down.

But then he twisted to look back at Tsunami, and so he didn't see the whale that suddenly loomed out of the deep in front of him.

Tsunami waved her talons and pointed. "Watch out!" she shouted in a cascade of bubbles.

The SeaWing smacked into the whale's side and careened backward. The whale was only slightly bigger than the dragon, with ridges all along its back and a flat, mild-mannered face. It made a weird squeaking groan and blinked at the SeaWing in confusion.

The dragon was still shaking his head, trying to reorient himself, when Tsunami caught up, grabbed his tail, and pinned him to the sand.

The whale blinked again and swam on. Eddies rippled around the two dragons as it powered away through the water.

Now what do I do? Tsunami thought. *I have to get him to the surface to talk to him, but if I let him go, he might try to escape again.*

She frowned down at the dragon and pointed at the surface again. Flashes of sunlight shimmered up above them, like pieces of broken gold-white glass floating on the water.

The other dragon tipped his head to one side. Luminescent stripes lit up along his wings, flashing fast, then slow.

All right, Tsunami thought. *I can do that, too. Maybe he's testing me.*

She lit up her own stripes, illuminating the ones on her snout, then the ones along her tail, and finally her wings. *See? My stripes flash, too. I'm a SeaWing. Now let's go up and talk.*

Slowly she spread her wings and lifted up, prepared to grab him if he tried to bolt again. He scrambled upright but stayed with her. Encouraged, Tsunami swam a bit closer to the surface. He followed, but only for a bit before he stopped and looked around.

His stripes flashed again, this time along his neck and tail.

Impatiently Tsunami lit up her stripes one more time, mirroring what he'd done.

The SeaWing's wings flared open with a whoosh that scared fish into the reef. He lunged toward Tsunami, fast as a minnow. His front talons reached for her.

Tsunami roared, blasting him in the eyes with bubbles, and sliced her claws across his snout. She didn't know why he was attacking. Maybe he was a traitor SeaWing. Or maybe he was guarding his territory or treasure. Perhaps he thought she was an intruder, although he wasn't much of a guard if his first instinct was to run away, and his second was to attack with no reason.

He'll be sorry when he finds out who I am! she thought fiercely.

She kicked his underbelly hard with her back legs. He coughed up a stream of bubbles and fell back. Tsunami spread her wings, snarled at him one more time, and shot to the surface.

She burst into the air and kept beating her wings to rise into the sky. In the distance, she could see the cliff-side cave and the worried faces of her friends poking out.

An enormous splash sounded behind her. The other SeaWing surged out of the ocean. His massive tail whacked the water twice as he lifted into the air, sending giant waves rushing in all directions.

He looked even bigger out here in the air. His hooked claws gleamed sharply in the sunlight. His dark blue eyes were fixed on her wings.

The first true citizen of her kingdom she'd ever met, and he was coming to kill her.

CHAPTER 4

Tsunami shot toward the island where her friends were. The SeaWing was close on her tail. He roared something, but the wind whipped it away so she couldn't hear it.

She saw Clay wriggle out of the cliff and take to the air. That's what she needed — backup. With a quick twist of her wings, she aimed for the strip of white sandy beach where she'd wanted to sleep the night before. The other three could stay safely in the cave. She and Clay together could handle this SeaWing.

She hoped.

"Wait!" her pursuer yelled. "Where are you going? What's wrong?"

Tsunami's wings missed a beat, and she nearly dropped into the ocean. She swung around, hovering over the sea between the cliff and the beach. Out of the corner of her eye, she saw Clay veer into a circle in the air, waiting to see what she would do.

The other SeaWing paused as well. He kept the length of

two dragons between him and her. The scratches on his snout were bleeding.

"What's wrong?" Tsunami cried indignantly. "Didn't you just attack me?"

"I certainly did not!" he protested. Glowing lines flickered along his snout. "I thought you — that's the normal —" He seemed to be getting more and more embarrassed. "*You* said you liked me!" he finally burst out.

"I didn't say anything of the sort," Tsunami said, astonished.

The SeaWing's brow furrowed. "You very clearly said you liked me, and you'd followed me all the way out here to tell me that."

Tsunami just about fell out of the sky. "You are a delusional squid-brain," she cried.

"Well, maybe not in those exact words!" he said. "All right, it was a little confusing. Maybe a lot confusing. But the message was in there. And why else would you be chasing me?"

"When, exactly, do you imagine I said all this?" Tsunami demanded. "Shortly after you attacked me, perhaps?"

The other dragon touched his snout gently and winced. "You were the only one doing any attacking," he said. "*I* was being friendly after what *you* said."

"Stop," Tsunami said. Maybe she'd misunderstood his actions. Maybe his approach had been a SeaWing greeting ritual she didn't know. In which case . . . his poor snout. She winced guiltily. Perhaps she shouldn't have gotten defensive so quickly. "Tell me exactly what you think I said."

He sighed. "I said, 'What are you doing all the way out here?' and you said —" He paused, rubbing his front talons against his head. "You said, 'Hey, sparkling teeth, I totally love three of your claws but not the others, and I wish your nose was a herring so I could eat it, and also your wings sound like sharks snoring.'"

Tsunami burst out laughing.

"All right, I get it," she said, although she didn't really. Did all SeaWings have a strange sense of humor? Would she have to develop one, too? "You're making this up."

He stared at her. "Are you seriously going to pretend you didn't say any of that?"

"Of course I didn't," Tsunami said. Maybe he wasn't kidding. Maybe he was mentally unbalanced. "I didn't say anything at all — we were underwater, remember?"

The strange dragon hovered for several wingbeats, glowing stripes lighting up along his blue scales. His face slowly went from confused to angry as he frowned at her.

"Who are you?" he demanded.

"I'm a SeaWing," she said hotly. "Just like you, so no need to get hostile."

"A SeaWing who doesn't speak Aquatic?" he growled. "Not likely. What are you really? How did you make yourself look like a SeaWing?"

Tsunami's heart sank. *Aquatic?*

SeaWings have their own language?

Of course they do, she realized. It felt like the tide was going out inside her, leaving nothing but stretches of bare sand. *And of course nobody ever bothered to teach it to me. Just one more creative way the Talons found to ruin my life.*

Why hadn't she thought of that before? Three moons, she was as thick as Clay. The dragons of the sea had a whole palace underwater — of course they needed a way to communicate down there. They couldn't just pop to the surface every time they needed to chat.

She glanced down at her webbed talons and remembered the gestures she'd seen the two SeaWings making while their luminescent stripes flashed. Talon signals and glowing stripes — she must have said all that nonsense with her stripes without realizing it.

But how can I be queen of the SeaWings if I don't even speak their language?

And why didn't anyone ever tell me about this?

Clay had never met a dragon of his own kind before. That's why he knew nothing about MudWings. But Tsunami didn't have that excuse: one of the guardians who'd raised them had been a SeaWing.

So why, *why*, had Webs never taught her the SeaWing language or even told her they had one?

All those scrolls about SeaWings . . . now that she thought about it, there was plenty of dialogue in the underwater scenes, like in *The Missing Princess* when the lost daughter found her parents. Tsunami had always assumed that was a storytelling technique, not an actual underwater language.

She looked up and met the SeaWing's dark blue eyes. His head was tilted curiously.

"You don't look guilty," he observed. "You look sad. And I imagine it would be hard to fake those." He nodded at the webs between her claws. "So where did you come from, and what's wrong with you?"

Tsunami bristled. "There's nothing wrong with me," she snapped. "I just happen to have been raised by idiot —"

His gaze suddenly shifted behind her. "Look out!" he yelled. His tail whipped around and slammed into her, knocking her aside. She spun toward the water, dizzy and shocked. Her wings brushed the ocean waves as she righted herself and turned around.

The strange SeaWing was grappling with Clay up in the sky.

Tsunami gasped. The SeaWing was full-grown, bigger than Clay, and he was not afraid to lash out with teeth, tail, and claws. But she could tell Clay was holding back, worried about hurting a possible ally. He ducked his head between his front talons and tried to dive away, but the SeaWing seized Clay's tail and dug his talons viciously into Clay's scales. Clay howled with pain.

The other dragon started to drag him down to the ocean, where he would have all the underwater advantages of SeaWings, and Clay would eventually drown.

"Clay!" Sunny shrieked, launching herself out of the cliff-side cave.

Tsunami got there first. She smacked the SeaWing over the head with her tail, seized his wing in her talons, and yanked him away from Clay when he turned around in surprise. He tried to spin around her to get back to his prey, but she blocked him with her wings and lashed out at his snout again. He flinched back, and that was enough time for Clay to scramble out of reach.

"What are you doing?" the SeaWing yelled at Tsunami. "I'm saving you from that MudWing!"

"Well, don't!" Tsunami yelled back. "He's my friend!"

"But —"

Sunny slammed into the back of the SeaWing, landing between his wings and wrapping her talons around his neck. "Leave him alone!" she panted.

The SeaWing looked more astonished than alarmed. He wriggled his shoulders and twisted his neck, trying to see what was on his back. Sunny kicked his wing, and he yelped.

"That's my other friend," Tsunami said. "Sunny, try not to hurt him too badly. We need his help."

"I hardly think this gnat is going to hurt me," the SeaWing growled.

Sunny kicked him again. "Promise me you won't attack Clay," she said.

His eyes went to the brown dragon circling just above them. Clay rubbed his head anxiously.

"The MudWings are our enemies," the SeaWing snarled at Tsunami. "If you don't know that, then you'd better leave the Bay of a Thousand Scales before Queen Coral's army finds you and does what they always do to traitors."

"I'm not a traitor," Tsunami said. "And Clay is not your enemy." She glanced up at him, then back at the SeaWing. "You'd better learn some respect, squid-brain. We're the dragonets of destiny."

— CHAPTER 5 —

"Riptide," Sunny said again. "That's a funny name."

"I like it," Tsunami said. "Fierce and scary, like mine."

Riptide was pacing the beach, lashing his tail in a long swooshing trail through the sand. His sky-blue scales glinted metallically in the morning light. He had claw-mark scars along his pale underbelly and what looked like an old bite mark on his tail. Tsunami was pretty sure he was only a couple years older than she was. The scratches she'd given his snout had finally stopped bleeding. She hoped those wouldn't leave scars, too — he had a very handsome snout when it wasn't all clawed up.

"All right," he said. "So the Talons of Peace are real."

"Unfortunately," Glory muttered.

Riptide glanced at her, and Tsunami felt a weird tingle of jealousy run through her scales. Glory had found a large rock to perch on, spreading her wings open to the sun, and her scales were shimmering silver and rose.

"I thought everyone knew about the Talons," Sunny said.

"Just rumors and whispers," said Riptide. "None of the tribe queens would be pleased to find a member of the peace movement in their midst. Conspiring with other tribes? Stealing eggs?" He shook his head. "Queen Coral would kill any dragon she found working with the Talons." He gave Tsunami a searching look she didn't understand.

Clay was sitting with his tail in the water. He had muddy sand packed over the spot where Riptide had clawed him. Sunny sat next to him, giving Riptide fierce looks whenever he paced too close to Clay.

"And you're *the* dragonets of destiny. For real. The ones in the prophecy. That's real." Riptide stopped, inhaled deeply, and blew out again. "And you're here. In SeaWing territory. Just like —" He glanced at Tsunami again, then went back to pacing.

"I know it's thrilling," Tsunami said. "But we're really looking for somewhere safe to go. The Talons of Peace treated us terribly, and I figured the SeaWings would welcome and protect us."

"I suppose," Riptide said not very reassuringly. "So you were all raised in a cave?" He stopped in front of Tsunami. "With no ocean? Never? You never went into the ocean?"

This seemed to be the hardest part for him to believe. "Not until we escaped," Tsunami said.

"But that's *awful*," said Riptide.

"*Thank* you," Tsunami said, flaring her wings. "I know it was. I've always said our life was miserable, but these dragons keep arguing with me."

"Not me," Glory said.

"I can't believe the Talons did that to you," Riptide said, clawing the sand.

"Tell me about it," Tsunami said. "They really are the worst."

"Even Webs — Webs didn't take you to the ocean?" Riptide asked.

"You know about Webs?" Sunny asked.

Riptide ducked his head and frowned at his talons. "He's pretty infamous in the tribe. We all know he deserted during a battle, and later he came back and stole one of the queen's eggs. At least, Queen Coral was sure it was him. But nobody knew if he stole it for the Talons of Peace or for his own reasons. We're not really supposed to talk about the Talons of Peace rumors."

"Didn't anyone think he might have stolen the egg to be part of the prophecy?" Starflight asked.

Riptide nodded. "Some of us did. But again, nobody talked about it. Queen Blister doesn't like hearing about the prophecy, so that's also been a forbidden topic."

Tsunami wrinkled her snout. "Blister gets to decide what SeaWings can talk about?"

Riptide shifted uncomfortably and picked up a large conch shell. He twisted it between his talons. "You'll want to call her *Queen* Blister when you meet her," he said.

"Not until we decide she *should* be queen," Tsunami said stoutly. "That's up to us, remember?"

It looked for a moment like Riptide was trying not to smile.

"Well," Starflight stammered, "she is a pretty good — I mean, she's the smart one — I think we'll probably —"

Tsunami tilted her head at him. What was he rattling on about? He snapped his mouth shut and went back to picking sand out of his scales.

"Did you know Webs?" Clay asked Riptide.

The SeaWing dropped his gaze. "Not really. He ran away during a battle when I was only two years old. But I've been hearing about his treachery my whole life." He sighed. "I really can't believe he never took you to the ocean in all that time."

"It's true," Tsunami said. "*And* he never taught me Aquatic. I wish I had all the Talons of Peace here so I could *bite* them."

"To be fair, the Talons were just keeping us safe," Sunny interjected. "They needed us to survive to fulfill the prophecy."

Tsunami snorted, and Sunny gave her an injured look.

"But the prophecy," Riptide said. He pointed at Glory. "It calls for a SkyWing. She's not a SkyWing."

"It's a little complicated," Tsunami said as a hint of sea green rippled across Glory's scales. "Anyway, I'm not sure we really care about the prophecy. But we do care about finding the families we were stolen from."

"I care about the prophecy!" Sunny protested. She poked Clay's side, and he nodded agreeably.

Starflight cleared his throat, but Tsunami hurried on before he could start lecturing again. *His* egg hadn't been stolen; the NightWings had handed it right over. So maybe he didn't care about getting home, but she certainly did.

"Only a few days ago, I found out I was stolen from the Royal Hatchery," Tsunami said. "So . . . so I thought maybe my parents were looking for me. Like in *The Missing Princess*? Do you know that scroll?"

Riptide definitely squashed a smile this time. "I do," he said. "It's required reading in school."

"School," Starflight said in the wistful tones Clay used to talk about food.

"Required reading?" Tsunami echoed. That was odd. It was a fairy tale, not a historical document. And not, perhaps, the best-written scroll she'd ever read, although it was still one of her favorites because of the story.

"But I can't take you to the palace," Riptide said firmly. "Not with him along." He jerked his head at Clay.

"Weren't you listening?" Tsunami said, exasperated. "He's not a regular MudWing. He's certainly not allied with Burn or the SkyWings. You can trust him."

"Perhaps you should stay here," Riptide suggested, "and I'll bring Queen Coral back to you." He glanced across the water at the other island, where he'd met the green dragon with the black spiral patterns. Tsunami wondered if he was wishing for reinforcements.

"Nope," she said. "We're all coming with you."

"I'm in enough trouble with Queen Coral," Riptide protested. "That's why I'm stuck patrolling all the way out here. If I bring a MudWing back to the palace, I might as well pull out my own teeth."

"Ew!" Sunny cried. "That's not a real punishment, is it?"

Tsunami didn't want to know the answer to that. She wanted to meet her mother without images of horrible things in her head. "Think of it this way," she said quickly. "What happens if Queen Coral finds out you met her missing daughter and *didn't* bring her back to the palace?"

Riptide squirmed and wrinkled his snout. "Can't I bring you and leave the others?" he asked. "At least until Queen Coral gives her permission?"

"No," she said stoutly. "We all go together. She'll understand once she realizes we're the dragonets of destiny."

Riptide sighed. "All right, but he has to be blindfolded." He looked at the other three, rubbing his chin. "It'd be better if they could all be blindfolded."

"What am *I* going to do?" Glory asked. "Round up some scary RainWings to come sleep on your roof? I thought no one was afraid of my tribe."

"We're not," Riptide objected. "Afraid of RainWings. Pffft. What a thing to say."

More streaks of pale green appeared along Glory's scales and then faded away. "Wonderful," she said. "So no blindfold for me, then." She tossed her head and turned back to the ocean.

Riptide looked doubtfully at Starflight and Sunny.

"The NightWings know everything," Starflight said loftily. "It's no use trying to keep secrets from them. I mean, us. I could just use my powers to figure out where your palace is."

Tsunami rolled her eyes. Starflight had no powers whatsoever, as far as any of the dragonets knew. But if he wanted the SeaWings to think he did, maybe that could be useful eventually.

"Please don't argue with him," Tsunami said to Riptide. "Once he starts yammering on about how amazing NightWings are, we'll never get him to shut up."

Starflight ruffled his wings in outrage. Riptide muttered something under his breath and started poking around in the shallow water below the rocks.

"You can blindfold me," Sunny offered. "I don't mind."

"If you do that, she can ride on my back," Tsunami suggested. She missed having the little SandWing come lean against her trustingly. Sunny was still acting jumpy and nervous around her, four whole *days* after her fight with the SkyWing soldier, as if Tsunami might suddenly attack someone out of nowhere, for no reason.

"Or my back," Starflight jumped in quickly. Tsunami frowned at him. Why was he trying so hard to take her place?

"You think you're strong enough?" she challenged.

"Sure he is," Sunny said. "I'll ride with him, and you can lead Clay."

Well, fine, then, Tsunami thought. *I guess everyone's giving the orders now.*

Riptide came stomping back with several long strands of thick black seaweed. Sunny immediately looked like she was regretting her offer. But she let the big SeaWing wrap the seaweed tightly around her head, covering her closed eyes.

"Ew," she said, shivering. "It's all wet and slimy."

"I like wet and slimy," Clay said, ducking his head to make it easier for Riptide to blindfold him.

"That's weird, Clay," said Glory.

Riptide's attention was focused on plastering seaweed all over Clay's broad head. When he was done, it looked more like an octopus trying to eat Clay's brain than a blindfold. But of course, Clay didn't complain. He never complained about anything except being hungry. It was one of the things Tsunami loved about him.

Tsunami helped Sunny climb awkwardly onto Starflight's back, balancing in the narrow space between his wings. The SandWing was small, but Starflight wasn't as burly as Tsunami or Clay.

"If you can't handle it, tell me and I'll take her," Tsunami said to him.

Starflight nodded, breathing deeply. His wings curled in, and he shivered as Sunny lay down, rested her head on his neck, and clasped her forearms trustingly around his shoulders.

Tsunami turned to Clay and brushed one of his wing tips with hers.

"Can you feel that?" she asked. "If I do that in the air, can you stay with me?"

"I think so," Clay said doubtfully.

"I'll fly on your other side," Glory said, hopping down from her rock. She reached up and nudged his other wing. "That way we can steer you together."

Clay shook his head a little and a loose flap of seaweed went *glop flop* against his neck. "This is really strange," he said. "It's as dark as the underground river. Only with breathing, so, better. I'm in favor of breathing. Definitely better than not breathing."

"Just don't go too fast. And listen to me," Tsunami ordered.

"To *us*," Glory chimed in. "And we promise not to drown you." She gave Tsunami an arch look.

If I do decide to drown somebody, I know who's at the top of my list, Tsunami thought, shooting a glare back at her. "All right, let's go," she said to Riptide.

The sky-blue SeaWing waved his talons in front of Clay's face to make sure there was no reaction. Finally he sprang into the sky with the dragonets close behind him.

Tsunami forgot to be mad at Glory and Starflight as they flew over the bay. Green-and-white islands glowed like scattered jewels in the ocean below them. Several of them were shaped like claws, curving neatly through the water. From up by the clouds, she could see part of the spiral pattern in the archipelago. And when they swooped down close to the sea, she saw pearlescent pink dolphins leaping in the clear water.

Glory told Clay about the dolphins, and his head went up hopefully. "Can we eat them?" he asked.

"No," Riptide called back over his shoulder. "Queen Coral has forbidden it. She thinks they might be distantly related to us."

Tsunami glanced down at the sleek darting shapes. Related to dragons? What a bizarre idea. It didn't really fit with how she'd imagined her mother.

Well, I can stop imagining soon, she thought.

She had no idea how the SeaWings had managed to hide a palace on one of these islands. From the air, it seemed like you could see everything — the white sand below the azure waters around the islands, every hole in the twisting rock formations, every palm tree and cormorant nest and scraggly bush on every cliff. There were a lot of small islands, but surely the enemy had searched every one by now, after eighteen years of war.

"Here comes our welcoming committee," Riptide said, just loud enough for Tsunami to hear.

She spotted a formation of blue and green dragons flying toward them — fifteen or more, with huge wings and bared teeth. She could hear them hissing from a distance.

"Uh-oh," Riptide muttered.

"Clay, stop and hover," Tsunami instructed. He paused in the air, with Glory close beside him.

"What's happening?" Sunny asked, lifting her head from Starflight's shoulder as they caught up. Starflight, for once, didn't say anything. His jaw was set, and it looked like he was using all his energy to stay aloft with Sunny.

"The advance guard," Riptide said. He swung in a slow circle around the group and stopped in front again, facing the incoming dragons. "They make sure no one even gets close to the Summer Palace."

A few moments later, they were surrounded. The flapping wingbeats filled their ears and pushed the air currents around.

"Rrrriptide," growled the dragon in the lead. His scales were a green so dull it was almost gray, like stone where moss had been scraped away. He had tiny bone-pale eyes that never seemed to blink under a knobbly protruding forehead, and his horns twisted strangely toward each other. Tsunami noticed that, unlike Riptide, the new dragon had no battle scars. Which either meant he stayed away from the fighting — or he was a very skilled fighter.

"What are you dragging home now?" he snarled.

Riptide looked him straight in the eyes. "I've found the missing princess."

That's not how I would have put it, Tsunami thought. *I was the one doing all the finding out there.*

A ripple of shock went through the other SeaWings. Tsunami's scales felt like insects were crawling under them as the guards all stared at her. She lifted her snout and tried to look regal and imposing.

"Oh, really?" said the leader. "You, Riptide? Of all dragons? What an unusual coincidence." His unsettling eyes scanned Tsunami from wing tips to claws, as if she were a dead eel someone had left half-eaten on the beach. Tsunami wanted to shred the skeptical, arrogant look right off his face.

"And who are you?" Tsunami demanded.

Riptide winced. "This is Shark," he said. "Commander of palace defense and brother to the queen."

"Oh, *really,*" Tsunami said, deliberately making her tone even more insolent and challenging than Shark's. She was not about to start her life with the SeaWings by kowtowing to every soldier dragon who came along. Even if he was her uncle.

Shark narrowed his eyes until they nearly disappeared into his scales. "What makes you believe this snip of a dragon comes from the stolen royal egg?" he asked Riptide.

"Why, do you lose a lot of eggs?" Tsunami jumped in. "Maybe whoever's in charge of defense isn't doing such a good job, then. Oh, wait, that's you, isn't it?"

"Her story makes sense," Riptide said desperately. "She knew about — about Webs. He raised her. And look at the glow patterns under her wings."

All of the SeaWings craned their necks to stare at Tsunami's wings. She snapped at a couple who got too close, then peered around to see what they were seeing.

Under her wings, when she lit them up, the luminescent stripes formed spirals around the outer edges. Starbursts shaped like webbed dragon footprints branched away from the lines in the middle. Was that weird? She glanced at the other SeaWings. Most of them had smaller starbursts and no spirals. Only Shark's patterns matched her own.

Because we're both royal. She lifted her head and met his gaze triumphantly. *But one day I shall be queen, and you will always be nothing but a soldier.*

Shark let out a long hissing breath. "Very well," he said. "Kill the other four and bring her."

CHAPTER 6

"Don't you touch them!" Tsunami yelled. She whirled and smacked a SeaWing out of the sky as he reached for Clay. Starflight had already ducked below Clay's massive wings. Glory drew her neck back and bared her fangs.

"I am the queen's daughter, and I order you to leave these dragonets alone," Tsunami shouted.

The guards looked from her to Shark uncertainly. His eyes were pale reflecting pools, hiding his thoughts. He slowly raised one talon and made a strange circling motion with it — a sign in the SeaWing language, Tsunami guessed. Whatever it was, it worked. To Tsunami's relief, the guards backed away.

But when she glanced at Riptide, she noticed that he still looked tense and unhappy. *Maybe he's just afraid of Shark,* she thought.

"Very good," she said, trying to sound like she was in command. "Now take us to my mother."

"The queen is conducting business at the Deep Palace," Shark said flatly. "We will take you to the Summer Palace, where you may wait for her." He made another talon signal, and two of the guards broke away from the group, winging off across the water. *Taking the message to my mother,* Tsunami thought, her wings expanding with joy. They were so close to everything she'd always imagined. *I'm going to meet my parents today.*

Islands flashed by below them as they flew on, now with a tight guard of SeaWings. Some of the islands were small patches of sand, barely big enough for one dragon to land on, and others were towering, jagged rocks shooting out of the water. Ahead, Tsunami saw one that looked like a huge dragon skeleton, with holes and gaps all through the pale stone.

The stone skeleton's nose pointed toward another island, this one ringed with forbidding-looking rocks and presenting only a high, sheer cliff face on all sides. The top was a rioting jungle. Thick green vines and trees pressed so close together that there was not a single spot clear enough to land on.

Tsunami was startled when Shark suddenly swerved and dove toward the base of the cliff. He splashed down between two spiraling rocks, sharp and evenly matched like dragon horns, and vanished into the azure water.

She blinked. Where had he gone? The water was so clear here that she could see fat black turtles strolling across the sand at the bottom of the sea.

But then, one by one, half the guards around them dove for the same spot, and each of them disappeared the same way — gone before the bubbles of their splash had cleared.

"Clay, stop," she said, brushing his wing. "Riptide?"

"It's the entrance to the Summer Palace," Riptide said. "There's no other way in. You'll all have to swim."

Sunny let out a small, unhappy noise. "How far?" she asked Riptide.

"You only have to stay underwater for short swims," he answered. "It has been redesigned so Queen Blister in particular can visit."

"And she hates water," Sunny said hopefully, "since she's a SandWing, too."

"Is she, uh — is she here now?" Starflight asked.

Riptide shook his head. "She is not fond of swimming, and even after all the changes we've made, she rarely visits."

Tsunami was secretly a bit relieved to hear that. After meeting Burn, she wasn't looking forward to encountering the other two rival SandWing sisters. What if they were all equally dangerous and crazy and controlling?

But eventually the dragonets would have to choose one of the three to win the war. To be fair, Tsunami thought they probably needed to meet both Blister and Blaze.

Then again, if Tsunami's mother liked Blister — enough to alter her palace to accommodate her — surely that was a sign in Blister's favor, wasn't it? Maybe they didn't have to meet Blaze. Maybe supporting the SeaWings and Blister would be the obvious right thing to do.

"Stay close behind me," Riptide said. "I'll light up my stripes so you can follow, and I'll flash them to signal you to surface at the breathing spots."

"Um," Clay said. "So . . . about this blindfold, uh . . . any chance —"

"Once we're in the tunnel," Riptide answered. He turned and dove for the dragon-horn rocks.

Tsunami flipped her tail into Clay's front talons and dove after Riptide, towing Clay behind her. Her scales tingled with excitement.

"Deep breath, Clay," she called.

She was not far behind Riptide when he dove into the water, but even so, she nearly lost him in the fizz of bubbles that swarmed up in her face as she splashed down. She blinked frantically, searching for a hole or a tunnel entrance.

Long, sun-colored tendrils of kelp grew up from the sandy floor, glowing an orange gold in the light filtering down from above. They were clustered around the base of the cliff, waving like a forest of octopus arms as tall as the five dragonets laid end to end.

The hole in the cliff must be hidden by the tendrils, but where?

Then Tsunami saw Riptide's glowing tail knocking the golden kelp curtain aside, and she plunged after him. It was hard to swim as fast as she wanted to with Clay clinging to her tail. She could feel him trying to beat his wings and kick helpfully, but he kept accidentally whacking into underwater boulders and slowing her down.

She poked her head into the forest and felt the tendrils of kelp slide and slither around her snout. Up close she could see little clear globules growing on them. These were surprisingly sticky, while the rest of the tendril was slippery smooth. It felt like gigantic golden inchworms were swarming around her.

She had to swim through a thick patch, following the glimmer of Riptide's lit-up tail, before reaching the cliff wall. Suddenly the tendrils slithered away and popped her out into a dark underwater tunnel.

Not entirely dark — Riptide was directly in front of her, his luminescent stripes all glowing. He reached around her, guided Clay into the tunnel, and unwrapped the seaweed blindfold. Clay blinked and rubbed his talons against his eyes, then immediately turned back toward the faint sunlight, searching for the others.

Glory came through next, her snout wrinkling as she pushed tendrils off her wings. Tsunami noticed that her scales had ripples of the orange-gold color crisscrossing the silver that had been there before. She wondered if Glory had done that deliberately or if her scales automatically tried to match their environment when she was stressed.

After a long pause, Starflight burst through after her. His face was puffed up like he was about to explode and, on his back, Sunny was shivering violently.

Riptide flashed the lights in his tail and shot upward, aiming for a hole in the tunnel roof not far inside the entrance. Tsunami was expecting more of a swim and was surprised when her head almost immediately popped out into air.

It wasn't much air — a tiny cavern, barely lit by a far-away gleam of sunlight up a long narrow chimney. The dragons' bodies were still in the watery tunnel below. There was only enough room in the cavern for their heads, all gathered closely in the pool. Tsunami could see right away that there was nowhere to climb out. This was a place to stop and breathe, nothing more.

Sunny and Starflight both gasped for air like they hadn't breathed in months. Clay fumbled in the dark to pat Sunny's head and pulled her blindfold off as well.

"Good thing this breathing hole is here," Clay remarked to Riptide. "So close to the entrance, I mean."

Riptide inclined his head in a sort of nod. "Queen Blister insisted on it."

Tsunami felt the whoosh of several SeaWing guards swimming past below them. She knew there would be a few of them bringing up the rear, making sure none of the dragonets ran off to spread the news of the Summer Palace's secret location.

She couldn't keep her wings still. They thrummed like trapped dragonflies, wanting to spring loose. She was *so close*. This was her palace! Her dragons were only a few wingbeats away! After six years of imagining what this would be like, she didn't think she could stand another minute of waiting.

"Let's go, let's go," she said, splashing the others enthusiastically with her tail.

"Good grief," Glory said with a shake. "It's like you've been possessed by Sunny or something."

"Come *on*, we're almost there." Tsunami flashed her stripes happily, and the other dragonets covered their eyes.

"I can swim from here," Sunny said to Starflight. "Or I'll hold on to Clay if you all go too fast."

Starflight looked disappointed and relieved at the same time.

Riptide sank below the surface, and Tsunami ducked after him, too excited to wait for the others.

Now it was easy to follow Riptide's glowing scales. The tunnel twisted up and down and around corners, with frequent stops like the first for breathing. Too frequent, if you asked Tsunami; each one made her want to bang her head into the cliff walls. She lost count after the fourth stop, but there had to be at least ten. How long was this tunnel?

Then suddenly, finally, there was light ahead — real light, not glowing scales. A moment later they swam out of the tunnel into an open lake, lifted their heads above the water, and breathed in deeply. Green-tinted sunlight dazzled their eyes at first, but as her vision cleared, Tsunami saw dragons.

Over a hundred blue and green dragons surrounded them, all of them staring expectantly at Tsunami.

Her tribe. Her dragons. Her future subjects.

They had reached the Summer Palace of the SeaWings, in the heart of the Kingdom of the Sea.

Ice Kingdom

Sky Kingdom

Burn's
Stronghold

Under the Mountain

Kingdom of
Sand

Scorpion Den

Jade Mountain

PART TWO

INTO THE DEEP

— CHAPTER 7 —

Overwhelmed, Tsunami spread her wings to float on the water and gazed around.

They were inside the island, surrounded by towering cliffs on all sides. Far above them, sunlight filtered through a thick green canopy — the vines and treetops she'd seen from the sky, woven so thickly it looked like a jungle from above. Like an emerald umbrella over the island, the canopy protected the Summer Palace from view and gave the light a sea-green quality that made Tsunami feel like she was still underwater.

Waterfalls cascaded down from several holes in the cliffs, like slender dragon tails of silver, bursting into spray as they hit the lake. The only exit Tsunami could see was the tunnel behind her.

Four pillars of blue-tinted white stone spiraled out of the water, winding toward one another until they formed a towering pavilion in the middle of the lake. The pavilion had twelve circular levels, each one smaller than the one below. There were few walls, most of them very low, and the whole structure was latticed with curving shapes and holes and little wading pools. It didn't look like it had been built; it looked as if it had grown that way, although Tsunami was pretty sure that was impossible.

Dragons were clustered along the edges of the pavilion, on ledges of the cliffs, and all across the water. She'd never seen so many faces like her own, dark blues and pale greens and sharp see-in-the-dark eyes staring.

The only sound was the splashing of the waterfalls, the soft hush of dragons breathing, and the quiet lapping of waves on the beaches around the lake.

After a moment, Starflight spotted the nearest stretch of sand and set off for it in a frantic paddle that sounded horribly loud in the silence. Sunny and Clay and Glory followed him.

Tsunami stayed where she was, ignoring the tiredness that was flooding her scales. She wanted to make a good impression on the dragons of her kingdom. Many of them were floating on the water, like she was, but many more were perched in cave openings all along the cliff or on rocks that jutted out of the water, while others lined the shallow beaches. Tsunami wondered what they'd all been doing before she appeared to capture their attention.

She spotted Shark hunched on one of the spirals of the closest pillar. She rather thought he should have given some sort of welcome speech, but he only stared at her with his pale, unblinking little eyes.

In the story, the royal parents had swept forward with a parade and a whole orchestra to welcome back their missing princess. But her parents weren't here yet, and now that she thought about it, dolphins playing harps would probably be a bit silly looking.

Well, she was a future queen, and she wasn't going to be intimidated by crowds of staring dragons. She shook her head and lifted her neck out of the water.

"Hello, fellow SeaWings," she called, and then paused as her voice echoed off the rocks, much louder than she'd expected. "I'm Tsunami, and, um — I'm very happy to be home at last, and — and I look forward to meeting each of you."

Three moons, was that the most awful speech in the history of Pyrrhia? What were all these still, silent faces thinking? Could the dragons see Tsunami's natural royalty? Were they excited that she'd be their queen one day?

She remembered her royal stripe patterns and lifted her wings out of the water so everyone could see them. To be sure they were visible, she lit them up, and then, with a sinking feeling, remembered what she'd accidentally said to Riptide. She really, really hoped she hadn't just told her entire kingdom that they had delicious fish breath or something.

A murmur ran around the gathered dragons, but she couldn't tell if it was good murmuring or bad murmuring. She turned to Riptide, who was watching Shark with a grim expression.

"I think you should take me somewhere I can wait for my mother," Tsunami suggested in a low voice — or she thought it was low, but the echoes still skipped back to her across the water. And now there was more murmuring. Tsunami wished she had NightWing powers so she could hear the dragons' thoughts.

"Up there," said Riptide, nodding to the top of the pavilion. He glanced at Shark again. "You should bring your friends."

The other dragonets were sprawled on the white pebbles of the beach, in front of a tall cave opening lined with sand. They had their wings spread out and were gasping in a rather undignified way. All except for Glory, who was sitting neatly by the cave, peering in. Her silver scales were now mottled with azure blue. Any SeaWings who weren't staring at Tsunami were staring at her.

Tsunami thwacked the water with her tail to get their attention. When Clay finally looked over, she pointed to the pavilion. He nodded, and she lifted into the air. Her wings felt heavy out of the water, and it took a few beats to get her balance. She wished the SeaWings would go back to whatever they were supposed to be doing.

Riptide flew up beside her. He looked uncomfortable with all the scrutiny as well.

"Tell me about the Summer Palace," Tsunami said, trying to distract herself.

He flicked his tail at the cliffs. "Guest rooms are in the caves. Queen Blister usually stays in the one closest to the tunnel. We brought in extra sand to line the floor for her, and it's the only cave where fire is allowed." His snout turned toward the pavilion as they flew higher. "She meets with Queen Coral on the second level from the top, which is only for visiting royalty. Each level has a different purpose — for instance, there's a floor for dragonet school visits, one for celebration spectacles, and one for war planning. When they are here instead of the Deep Palace, the Council meets on this level, halfway up."

He paused, beating his wings, so Tsunami could look across the middle level. Twelve dragon-sized pools were arranged in a circle with small channels running from one to the next and crisscrossing the center. Glittering emeralds the size of fish eggs, which were embedded in the stone, spelled out words by each pool. Tsunami saw one marked TREASURY, one labeled DEFENSE, and another that said SECRETS & SPIES. Before she could read any further, Riptide turned to fly higher.

"Council?" Tsunami said, catching up to him.

"They prefer the Deep Palace, as does the queen," Riptide said. "Only Shark and Lagoon are here at the moment."

Tsunami had no idea what he was talking about, but she didn't want to reveal how ignorant she was of SeaWing politics. She wondered if there was anything about a council in Starflight's favorite scrolls.

"So which level is for missing princesses?" she joked.

"I think the top pavilion would be best," Riptide said. "That's for new visitors, and we hardly ever have any of those. Queen Blister was probably the last — oh, no, it was that NightWing." He landed gracefully on the uppermost ledge of the pavilion, his claws catching on polished ridges in the bluish-white stone.

"What NightWing?" Tsunami asked, landing beside him. This level was bigger than she'd expected. A spiraling starburst of webbed talon-print shapes was carved into the floor and filled with glittering water, lined all along the bottom with tiny pearls. Tsunami realized the pattern was the same as the one on her wings.

"I don't know," Riptide answered her. "He only spoke with Her Majesty and Queen Blister, and all I heard was that he wanted to fly out through the canopy instead of the tunnel — but of course they wouldn't let him do that. He looked big and bad-tempered."

"Sounds like Morrowseer," Tsunami muttered, although she didn't exactly have a lot of other NightWings to compare him to. But he seemed more meddlesome than the rest of them. While most of the tribe hid in their secret location, being all mysterious and unhelpfully powerful, Morrowseer kept turning up . . . delivering the dragonet prophecy, inspecting the dragonets, trying to get Glory killed, saving Starflight (but no one else) from the SkyWings, then giving him back once everyone had escaped. Tsunami could easily imagine him poking around here, although she couldn't guess why.

Riptide glanced down at the dragons below, including Shark, who hadn't moved from his spot on the pillar. "I can't believe you spoke to Shark like that," he whispered. "I've never seen *anyone* talk back to him, apart from the queen and Queen Blister."

"He deserved it," Tsunami said, settling her wings. "Arrogant blowfish-head. When I'm queen, I'll make him go sit in a lagoon and grow seaweed."

Riptide coughed hard to cover a laugh. "Don't *talk* like that!" he whispered. "Don't you know the difference between brave and reckless? Shark will eat you and your friends for lunch if he thinks you're a threat to him."

"Pfft," Tsunami said. "He can try." She shoved away the creepy memory of Shark's unblinking, malicious eyes.

"By the moons, you make me nervous," Riptide said.

One end of the top floor was raised and carved into a magnificent dragon throne, studded with emeralds and sapphires and shot through with gold lines in the shape of waves. Beside and below the throne was another, smaller throne carved to match, with the same patterns made of tinier gemstones.

Tsunami tilted her head at the second throne. It looked too small to be for a king. So was this for her? Had Queen

Coral prepared a throne for her missing daughter, waiting all these years for her to come fill it?

She took a step toward it, her heart pounding with excitement. A throne of her own! Already!

The arrival of her friends stopped her, as the four dragonets crashed down around the ledge. Sunny landed lightly, avoiding the channels of water, but Clay somehow stumbled as his claws hit the stone and nearly somersaulted right off the other side. Glory darted in his way and pushed him back, then made another loop around and landed close to the throne. Her green eyes studied it closely; she looked almost ready to climb onto it herself.

Starflight arrived last, catching on to the side and pitching forward as if his wings had barely been strong enough to carry him. He lay there like a woeful black puddle for a moment, taking deep breaths. Sunny hopped over a watery footprint to nudge his wing gently.

Tsunami managed not to roll her eyes, but really. Couldn't everyone at least *try* to act a *little* more impressive?

"This is a really big thing!" Clay said to her and Riptide. His tail accidentally splashed Glory, but she was too busy looking at the throne to snap at him. "I mean, this thing we're standing on. What do you call it? It's really tall — taller than our prisons in the Sky Kingdom, I think." He peered over the edge, missing Riptide's sharp look. Tsunami realized they hadn't told him about being captured by Queen Scarlet and the SkyWings.

"I like it," Clay went on, sitting down and splashing Glory again. "Of course, it's much nicer to be this high when your wings are free. But at least the SkyWings gave us a pig sometimes. Do you have pigs? Octopi would be all right instead if you don't. Or squid. Or manatees. I could go for a manatee right now. Or a whale. I'm not fussy, is what I'm saying. Say, how did you make this big thing? Did it take forever to build?"

Riptide blinked for a moment, following Clay's train of thought. "The pavilion? An animus SeaWing designed it, many generations ago, and magicked the stone to grow this way," Riptide said. "Even so, it took nearly ten years to reach this form."

"Wow," said Clay, and Tsunami couldn't help being impressed, too. She hadn't realized animus dragons had that kind of power. In their lessons, Webs had told them animus dragons could enchant chess pieces to play themselves. Sometimes they left curses on their jewels to poison anyone who tried to steal them. But making a whole pavilion grow from stone — that seemed like strong magic, more powerful than anything the NightWings could do.

Starflight was clearly thinking the same thing, judging from his disgruntled snout. Tsunami hurriedly interrupted before he could begin a lecture.

"This top level is where Queen Coral meets new visitors, like us," she said importantly to her friends. "So when she arrives, everyone *please* act like dragonets of destiny instead of half-drowned seagulls, for goodness' sake."

Sunny looked wounded, and Starflight sniffed loudly while Glory turned up her snout like she wasn't taking any orders from Tsunami. Clay poked his nose over the edge and blinked at the lower pavilion tiers.

"Which level is the feasting on?" he asked. "You do have feasting, right?" His wide brown eyes turned to Riptide. "No reason. Just wondering."

"Sure, sometimes we have feasts," Riptide said. "Especially when Queen Blister is —"

A commotion from below interrupted him. Tsunami sprang to the edge and gazed down at the lake.

A huge blue SeaWing, exactly the color of Tsunami's scales, burst out of the tunnel. Vines of pearls were woven around her horns and neck and wings, and a twisted white horn with a wicked-looking point was attached to the end of her tail. She had odd black stains on her claws, but she was the most beautiful sight Tsunami had ever seen.

All over the palace, dragons were folding down into low bows.

This had to be her mother — queen of the SeaWings. Tsunami reached to grab Riptide's forearm, feeling dizzy with joy.

But as Queen Coral shot out of the water, Tsunami saw that she wore a thin, webbed harness with a long cord . . . which led to a harness on another dragon, flying close behind her.

The second dragon was much smaller — a dragonet only about a year old, perhaps. She flapped her wings frantically, trying to keep up. With a jolt of shock, Tsunami spotted the royal pattern of stripes on the underside of her wings.

"Who is that?" she hissed at Riptide. He was backing away to the edge of the floor, the farthest spot from the throne.

"That's Anemone," he said, blinking in surprise. "Your sister."

— CHAPTER 8 —

An enemy.

Anemone.

An enemy.

It took Tsunami a few moments to realize what Riptide had actually said. Her skin prickled, hearing *an enemy, an enemy*, until it sank in that he'd been saying a name.

Anemone. Tsunami's sister. Another heir to the throne.

So much for being special. So much for her guaranteed future kingdom.

"Uh-oh," Glory said, echoing her thoughts. "Looks like you've got some competition. Maybe you're not destined to be queen after all."

Tsunami whirled toward Starflight, her gills flaring. "You said I was the only one," she cried. "You said none of the others survived."

"That's what I read," he protested. He spread his black claws. "Blame the Talons, not me. Our scrolls were often old and outdated. *The Royal Lineage of the SeaWings, from the*

Scorching to the Present must have been written before this one was hatched." He nodded at the little dragon flapping behind the queen.

Anemone was a pale, pale blue, almost white like an IceWing, with hints of pink along her wings and ears and horns. She looked a little bit like the dolphins they'd seen earlier, and Tsunami wondered grumpily if that was really why Queen Coral had forbidden SeaWings to eat them — in case one of them ate Anemone by mistake. Anemone's eyes were large and blue, and tiny strands of pearls were woven around her neck and tail as if to match her mother's.

That could have been me, Tsunami thought. *I could have been the one with matching pearls and a matching throne and a mother who loved me, if the Talons hadn't stolen me from my home.*

She didn't have a chance to notice anything else, because suddenly Queen Coral was landing and running toward her.

"My baby!" Coral cried. Enormous blue wings whooshed around Tsunami, enveloping her in a hug that smelled of sea air and starfish. Pearls pressed into Tsunami's face as Coral cuddled her close. Her wet scales were warm and her talons were gentle as she stroked Tsunami's head and back and wings.

"I knew you'd come back to me," she said. "I knew you were out there, trying to find your way back. I never stopped searching for you."

It was exactly what Tsunami had always wanted to hear.

Actually it was word-for-word what the queen said in *The Missing Princess*, but Tsunami shoved that thought aside.

She leaned into her mother, feeling elation flood her from horns to claws. *Someone* does *want me. I have a place in the world.*

"*Mother*," whined a tiny voice from behind them. "*Ow.* That was too fast. I think I hurt my claws."

Queen Coral let go of Tsunami, whirled around, and tugged Anemone closer with the harness cord. The little dragonet crept under her wing and held out her front talons with a pitiful expression.

"I'm sorry, sweetheart," Coral said, carefully examining Anemone's claws and then giving them a quick lick with her forked tongue. "Is that better?"

"I guess," Anemone said, flexing her talons mournfully.

"Look, darling, it's your sister. The one I told you about, who was stolen six years ago." Coral reached out and slid one webbed talon over Tsunami's snout. "Isn't she gorgeous?"

Anemone blinked at Tsunami. She was really tiny, no taller than a scavenger, and she didn't look very strong. *Maybe I don't have to worry about her,* Tsunami thought. *She'd be easy to defeat, and obviously I'd make a better queen.*

Then she felt a stab of guilt for thinking about something like that on her first meeting with her real family. She held out one of her front talons to Anemone, and after a small pause, Anemone pressed her own talon against it.

"Hi," Tsunami said. "I'm Tsunami."

"Ah," Queen Coral said. "A good name. Webs did one thing right." Her green eyes narrowed. "Where is he now? I have been planning his punishment for years." She glared over Tsunami's shoulder, but when Tsunami looked around, the only dragon there was Riptide. He had his head ducked and his wings folded as low as he could get.

"I knew he was a coward and a deserter," Coral said, "but after he returned to steal my egg . . . well, let's just say it won't be a quick death."

"Oh, no," Sunny squeaked. "Please don't hurt him. He was the only one who was really nice to us."

"We don't know where he is anyway," Tsunami said as Queen Coral turned to stare at Sunny. "He escaped when —"

"What are *you*?" Coral asked Sunny. Her gaze fell on the other dragonets, and her tail lashed dangerously. "WHY IS THERE A MUDWING IN MY SUMMER PALACE?" She took a step toward Clay, gills flaring.

"These are my friends," Tsunami cried, leaping in front of Clay. "You can trust them, I promise. We were all stolen from our homes as eggs. We're the dragonets of destiny, from the prophecy."

"Ha," muttered a voice, and Tsunami realized that Shark was now perched on the rim of the ledge along with nine other very large dragons.

"Oh," Queen Coral said slowly. "Oh, I see." She studied Clay suspiciously, then turned her gaze to Starflight, Sunny, and Glory. "Yes, that was the rumor. If you believe in things like prophecies, of course. Dragonets of destiny. Well, Queen Blister will be so interested to meet you. We'd better make sure you don't go anywhere." She flashed the royal patterns along her wings and clapped her front talons together. Seven burly SeaWings rose up behind the dragonets, claws twitching ominously.

"Put these four in Blister's cave," Queen Coral commanded, "and set a guard so they stay there."

"What?" Sunny cried. "But we came here to be safe! Not to be prisoners again!" She squeaked in terror as one guard snatched her into the air. Starflight stared after her, frozen in place with his claws half outstretched.

"Nobody touches me," Glory snarled at the SeaWing who was reaching for her. Black clouds billowed up in her scales.

"Don't hurt Sun — ow," Clay yelped as three SeaWings landed on him at once, pinning him down. "Ouch! Ow!" One began lashing woven seaweed ropes around his wings and claws and snout.

"Wait," Tsunami said. She clasped her talons pleadingly. "Your Majesty . . . Mother." The word felt so odd on her tongue, even though she'd imagined saying it a million times. "You don't have to do this. They're my friends, and I brought them here so you could protect us. I swear they're trustworthy."

"It's for their own safety, too, dear," Coral said, stroking Tsunami's head again. "We won't hurt them, of course. You've come to the right place for protection. But they shouldn't wander the palace unsupervised — most of my dragons will attack MudWings and unfamiliar SandWings on sight."

"Or whatever that is," Shark muttered, sniffing at Sunny. Starflight shot him a glare, then looked away quickly as the SeaWing turned his gaze to him.

"I guess this means no feast?" Clay said mournfully. He rested his snout on the stone with a sigh.

"Food can certainly be arranged," said the queen. "Lagoon, make sure our guests are well fed." A plump turquoise dragon bowed and dove off the ledge. "See, darling, we'll take good care of you all. Please tell that one to stop looking so fierce." Coral flicked a claw at Glory, who was still facing off with a nervous-looking SeaWing guard.

Tsunami thought, uncomfortably, of Glory's secret weapon. In the SkyWing palace, they'd discovered Glory could spit a deadly venom, which seemed to be a RainWing skill most dragons didn't know about. It certainly hadn't been in any of the scrolls, which rarely mentioned RainWings at all.

But Tsunami hoped Glory would decide to keep her venom a secret for now. Melting one of the queen's guards probably wasn't the best way to introduce the dragonets of destiny to the SeaWings.

"You don't have to tie them up," Tsunami said. "They'll go with you."

"Speak for yourself," Glory growled.

"Calm down, Glory," Tsunami said. She hoped her mother and the other dragons would see her as the leader of the dragonets. "You heard the queen. It's for your own safety. You'll be fine."

Please don't argue with me in front of my mother, Tsunami prayed.

Glory glared at the SeaWing guard for a moment longer. "All right," she snarled. "I'll go with you. But I still say nobody touches me."

"Fair enough," Queen Coral purred with another gesture and flash of her stripes. "Off you all go, then. Tsunami, darling, come sit with me and let's talk." She swept over to her throne, towing Anemone behind her. The tiny dragonet settled onto the small throne, flicking her pearly wings and watching Tsunami's friends with big eyes.

"It'll be all right," Tsunami said to Clay as the guards hefted him into the air. "I'll come join you very soon." He nodded, still looking rather anxious. Another guard tentatively tried to shoo Starflight off the edge. The NightWing backed away from him unhappily, then turned and flew after the guard who had Sunny.

Tsunami watched her friends spiral down to the cave by the entrance — brown and gold, black and silver, all of them so out of place here. She saw them vanish into the dark hole, and then the guards emerged and planted themselves outside. It didn't look like the way you'd treat guests.

At least it's better than the SkyWing palace, she thought. *At least we're not being forced to fight to the death. My mother is keeping us safe. She's really being welcoming, in her own way.* She glanced up at her mother's warm eyes. *Especially to me.*

Her mother reached out her talons to her, smiling. She was perfect — just what Tsunami had always imagined.

Her friends would be all right, Tsunami was sure. They were in the SeaWing palace now. She was home with her family. This was her lifelong dream.

There's nothing to worry about, she told herself. *Nothing at all.*

CHAPTER 9

"Here," Queen Coral said, taking a strand of pearls off her own horns. "You're so unadorned, my beautiful dragonet. I have to start making up for all the presents I missed giving you." She leaned forward and draped the pearls around Tsunami's neck. They were heavy and smooth, sliding coolly across Tsunami's scales.

My first treasure.

It was a strange thrill, having something of her very own. All dragons loved treasure — it was the only thing they had in common with scavengers. But this was more than a shiny, beautiful thing. It belonged to Tsunami and nobody else. And it made her look even more like her mother.

Tsunami stroked the pearls with her claw and tucked her tail around her back talons. She wished Anemone would stop staring at her. *She must hate me,* she thought. *I would if I were her. She must know I want the throne she thought was hers.*

But not yet. Now was the time for getting to know her mother.

"Can we talk alone?" Tsunami asked. The ten dragons were still perched like creepy sentinels, with Shark the creepiest of all.

"Of course," said the queen. "Council, you are dismissed. Moray, send a message to Queen Blister and see how quickly she can get here. As for you, creature, go back to your guard outpost and stay there until someone actually wants to see you."

Riptide crouched, nodding, and dove over the edge. Tsunami leaned out to watch him swimming into the tunnel.

"What's wrong with Riptide?" she asked as the other ten dragons also flew away in a thunderclap of wingbeats. "I thought he was nice."

"Oh, *no*," Queen Coral said with a shudder. "He can't be trusted. Webs is his father. Their bloodline is tainted with betrayal."

Tsunami felt like a giant wave had just knocked her over. "Webs is his *father*?" But she'd liked Riptide — and all along he was the son of her kidnapper. Which he'd carefully never mentioned. What else hadn't he told her?

"Nasty family," Coral went on. She lashed her tail, nearly hitting Anemone in the head. "Not fitting company for royalty by any means. We keep him as far away from us as possible."

Poor Riptide, Tsunami thought. It wasn't his fault his father had turned traitor, but he suffered for it anyway.

And yet, he *had* hidden the truth from her, and she didn't like that at all.

Was Queen Coral right about him? Surely she knew her own subjects better than Tsunami did.

But there was still a part of Tsunami that hoped she'd see him again.

She glanced at Anemone. "So — we were saying — alone — ?"

"Oh, no, Anemone never leaves my side," Queen Coral said. She reached over and lovingly patted the little dragonet's head. "I finally got a living daughter, and I'm keeping her that way."

"By watching me *every second*," Anemone said. She widened her eyes at Tsunami, who wondered if she'd imagined a hint of sarcasm in her sister's words.

"And now I have two daughters!" Queen Coral said proudly. "Possibly four by the end of next week, if Tortoise does her job right." She gave Tsunami a worried look. "Maybe we should make a harness for you, too, dear."

"Oh, no, that's all right," Tsunami said, eyeing the straps that lashed Coral and Anemone together. "I've managed to take care of myself up to now. I promise I'll stay alive." Much as she already loved her mother, she could not imagine being attached to anyone every moment of every day.

"Hmmm," said the queen. "Well, we'll think about it." She studied Tsunami's shoulders as if she was mentally measuring her for a harness anyway.

"I have to tell you something," Tsunami said, hoping to change the subject. "I — I don't know the underwater language. Webs never taught it to me."

Queen Coral stared at her. "What is wrong with that dragon?" she growled. "It's all right, sweetheart. We'll have Whirlpool teach you — he's a terrific teacher. Right, Anemone?"

Anemone shrugged.

"So what *do* you know?" Queen Coral asked. "Did they teach you anything?"

"Of course!" Tsunami said. She didn't want her mother to think she was unfit to be queen. "We had lots of battle training. And Webs taught us the history of Pyrrhia. We learned all about the Scorching and how the tribes were founded and how we nearly wiped out the scavengers. Um, and he did geography, too. Dune taught us hunting. Kestrel was supposed to teach different tribe strengths and weaknesses, but mostly she just yelled and tried to set us on fire a lot."

Anemone's eyes were bright with interest. "Why don't I get to learn those things, Mother?" she asked.

"You will, dear," said Queen Coral. "When I think you're ready."

"What do you study?" Tsunami asked.

Anemone glanced up at her mother. "How the Council works," she said. "Aquatic, of course. How to interpret battle reports and order our defenses. Managing the food supply and the treasury, although the Council commanders really do all that."

"It's still important to stay on top of them," purred the queen. "Dragons do their best work if you watch them closely the whole time."

"But mostly I'm stuck in training sessions with Whirlpool," Anemone said. Her wings drooped.

"For what?" Tsunami asked. "Aquatic?"

"Never mind, dear," Queen Coral interrupted. "You'll see eventually. Were the Talons of Peace very cruel to you?"

"Terribly!" Tsunami said. This was one of her favorite topics. "They never let us out of the caves at all! They acted like we were brainless snails! Nobody ever listened to me. And they wouldn't tell us anything about our families or where we came from. I only found out about you a few days ago."

"My poor, poor baby," Queen Coral said, stroking Tsunami's head again.

Exactly, Tsunami thought. This was the sympathy she'd always wanted. Although she didn't appreciate the skeptical look on Anemone's face.

"What are these?" Tsunami asked. She leaned forward and touched the dark stains on the queen's talons with one claw. They looked too dark to be bloodstains, but she couldn't guess what else they were.

"The perils of my job!" Queen Coral said with a laugh.

"Well, my hobby. My art, you might call it. I should show you." She sprang to her feet, tugging Anemone up with her. "And then you can meet Whirlpool. You'll adore him. He's just the most wonderful, brilliant young dragon."

Tsunami was nearly certain she caught Anemone rolling her eyes. She followed the two of them down four levels to a floor with low walls and several shapes like large cauldrons molded into the stone. Black and blue webbed talon prints trailed all around the floor, and a raised podium stood at one end with space for an audience of thirty dragons in front.

At the other end was a long gray stone table with a scroll spread out on it, held down at either end by a small seahorse carved of dark brown wood. Tsunami peered at the scroll, which looked only half written.

"That's my work in progress," Queen Coral said proudly. "Whirlpool, come here!" She bustled over to one of the cauldrons, and Tsunami realized they were all packed with neatly rolled scrolls.

"This is beautiful," she said, lifting one of the carved seahorses. They were heavy and intricately detailed, with curiously dragonlike expressions on their tiny faces.

"Orca made those," Queen Coral said sadly. "My first daughter. She was a very talented sculptor."

First daughter? What happened to her? Tsunami hadn't thought any of them lived long enough to become artists. She gave Anemone a quizzical expression, but her sister was watching the queen intently. *I'll ask Starflight later. Orca must be in that lineage scroll he was going on about.*

A dark green dragon with pale green eyes rose up from the Council level. He had a remarkably large gold hoop piercing one ear and dappled, light green scales in wave patterns along his back. He also had the same dark stains on his talons.

"Your Majesty," he said with an elaborate bow. "And Your Smaller Majesties." His voice was oily and slow, like squids creeping into Tsunami's ears. She guessed this was Whirlpool, although he didn't *look* particularly "wonderful" or "brilliant."

He bowed to Anemone and Tsunami as he settled onto the floor behind the stone table. His eyes almost immediately went from them to the scroll in front of him, and he tilted his head thoughtfully. After a moment, he reached forward and dipped one claw into a small pool of black ink in the top corner of the table. With the ink, he scratched a few more words at the point where the scroll went blank.

"Oh," Tsunami said, glancing from his talons to her mother's. "Oh, it's *ink*."

"Yes, dear," said Queen Coral. She pulled an armful of scrolls out of the cauldron. "It's a special formula made of squid ink and a touch of whale blood, so it never fades. Immortality is worth a few claw stains, don't you agree?

Whirlpool invented it. He's terribly clever." She peered at the words he'd written. "Exactly what I was thinking! This is an exciting one, isn't it?"

"Certain to win all the awards in the kingdom, Your Majesty," Whirlpool oozed.

Queen Coral piled four scrolls into Tsunami's talons. "These are my favorites. You can read them all tonight, and tomorrow I'll give you four of my other favorites."

"Read all these tonight?" Tsunami echoed, dismayed. Reading was Starflight's specialty. She liked it fine, but only if there were exciting stories and female warrior dragons. She didn't read very fast, and really she'd rather be fighting something.

"Start with this one," Queen Coral said, plucking one of the scrolls free.

It was *The Missing Princess*! Relief flooded through Tsunami. "I've read that one!" she cried. "That was my favorite story ever."

"Really?" Queen Coral looked delighted, and Tsunami was pretty sure Anemone had rolled her eyes again. "I wrote it for you!"

"You —" Tsunami looked from Queen Coral to Whirlpool and the scroll on the table. "You *wrote The Missing Princess*?"

"I wrote all of these." Queen Coral waved her talons at all the scrolls in the cauldrons. "I'm really quite prolific. Whirlpool makes sure hundreds of copies are instantly made and distributed all over SeaWing territory — and wherever else on Pyrrhia we can send them. My communications herald, Moray, is in charge of the printer dragons who make the underwater copies. She also makes sure they go to all the schools. But Whirlpool organizes my readings here. Isn't he brilliant?" She lowered her voice and winked at Tsunami. "And don't you think he's very handsome?"

Whirlpool looked up and gave Tsunami a toothy smile that didn't reach his eyes. His teeth were weirdly small, and his eyes were too pale and blobby, like frog eyes. Tsunami couldn't help thinking of Riptide, who was much more hand-some, if you asked her — although she knew better than to tell Coral that.

"He'll make a fabulous king one day," Queen Coral added in a loud whisper.

Oh dear. Tsunami hid her shudder. *Is Queen Coral throw-ing him at me?* She glanced at Anemone and saw the little dragonet quickly erasing a hopeful expression from her face. *Hmmm.* She bet Anemone could clear up a lot of mysteries, if Tsunami could get her alone for a moment. Too bad that was impossible.

"Your Majesty." They all turned and found another Council dragon hovering in the air behind the queen, with a smaller dragon beside her. "I'm sorry to interrupt, but Urchin just arrived with strange news. I knew you'd want to hear it right away."

"Of course, Moray," said Queen Coral. "You always know what's best."

Moray's scales were the same dull gray green as Shark's, and her eyes were also small and colorless. Tsunami wondered if they were related. The Council dragon pressed her snout into a brief smug look. "That's because I have had excellent training at the side of the most wonderful queen in Pyrrhian history," she said.

Oh my word, Tsunami thought. This time she was able to catch Anemone's eye, behind the queen's back, to make an "Is she serious?" face. Anemone looked startled for a moment, then made a face back that Tsunami was pretty sure meant "Believe me, it gets worse."

Moray went on. "Apparently a dead dragon has been found only a few islands from the Summer Palace."

"Oh, how sad," said Queen Coral with a little yawn. She glanced at her scrolls as if she wanted to get back to them. "What happened to him?"

"Her," said Moray. "And we don't know yet. But the strange part is that it's not a SeaWing. It's a SkyWing."

"WHAT?" Queen Coral leaped to her talons. "That close to the palace?" She snapped at the air and spread her wings. "Get Shark and Piranha and take me to the body. Now."

The queen shot into the air with Anemone flapping wildly to keep up. Tsunami dropped the scrolls and jumped after them, flying in a tight spiral down to the water. This was her chance to see the queen in action!

She thought she heard someone shout her name as she splashed down. Sunny or Clay? The water rushed into her ears, muffling the cry. They didn't have to worry; she wouldn't be gone long. They'd be safe here.

Shark whipped past, churning up the water as he charged into the tunnel ahead of her. He was between her and Coral now, but Tsunami wasn't going to let that stop her. She swam after them as fast as she could. She felt another dragon close on her tail, but didn't turn around or slow down.

It felt like only moments later when Tsunami's snout emerged into the golden kelp curtain. She followed the eddies left by the dragon tails ahead of her and realized they weren't going to the surface.

So they weren't flying to the body; they were swimming there. Which made sense. They were SeaWings, after all.

All right. I can do this. Tsunami ignored how tired her wings felt and beat them harder, determined to keep up. Even so, the two dragons behind her quickly passed her — Moray and another from the Council, who she guessed was Piranha.

She saw both dragons dip down in the water and suddenly speed up. Despairing, she tried to do the same thing — tipping her wings to dip down to the same level. A fierce current immediately caught her up and shoved her along after them.

For a moment, Tsunami struggled against it. She didn't like being caught by anything stronger than her. But then she realized the other dragons were using it to travel faster, and she'd have to do the same thing if she wanted to stay with them.

Slowly she relaxed and let the current sweep her along. It gave her a chance to look around. A school of black fish with silver speckles shot by overhead, like a flock of crows or NightWings, spinning and whirling in shifting formations. Large translucent mushrooms sprouted from the ocean floor, with tiny orange fish clustered around them.

A pulsing reddish-pink octopus wobbled by, and Tsunami wondered if they were delicious; they were definitely slow enough to catch.

Out of the corner of her eye, she spotted movement behind a swarm of iridescent jellyfish. She squinted and realized it was Riptide, following her from a distance. She lifted one of her wings and waved to him, and after a moment, he sheepishly waved back.

She didn't know what he was *supposed* to be doing, but this probably wasn't it.

Still, she kind of liked having him there, so she wasn't going to tell Coral on him. Not until she decided how mad she was about the "Webs being his father" secret anyway.

They swam for what felt like miles, over wide stretches of algae-covered coral reef that looked like ancient stone ruins: palaces and temples that had collapsed long ago. Occasionally a large greenish-silver fish would dart up, swim alongside Tsunami for a moment, notice her with a start of alarm, and flash away again. She was hungry but too tired to try eating any of them.

Even with the help of the current, Tsunami felt ready to collapse. Finally, up ahead, she saw Moray and Piranha sweep up to the surface. Relieved, she struggled out of the current and followed them into the air.

Queen Coral was already standing on a large, craggy boulder that jutted out of the sea at the base of an enormous cliff. Anemone was crowded onto a tiny outcropping beside her. Not far away, a seal edged nervously into the water, trying not to attract their attention.

Waves pounded the rocks, roaring like angry dragons and spraying salt water over everyone who was clustered around the queen on smaller rocks.

Tsunami found a jagged black rock the right size for her and clambered up. For a moment she just breathed, happy not to be moving. She had no idea how she'd make it back to the Summer Palace. *Deal with that later.* Far off to the north, she saw a bank of dark clouds huddled on the horizon, muttering and flashing.

"She's been dead a day or two," Shark said grimly. "Killed quite violently, by the looks of it."

Tsunami glanced down at the broken red body snagged on the rocks. Shark was leaning over the corpse, inspecting the deep slashes across the throat. He shook his head and stepped back.

A bolt of shock and terror shot through Tsunami.

She *knew* this SkyWing.

It was Kestrel, the dragon who'd raised them.

Kestrel was dead. And somebody had clearly murdered her.

CHAPTER 10

Tell.

Don't tell.

Mother needs to know who it is.

But what if she thinks we killed her?

Tsunami didn't know what to do. It was too strange a coincidence, Kestrel turning up dead a few islands away at the same time as the dragonets arriving at the Summer Palace. If Tsunami admitted she knew her, wouldn't her mother's first thought be that the dragonets had killed her themselves?

After the way her friends had been looking at her lately, Tsunami didn't want to risk getting a similar reaction from her mother . . . the "What kind of dragon are you really?" and "Can you be trusted?" and "Who else might you attack?" looks.

She worried about it all the way back to the Summer Palace — mercifully, they flew back, giving Tsunami's swimming muscles a rest — but in the bustle of orders and flying messengers, there wasn't a moment to talk to the queen on her own anyway.

Back at the palace, Queen Coral told Tsunami to wait for her and took a few Council dragons off for a war meeting. Tsunami sat on one of the pavilion pillars, watching dragons dart about.

Who would kill Kestrel? Apart from Glory or me, that is?

She glanced at the cave where her friends were being held, where guards were still posted outside. She knew she should go check on the other dragonets . . . but what would *they* think when they heard about Kestrel?

What if her friends decided it wasn't safe here? Starflight might convince the others that Kestrel's murderer could be nearby, waiting to kill them, too. He'd talk them into leaving the Kingdom of the Sea, and Tsunami wasn't ready for that.

They were all too mad at her right now to listen to sense. And they were probably pretty grumpy about being stuck in a guarded cave all afternoon, too.

It'd be better to wait and tell them everything after they had a chance to see how wonderful it could be here. Tomorrow she'd ask her mother to bring them out for a feast or something, and that would cheer up at least a couple of them.

Yes. That's a better plan. Avoid them until tomorrow, then tell them everything.

Besides, she was so, so tired. Darkness had fallen as they

flew back to the Summer Palace, and now the cavern was lit only by trails of glowing jellyfish in the water below. Not that it mattered to SeaWings, who could see in the dark, but her friends probably wouldn't be too thrilled about having no light either. Another argument that could wait until tomorrow.

She was relieved when the queen finally came down from the Council level and led her across the lake. Queen Coral's chambers at the Summer Palace were in a vast underwater cave below one of the waterfalls, lined with waving tendrils of forest green and brilliant gold anemones. Stone carvings of dolphins danced around the entrance. The walls were studded with emeralds and pearls, and the beds were soft expanses of bubbly seaweed.

A bed was already made up for Tsunami next to Anemone's. She collapsed onto it with a sigh. Sleeping underwater on comfortable seaweed instead of a hard ledge of stone was even more wonderful than she'd ever imagined.

She fell asleep to the sound of the waterfall splashing overhead and didn't wake up until the next morning.

When she opened her eyes, she found the pale pinkish-blue head of Anemone leaning over her. Tsunami yelped and leaped back, crashing into the stone wall and bouncing off it in a stream of bubbles. She had a wild, brief moment of thinking Anemone had been about to kill her, and then her sister waved her talons and made a shushing gesture.

Anemone pointed at Queen Coral, who was still asleep. She clasped her talons in front of her and flashed some of the stripes along her wings and tail.

Sorry, little sister. Tsunami spread her front talons and shook her head. *I wish I could.*

Anemone flashed her stripes again, then smacked her head, remembering that Tsunami didn't know Aquatic. She frowned in frustration.

Tsunami felt equally frustrated. They couldn't sneak off to the surface to talk; Anemone was trapped here by the harness tethering her to the queen. And Tsunami couldn't communicate underwater. They'd never have a chance to talk privately.

She swam over to her sister and studied the harness. It was made of a stretchy, gummy, clear material that seemed to cling to Anemone's scales, as if it had grown along with her. *It probably has,* Tsunami thought, wondering if the poor dragonet would have to wear this until she was Tsunami's age, or even older.

When Tsunami tugged on it lightly, Anemone shook her head. She mimed trying to wriggle out of the harness and pointed to the queen again. *Not possible without waking her up,* Tsunami guessed. *If it's even possible at all.*

Anemone carefully eased toward the entrance, glancing back at the queen. The cord between them uncoiled. The little dragonet lifted off the floor and swam up toward the top of the door, stretching the leash to its full length. She beckoned Tsunami after her.

Where the waterfall met the lake, just behind the cascade and right outside the cave entrance, there was a small pocket of air. At the end of her leash, Anemone was barely able to reach it with her snout. Tsunami popped her head out beside her.

"Clever," Tsunami said, glancing around. Here they were also hidden from view, if any SeaWings were out and about this early in the Summer Palace.

"I hope she doesn't wake up," Anemone said. She blinked at Tsunami for a moment, then burst out, "Oh, I'm so glad you're here!" She reached out one of her front talons, and Tsunami pressed it like they had the day before.

"Really?" Tsunami said, astonished. *But aren't we rivals? If I'm here, doesn't that threaten your chance at the throne?*

"Maybe you can make her less crazy," Anemone said in a whisper. "Or maybe she'll set me free now that she has you. Maybe you could talk to her. I need to get out of this harness. Tsunami, you have no idea how awful my life has been."

Tsunami stared at her, hearing the echo of her own words. "*Your* life has been awful?" she said. "You can't even imagine awful. Try being raised under a mountain with no ocean or proper sunlight and only a river to swim in. Try being raised by three dragons who hate you and treat you like a blobby tadpole."

"I *am* treated like a tadpole," Anemone protested. "Mother doesn't trust me to do *anything* by myself."

"You're only, what, one year old?" Tsunami guessed. "I'm sure that'll change." *Well, I'm mostly sure. Halfway sure.* "And at least she cares about you."

"She cares about me *way* too much," Anemone said. "I never get to do anything except whatever she's doing. At least you have friends. I never even see any other dragonets."

"Well, I was sort of stuck with those four," Tsunami said. "And they're always arguing with me or getting mad about something." She felt a pang of guilt about not visiting them the night before. They must be wondering where she'd gone.

Well, maybe if they miss me for a while, they'll be more pleased to see me when I do show up.

"They seem great," Anemone said wistfully. "I always wanted brothers and sisters."

"Don't you have brothers?"

She snorted. "Yes, but Mother thinks they play too rough, and she won't let them near me. My cousins are all possible suspects in her mind, except Moray, who's perfect and boring and old and can do no wrong. And nonroyal dragonets aren't special enough for me to play with." Anemone sighed, blowing bubbles across the water at Tsunami.

"I guess my friends are all right when they're not complaining," Tsunami admitted. "They complain a lot, though."

"I tried complaining *once*," Anemone said with a stab of venom in her voice. "Mother nearly got me a gag to match the harness."

"At least somebody loves you," Tsunami said. "And you're with your own kind. And you know your own stupid language."

"She loves you, too," Anemone offered. She paused, glancing down into the cave. Queen Coral was still fast asleep, her blue scales rising and falling smoothly. "I hope you'll take Whirlpool," Anemone blurted. "Three moons, I was so sure I'd have to marry him. But now you're here, and *you* can have him and that'll be *much* better."

"No way!" Tsunami said, lashing her tail. "No, no, *no*." An image of Riptide flashed in her head, which was ridiculous, because she hardly knew him either. "Absolutely not. First of all, I don't have time to get married. I have to stop the war and save the world." *And/or learn how to be queen of the SeaWings.* "Second of all, *that* dragon? No, thank you. I'd rather have my tail nibbled off by snapping turtles."

Anemone giggled. "He's dreadful, isn't he?"

"Your Smaller Majesties," Tsunami smarmed, imitating his fake grin and tiny bow.

Anemone had to stick her head under the water so her giggling wouldn't shake the harness and wake the queen.

"Anyway, Mother can't decide who we marry," Tsunami said.

"Really?" Anemone said doubtfully. "She gets to decide everything else."

"We're royalty," Tsunami pointed out. "Meaning we do whatever we want."

"Gosh, that is *not* what I've seen," Anemone said. "More like 'we're royalty, so we only get to do what historical SeaWing queens would approve of us doing, for the good of our subjects, for the honor of the throne, for the YAWN, CLAW ME TO DEATH ALREADY.'"

Tsunami laughed, but her gills felt choked and her scales prickled uncomfortably. She'd never thought of royalty that way. Did queens really have to worry about honor and other dragons' approval?

What would happen if a SeaWing queen — or potential queen — decided to, say, marry someone the rest of the tribe disapproved of? Or chose not to get married at all?

It would be harder to rule subjects who didn't respect you. Tsunami had enough trouble with her usual four. She imagined a whole grumbling tribe full of Glorys and Starflights. But no one would dare argue with the queen, would they? Maybe it depended on the kind of queen you were. No one argued with Scarlet in the SkyWings, that was for sure.

But Scarlet was murderous and insane. Not exactly the role model I want to follow.

She stretched her wings out to feel the splashing of the waterfall. Outside their hidden spot, she could hear the quiet noises of the Summer Palace waking up. Dragon wings fluttered overhead. Bubbles burbled up from underwater caves where most of the SeaWings were sleeping. Pots clattered on the kitchen level of the pavilion, reminding her of how hungry she was.

"Uh-oh," Anemone whispered, glancing down. "I think she's waking up. We'd better go back in."

Tsunami hesitated. Should she go visit her friends now? But what would her mother think if she woke up and found Tsunami gone?

"All right," she said, "but I have one more question. What happened to Orca?" If Anemone could tell her, she could put off going to ask Starflight about it.

Anemone's pink-tinted wings shivered under the water. "She challenged Mother for the throne when she was only seven years old," she whispered. "Everyone says it was horrible. She nearly won, but Mother killed her in the end." She glanced down again. "It's weird. Mother worships her and misses her, but lots of dragons still hate Orca for nearly killing their queen. Don't *ever* mention her name around Moray."

"Moray," Tsunami echoed. "She seems —"

"Drippy? Fatuous? About as interesting as sea slime?"

"I was going to say odd," Tsunami laughed. "But those work, too."

"Uh-oh!" Anemone vanished below the water. Tsunami followed her, swimming back to her bed a few moments before Queen Coral opened her eyes. The queen sat up and stirred the water with her wings as she stretched. She beamed at Tsunami and Anemone, reaching to stroke their heads gently with her talons.

The queen gathered her strands of pearls from the coral branch where they'd hung during the night. Carefully she draped them around herself again, then decorated Anemone the same way.

Tsunami hadn't taken off the one she'd been given the day before. Her mother smiled at this and produced another long strand of pearls, these a shimmering pale purple and oddly shaped instead of round.

With expert talons, Queen Coral wound them around Tsunami's chest and wings. They were beautiful, but it was strange to have something weighing her down. Tsunami felt almost as if she was wearing a harness of treasure. She wasn't about to complain, though. The Talons of Peace had never given the dragonets beautiful things.

Finally the queen beckoned for them to follow her to the pavilion.

Tsunami wasn't sure how she felt about being treated the same as Anemone, a one-year-old dragonet. But she did like how her mother kept patting her, as if she wanted to make sure Tsunami was real.

As they flew up to the pavilion, Tsunami saw several guards clustered on one of the lowest levels, half of them sleeping and half of them drinking something steaming out of handheld cauldrons. She noticed that they looked well fed, well rested, and content, not thin and grumpy like Queen Scarlet's guards in the SkyWing palace. *Proof that my mother is a better queen than Scarlet,* Tsunami thought.

When Queen Coral landed on the Council level, a flurry of wingbeats sounded all over the palace. Council members swept down from caves or surged up from the water below. Coral settled herself in the largest pool, which was labeled QUEEN. She tugged Anemone into the water with her, although it was a bit of a squeeze, and the little dragonet had to curl under the queen's wing.

"Mother," Anemone protested. "Quit *squashing* me." She wriggled around until there was a little more space for her.

Small turquoise dragons darted in with platters of food, laying them all around the pools as Council members slipped into their places. Tsunami stood awkwardly to the side. She felt like her tail and wings were in the way of everything.

"Oh," said Queen Coral, finally noticing. "Tsunami, you can sit there. Tortoise is guarding the hatchery at the Deep Palace, so she won't be joining us today." The queen pointed her claw at a pool two down from hers, labeled DRAGONET CARE in tiny emeralds. The wet stone was chilly under Tsunami's talons as she climbed into it.

The pools on either side of the queen said DEFENSE and COMMUNICATION. Shark splashed down in the first one, and a moment later, Moray landed in the other.

"Good morning, Your Majesty," Moray said, bowing and dipping her wings. "I know yesterday was a shocking day, but I hope you slept well. I worried about you all night."

"Thank you, dear," said the queen. Her eyes were scanning the rest of the Council. Whirlpool flew up beside Moray. His pool was labeled MAGIC & PUBLISHING. Tsunami tilted her head at him. How did one become an expert in either of those things? What kind of magic did he know anything about?

She glanced around, wondering if there was a pool for the king, but she didn't see one. Queen Coral hadn't said anything about Tsunami's father yesterday, and in all the excitement about Kestrel's body, Tsunami hadn't had a chance to ask. Maybe he was at the Deep Palace. Maybe she could meet him later today.

She remembered some of the Council from the day before — the plump dragon, Lagoon, who'd been sent to feed the other dragonets, sat in a pool marked AQUACULTURE. Piranha, the one who'd gone with Shark to examine and dispose of Kestrel's body, was in WAR. Tsunami didn't know any of the other dragons' names, but from where she sat she could see the labels TREASURY, JUSTICE, and HUNTING.

She didn't really understand this "Council" business. She wasn't sure what they did or why they were necessary.

Wasn't it enough to have a queen? Couldn't Coral just decide everything herself?

That's what I'd do, she thought. *I'll get rid of this Council and run the tribe like a proper queen.* Maybe it worked for Coral, but Tsunami didn't need or want eleven dragons following her around offering advice all the time.

Her stomach rumbled, and she tried to remember when she'd last eaten. The platters around her were loaded with raw ruby-red fish, most of it sliced and deboned and arranged into fancy rolls with seaweed. She'd only ever eaten fish raw and whole, or sometimes scorched when her friends decided to set their dinner on fire.

A few cauldrons held seething mountains of tiny green crabs. Three large bowls contained some kind of salad of octopus tentacles and herbs that Tsunami had never seen before.

She plucked out one of the tentacles and tasted it. It was rubbery but sweet, with a tang like lemons and salt. She reached for another one and realized the whole Council was staring at her. Nobody else had started eating yet.

Oops.

All the Council eyes swiveled toward the queen, who was staring at the bit of octopus in Tsunami's claws. Coral shook herself and smiled.

"It's all right," the queen said, clapping her talons together. "Naturally I forgive my long-lost daughter any accidental impudence. As we all know, she was raised by barbarians, so she couldn't know any better. I give you all permission to eat."

Tsunami crushed the tentacle between her claws. *Raised by barbarians!* Perhaps it was true, but what a thing to say to Tsunami's future subjects. They'd think of her as the dragon who knew nothing about SeaWing customs. How would she ever earn their respect with *that* reputation?

Was Coral deliberately making Tsunami look foolish in front of the other dragons?

Tsunami studied her mother while Coral helped herself to the largest pieces of fish and crunched through talonfuls of crabs. She dropped bits of food into Anemone's open mouth as she ate.

Maybe not. Maybe Tsunami was seeing problems where there weren't any.

But maybe it wouldn't hurt to be a little more careful from now on.

— CHAPTER 11 —

"Pearl, report," ordered the queen after the dragons had eaten in silence for a while.

"No change," said the elegant pale green dragon in the treasury pool. "All your jewels are safe, as always. No scavengers can get to them, and no dragon would dare to try."

"Splendid," said Coral. She upended the last of a cauldron of crabs into her mouth. "Shark, report."

"I am concerned about our defenses," snarled the gray-green dragon. He glared at Tsunami. "The intruders in our midst are a danger to us. We have no idea whether they might have led others to our palace, or what they might be planning."

"Now, now," said the queen. "Those are our guests, not intruders. If my daughter trusts them, then of course I do, too."

"Oh, good," Tsunami said quickly. "Because I was thinking maybe they could join us for breakfast. I'm sure they're hungry. And if they could see that they're really welcome here . . ." She trailed off as Coral shook her head.

"Only Council members and royalty are allowed at Council meetings, darling," Queen Coral said, running one claw along a strand of her pearls. "But they certainly won't go hungry. Lagoon, did you make sure they were served an ample breakfast?"

The turquoise dragon nodded.

"They can have the rest of this as well." Queen Coral waved her talons at the breakfast leftovers. The same small dragons from before darted up from the kitchen level, collected the platters, and flew down to the cave with them. Tsunami watched over the edge of the pavilion. None of her friends even poked their heads out. Were they sulking in there? Were they still mad at her?

Well, she was doing a fine enough job of embarrassing herself. She didn't need them to come out and help. Raised by barbarians, friends with other tribes . . . not the stuff most queens were made of.

"Whirlpool, report," said the queen, smiling at him.

Whirlpool touched the hoop in his ear and flared his wings. "Anemone's lessons are going wonderfully," he said. Tsunami wasn't sure why his voice was so irritating, but it felt like claws scraping on stone to listen to him. "And your scrolls have never been more popular. The latest has been bought by every single SeaWing in the tribe."

"Mostly the underwater editions," Moray jumped in. "Those tend to sell the best. Of course, I spend all my energy promoting them —"

"But I've organized another reading," Whirlpool interrupted. "Every high-ranking dragon is clamoring to attend. We're charging an emerald apiece this time."

Queen Coral waved her tail thoughtfully. "I want to be sure I'm reaching the eel-eating masses as well, though," she said. "I mean, my writing should be shared with everyone, not just those who can afford it."

"Of course," Moray said. "That's why the schools have all changed their curriculums again to be sure the dragonets have enough time to read everything you've written. It's the most important subject they study."

"You can't be serious," Tsunami burst out. "More important than how to fight the war?"

Cold silence.

Queen Coral pressed a talon to her chest, looking injured. "Darling, my writing is about *everything*. As you would know if you'd finished the scrolls I gave you yesterday. What did you think of them?"

Tsunami guiltily remembered the scrolls she'd tossed aside as they flew off to see Kestrel's body. She hadn't even gone back to the library to get them.

"Uh," she mumbled. "*The Missing Princess* is still my favorite."

A chuckle ran around the assembled dragons. Tsunami felt hot with embarrassment. Councils were so stupid! She would never ever have something like this when *she* was queen!

"That reminds me," said the queen. "Whirlpool, Tsunami needs lessons in Aquatic. Can you believe she never learned it, poor thing?" She tapped her claws on the stone in front of her. "Such a sad upbringing." Her face was sympathetic, but her stripes were flashing, and Tsunami wondered angrily if she was saying something different to the Council, knowing Tsunami couldn't understand.

"Of course, Your Majesty," Whirlpool said. He inclined his head toward Tsunami. "I would be happy to instruct the princess."

"Piranha, report." Queen Coral snapped her head around to the war pool.

The war commander was so clawed up that she seemed to be more scars than scales. One horn was snapped in half, and several of her teeth were broken.

"Still no information about the dead SkyWing," Piranha growled. Tsunami ducked her head. Eventually she had to tell her mother the truth — who Kestrel was, how Tsunami knew her. But she didn't want a harness attached to her, or some kind of permanent guard. And she felt like she should tell her friends first. *I'll tell her later. I will.*

"A war party returned early this morning," Piranha went on. "Do you want to hear their report?"

Queen Coral sighed and gestured with her claws.

Piranha called over the edge and two soldier SeaWings came flying up from a lower level. One was too injured to fly, so the other supported him. They spiraled in a jerking, awkward motion and landed heavily in the center of the Council meeting.

The SeaWing who couldn't fly had long burns along his side and one wing was scorched almost entirely black. Claw marks along his underbelly were still oozing blood, which dripped into the sparkling channels between the Council dragons, staining the pearls red. Tsunami saw the queen give her decorated floor a concerned look.

The other SeaWing had a scorch mark in the middle of his tail and a horrible gash in his neck. He was breathing heavily, and bubbles of pale red blood foamed out of his gills.

"Let's hear it," Queen Coral ordered.

"Something strange is happening in the Sky Kingdom, Your Majesty," said the one who couldn't fly. "The battalions — it's as if nobody knows who's in charge. We were patrolling the outer islands, and we were attacked by three separate wings. The first squadron was half SkyWings and half SandWings. During the second attack, we heard the SkyWings yelling, 'For Ruby!' and in the third, at least one dragon shouted, 'The queen is not dead! Long live the queen!'"

Queen Coral sat forward, splashing water over the edge of the pool and squashing Anemone over to the side. "For *Ruby*?" she echoed.

"One of Scarlet's daughters," growled Piranha. "Does that mean Queen Scarlet is dead?"

Tsunami clenched and unclenched her talons. How much should she tell the Council? She didn't want to reveal Glory's secret weapon. They never knew when they might need it. And they weren't even sure Glory *had* killed Queen Scarlet during the escape.

"We would have heard if there had been a challenge, surely," said Moray.

Queen Coral shot a stern look at the blue dragon in the secrets and spies pool. "Why don't you know anything about this?"

"None of my spies have reported in for days," he protested. "I had no idea anything strange was happening in the Sky Kingdom."

The soldier who couldn't fly was leaning more and more dizzily against his companion. Puddles of blood soaked their claws.

"Mother," Tsunami said. "Shouldn't somebody look at their injuries?" She pointed at the soldiers.

Coral eyed them up and down. "Anything else to report?"

"Twelve casualties," the soldier croaked. "All the rest badly injured."

"But nobody followed you back to the palace?" demanded Shark.

"We were careful," he promised, wincing with pain. "We took the longest routes back."

"Very well." Queen Coral waved her talons dismissively.

"You may go." She flicked her tail at the smallest Council member, in the DRAGON HEALTH pool, who ushered the soldiers away. Moray immediately jumped out of her own pool and started cleaning up the blood on the floor.

"If there is chaos in the Sky Kingdom, maybe this is the time to strike," Coral said. She wrapped one strand of pearls around her claws. "We should send the rescue mission now. We could get him back *today*."

"We don't know enough," growled the secrets and spies dragon. "If Scarlet is dead, how did she die? Did Ruby kill her, or is she fighting with her sisters for the throne?"

Moray hissed at the blood under her claws. "Like the SandWing rivalry all over again. Making the war even worse."

"Or has Burn taken over?" Piranha suggested. "She would, if she was there."

"But Scarlet's daughters might not listen to Burn the way Scarlet did," said Moray.

"What could have happened?" Coral said. "Queen Scarlet was so strong."

Tsunami shifted uncomfortably, feeling the cold water seeping through her scales. She couldn't hide what she knew, not when her mother needed the information so much. Or at least she could share some of the dramatic highlights. "Um," Tsunami said. The entire Council turned to stare at her. "That . . . might have been us."

There was a shocked pause.

"You!" barked Piranha.

"Ridiculous," snarled Shark.

"Queen Scarlet found us under the mountain," Tsunami said. "She held us prisoner in her palace, and when we escaped, we sort of might have killed her. Maybe. I'm not sure. I will say we *tried*." She quite liked the horrified look on Shark's face at that bit of news. *Starting to respect us a bit more?* she thought.

"You were at the SkyWing palace?" Coral lunged out of her pool, swarmed across the stone, and seized Tsunami's front talons in her own, clutching them so hard it was a little painful. Behind her, Anemone was yanked half out of the pool with a squeak of protest, but Coral didn't seem to notice.

"Did you see a SeaWing named Gill?" the queen cried. "Green scales, big and powerful, with brave eyes?"

Tsunami felt sick. Gill. Yes, she remembered Gill — but not the way Queen Coral described him. She'd been forced to fight Gill in Scarlet's gladiator arena after he'd been deprived of water for months and driven mad with thirst. He'd been covered in scratches, as if he'd tried to drink his own blood.

The sound of dragon bones snapping between my talons.

"I did see him," Tsunami said slowly. A gasp went up around her, whispers traveling from one Council member to the next. Shark's pale, unfriendly eyes were like octopus arms coiling around her neck.

"Can you tell us where he is?" Queen Coral asked urgently. "We've been planning a rescue mission, but he's not in the regular prison with the others. And we've got to get him back, Tsunami. You have no idea how important it is."

Tsunami curled her tail in close to her talons. She wanted to dive into the lake, crawl down to the bottom, and stay there forever with her wings over her head.

"He's —" Her voice cracked. She swallowed and started again. "He's dead."

She'd had no choice but to kill the desperate SeaWing in the arena. It was his life or hers. She hadn't wanted to kill him . . . at least, she was pretty sure she hadn't wanted to kill him. But when she did — the truth was, Tsunami had loved the look on Queen Scarlet's face when she broke Gill's neck. She liked the feeling of being powerful and dangerous.

Gill's sanity had been long gone anyway. It had been easy for Tsunami not to think about where he came from or what his life was like before he landed in the SkyWing prison. It was easier not to think of him as a real dragon.

She'd never imagined her own mother desperately planning to get him back — or that she'd have to explain his death to anyone.

"Dead?" Queen Coral released Tsunami's talons and staggered backward. Her claws splashed in the winding channels, slipping on pearls. "How?"

"Um," Tsunami stammered. Did she really have to admit this in front of all these dragons? "In the arena."

"But he refused to fight," Coral said. "We heard about it, through our spies. He convinced each of his opponents to lie down and refuse to fight along with him. He has — had a way with words. No one who met him would be able to kill him." A smile flickered across her snout and vanished. "Queen Scarlet was furious, I heard."

"She was." Tsunami swallowed again. "She punished him. It was — really awful."

"What do you know about his death?" Shark demanded coldly.

Tsunami stirred the water with her claws. "She drove him mad. She kept him away from water until he lost his mind and — and when he was crazy, he was dangerous. He was barely even a dragon anymore. He had to be killed."

"Really," Shark said, and Tsunami felt horribly sure he had guessed the truth.

"Why?" Tsunami asked. "Who — who was he? An important general?"

"More than that," said Queen Coral in a hollow voice. "Much more. He was my husband."

Darkness seemed to be rushing into Tsunami's vision, sucking away all her breath. She knew what Queen Coral was going to say next, and she would have fled back to the mountains to avoid hearing it if she could.

"Tsunami . . . Gill was your father."

——— CHAPTER 12 ———

Queen Coral dropped her head and slowly dragged herself back to her pool. "Dead," she said. "My Gill is dead."

"No more eggs," Moray whispered. She was still crouched in the center of the floor, scrubbing at the blood. Her eyes had a weird glow to them. "No more dragonets, no more challenges."

"Not necessarily. She *could* marry again," Whirlpool murmured. Moray shot him a glare.

Coral didn't seem to hear either of them. She pulled Anemone into her wings and clutched her tightly. The little dragonet wriggled a bit, then gave up and rested her head on Coral's shoulder. She blinked in a resigned way at Tsunami over their mother's back.

Tsunami felt like oceans were pressing against the back of her eyes. Her scales were heavy, as if they were clogged with seaweed.

But I didn't have a choice.

Did I?

He was my father. And I had no idea.

But he wasn't a real dragon anymore. He wasn't anyone, inside his parched scales. He was gone, and I had to survive. I had to survive to protect my friends and fulfill my destiny.

Nothing helped. She hadn't really thought about other options when she'd killed the SeaWing in the arena. It was impulse and wanting to prove something to Queen Scarlet.

Shark was still staring at her, unblinking. Tsunami bared her teeth at him.

"I must grieve," said the queen. "Council dismissed." She stepped to the edge of the pavilion and flew off to her cave, still holding Anemone.

The Council dragons peeled off to various caves and other levels of the pavilion. Tsunami buried her head in the pool and clutched her horns. Now what was she supposed to do?

She definitely was *not* in the mood for seeing her friends. It would not make her feel any better to face their remarks about what a terrible dragon she was. The kind of dragon who attacked other dragons for no reason. The kind of dragon who did what she thought was right, but was always wrong.

The kind of dragon who could kill her own father.

Something tapped her on the top of her head.

She emerged from the water and found Whirlpool rubbing his claws together. "Time for your first lesson," he said in his oily voice.

"Now?" Tsunami said.

"Why not?" He spread his talons. "It is never too soon to begin filling our minds with knowledge."

Tsunami hissed softly under her breath. This was not going to be fun. But perhaps it would be distracting.

"Come," he said, strutting to the edge and diving over. Tsunami reluctantly followed him into the cavern lake. He was hovering several lengths below the surface, flashing his stripes at her.

Tsunami sank to his level and watched him. She kept her own scales dark. She most definitely did not want to say something to him like what she'd said to Riptide. If Anemone was right about Coral's plans for him, Whirlpool did not need any encouraging.

After a few moments, Whirlpool swam up to the surface again. His pale green eyes seemed far too big for his eye sockets.

"What's the matter?" he said. "Don't your stripes light up?"

"Of course they do!" Tsunami snapped. "But you haven't told me what we're saying or anything."

"Just imitate me," he said officiously, and dove again before she could argue.

"Rrrrgh," Tsunami growled.

This time she imitated each flashing path of light — along her wings, her tail, her sides, alternating and sometimes flashing faster or slower. It seemed to go on for an eternity.

Finally Whirlpool nodded with satisfaction and rose to the air again.

"Excellent," he proclaimed.

"What's excellent?" Tsunami demanded, spreading her wings to float. "What did we just say?"

"We recited the first chapter of the queen's very first work, *The Tragedy of Orca*. It's extremely moving, glorious writing. You nearly repeated it perfectly."

Tsunami wanted to splash seawater up his annoying snout. "But I didn't learn anything."

"Oh, you will," he said. "With repetition comes perfection. Shall we go on to the second chapter?"

"No!" Tsunami said. "Teach me something I can use. How do you greet strangers? How do you warn other SeaWings of danger?" *How do you say "I'm sorry I killed my father?"* She shook herself. "For moon's sake, at least show me how to say 'I don't speak Aquatic.'"

"All knowledge can be found in the queen's writing," Whirlpool insisted. "If we recite three chapters a day, we should get through her entire body of work in about five years."

"I have to get out of here," Tsunami said. *Before I tie your stupid tail around your stupid snout and leave you in a bundle at the bottom of the lake.* She turned and swam toward the exit tunnel. It wasn't quite as dramatic as storming out of a cave, which she hoped would be the first and last time she missed anything about life under the mountain.

"I am not impressed with your work ethic," Whirlpool called. "This may take us closer to seven or eight years if you —"

Tsunami plunged her head under the water so she wouldn't have to listen to him anymore. The exit tunnel yawned ahead of her, and she shot into it as fast as her wings could beat.

Outside the Summer Palace, the sky was gray and overcast, which suited Tsunami's mood perfectly. Wind whipped the sea into white-tipped peaks, knocking Tsunami around even more than usual. She tried paddling away from the palace underwater, but currents kept flinging her into the jagged boulders.

She was sick of fighting with the ocean. Why wouldn't it welcome her, like it was supposed to?

Why couldn't she start over as a normal SeaWing with normal problems, instead of having her past mistakes suckered onto her tail like overgrown leeches?

Frustrated, she swam to the surface and flew into the sky. It didn't make sense that flying should be easier for her than swimming. What kind of SeaWing didn't love the sea? *The kind that shouldn't be queen, maybe*, Tsunami thought.

Looming out of the water ahead of her was the island of rocks shaped like a giant dragon skeleton. Tsunami banked toward it, studying the holes and gaps. She chose the cave where the eye should be and landed in cool semidarkness. The stone was smooth like pearls under her claws.

She flapped her wings to dry them and turned to look out the entrance.

A dragon head popped into her view, then vanished again.

"Wow," Tsunami said. "You are the *worst* at staying hidden. Has anyone ever told you that you should definitely never be a spy?"

Riptide slowly poked his head around the mouth of the cave. "I think I'd make a splendid spy," he said with dignity.

"Aren't you supposed to be patrolling the outer islands, where we met?" Tsunami asked.

"Perhaps, but as you can imagine, I don't have a very important job." Riptide made a wry expression. "Her Majesty can't trust me with anything vital."

"You do seem like a shady character," Tsunami said, remembering that she was supposed to be mad at him, too. She could yell at him. Her first instinct was to yell at him.

Maybe I should stop listening to all my first instincts.

She scooted back farther into the cave. "Come on in. I'm just recovering from an Aquatic lesson with Whirlpool."

"Oh, Whirlpool. Queen Coral's favorite instrument of torture," Riptide said. He climbed into the cave beside her, shaking water droplets from his scales. The cave was only big enough for three or four dragons, so they were closer together in the dark than Tsunami had expected.

When she was much younger, Tsunami had had fleeting crushes on Clay and Starflight — before she realized that Starflight could be massively annoying, and that sweet loyal

Clay saw the other dragonets as brother and sisters. But they were the only dragonets her own age that she'd ever met. Even though they weren't SeaWings, who else was she supposed to like?

Now here she was, alone with a SeaWing . . . a SeaWing who looked at her as if he didn't see a future queen, or a father killer, or anything but a dragon whom he liked very much.

"Coral told me Webs is your father," she said quickly, awkwardly. "Why didn't you say something when we met?"

"It's not how I usually introduce myself," he said. He coiled his tail around his talons. "It makes dragons see me a certain way. I'm sorry, I should have told you. I was hoping you might, um — I'd like to know more about him."

Tsunami shook her head, tempted to say, *No, you wouldn't*. "Is that why you've been hanging around watching me?" she asked instead.

His dark blue eyes caught the faint light from outside. "That and other reasons," he said. "I was worried about you. There aren't a lot of . . . outspoken dragons in the Kingdom of the Sea."

"I can say whatever I want," Tsunami said boldly. "I'm the missing princess. Mother loves me so much, she'll have a harness on me by the end of the day if I'm not careful."

Riptide snorted. "I'd like to see any dragon try to put a harness on you."

"Then they'd really find out how 'outspoken' I am," Tsunami said. She opened and closed her wings, accidentally brushing against his. *Oops. Say something, quick.* "Webs wasn't so bad," she blurted. "Not as bad as the other two."

He tilted his head.

"We had three guardians. The other two, Dune and Kestrel, hated everything," Tsunami said. "Except maybe Sunny. Nobody hates Sunny — she's too sweet and simple and lovable."

"She sounds frightful," Riptide said, and Tsunami laughed.

"But Webs — he wasn't just trying to keep us alive. He taught us everything he could, except Aquatic, I guess. He taught us history and geography and all about the prophecy, and he wasn't even that boring about it. When it was his turn to hunt, he tried to bring back prey he knew we liked. It would have been worse without him." She fell silent, thinking. She'd never tried listing good things about Webs before. It was a lot harder than complaining about him, like she'd done her whole life.

"It's all right," Riptide said. "You can tell me the truth." The end of his tail flicked up and down. "I want to hear the bad stuff, too. It's good for me."

Tsunami took a deep breath. "He should have protected us better," she said. "If he was the only one who cared, he should have stopped Dune and Kestrel from hurting us and telling us we were worthless. He should have fought for us, and he never did, except right at the end when Scarlet and the SkyWings attacked."

That's one thing I do, she thought to herself. *I fight for my friends, even if I'm doing it all wrong.*

Riptide nodded, looking down at the stone under his talons. "Weak and cowardly," he said. "That's how he's always been described to me."

Tsunami reached out and touched his wing with one claw. "That doesn't mean you're anything like him," she said. "It's not fair to punish you for what he did."

Something tingled in the air between them, like the sky outside, waiting for the storm. *This is MOST improper for the future SeaWing queen,* Tsunami thought. *But maybe I'd rather have this than a throne anyway.*

"Would you like a real Aquatic lesson?" Riptide asked with a smile.

"I *demand* one," she answered.

"It's dark enough in here," he said. "All right, here's what you say to Whirlpool next time you see him." The stripe on his tail lit up three times.

"Uh-oh," Tsunami said, copying him. "What did I just call him?"

"A squid-brain," Riptide said. "My new favorite insult, thanks to you."

"I'm not sure this lesson is teaching me much more than his did," Tsunami pointed out.

"Hey, now I'm offended," he said. "All right, you asked for it." He sat down and pointed to his snout. "These stripes usually indicate a question. Like this for *why*, and like this for *how*, and like this for *when*."

Tsunami mimicked him, memorizing the patterns of flashes. It was easier than she'd expected. Maybe there was one part of being a SeaWing that she wouldn't be a total failure at.

After she had the question patterns down, Riptide said, "Try this one: I. Will. Protect. You." Stripes flashed along his side, and he gestured at the same time.

"I don't need protecting," Tsunami said.

"I know," he answered, "but knowing you, you'll probably need to say it to someone one day."

Tsunami liked that. *I will protect you,* she echoed, flashing it back at him.

He smiled a little sadly. "I wish you could," he said.

"Why not?" she said. "I am a princess. I can do whatever I want."

"Not while someone else is queen," he pointed out. "All right, here's how you indicate different kinds of danger."

Riptide showed her other stripe patterns and some of the talon gestures as well. It was all fascinating, and Tsunami wasn't sure how much time had passed when she finally glanced out at the wind-whipped sea and realized she should be getting back.

"Mother might be looking for me," she explained. "But thank you. You have no idea how helpful this was." *All of this,* she thought, realizing she'd managed to forget about Gill for a little while.

"Has Blister arrived yet?" Riptide asked.

Tsunami shook her head. He took her front talons in his.

"Be wary of her," he said. "She has her own plans, and I don't think protecting SeaWings is high on her list."

"I will," Tsunami said. "Oh," she added, freeing her talons. "What does this mean?" She tried to imitate the circular gesture Shark had made yesterday.

Riptide tilted his head at her. "If you mean this," he said, doing it perfectly, "then it means something like *Not right now, we'll finish this later.*"

Tsunami stared at him. "Are you sure?"

"Pretty sure," Riptide said. "Why, who —"

"Yesterday, when I stopped Shark and the guards from killing my friends," Tsunami said, jumping to her feet, "that's the gesture he made to them. You're telling me he was saying 'we'll just kill them later'?"

Riptide rubbed his snout. "Maybe," he said unhappily. "But if Queen Coral hasn't ordered it, then I'm sure —"

"How would I know?" Tsunami cried. "What if she has ordered it, and I didn't understand her?" She ran to the mouth of the cave. "I have to go back. I have to check on them. I haven't even seen them since yesterday." She leaped into the air, catching the air currents.

"Be careful!" Riptide called after her. "I'll be out here if you need me. Just —" The wind yanked away his last words.

Tsunami dove into the water, between the spiral dragon horn rocks. She powered through the kelp into the tunnel, shooting between the rock walls. She was going so fast, she didn't see the dark shape waiting above her in one of the breathing holes.

She thought she was alone until talons slammed into her back and sharp claws closed around her neck.

CHAPTER 13

Giant wings smashed Tsunami to the rock floor of the tunnel. She tried to twist around, but her attacker kicked her in the head and then shoved a hood that smelled of seaweed over her snout so she couldn't see. Tsunami shouted and struggled, lashing out with her claws and tail. Her attacker was bigger than her, and heavier, so Tsunami could barely move under the weight. It seemed like he or she was wearing something to make them heavier; she felt something metallic clank against her spines.

Fishhook claws dug into her gills, and Tsunami shrieked with pain. She felt blood swirling away from her neck into the water.

I'm not going to die here! she thought ferociously. *Killed by a coward I can't even see! I don't think so!*

She remembered how Sunny always managed to wriggle free during their battle training sessions. The tiny dragonet used her small size to slip out of almost every hold Tsunami could think of.

Tsunami scrunched her legs and wings in close and ducked her head, rolling into a tight, spiky ball. Her attacker's grip loosened around her neck and, as the dragon fumbled for Tsunami's snout, Tsunami was able to squirm down and shove her opponent over her head. A blast of bubbles slammed into her as the dragon crashed into the wall.

Before she could pull her hood off, the talons were back, clutching her forearms. Tsunami kicked viciously at the underbelly that had to be in front of her and felt her claws snag painfully on metal rings. Her attacker made no sound, but a moment later the dragon's tail hit Tsunami so hard she thought she heard bones crack.

The other dragon's wings began to press her down toward the rock floor again. Whoever it was knew how to fight like a SeaWing; they had all the advantages of this world. *So use something they haven't seen before.* Tsunami thought of how Glory used distraction whenever she fought Kestrel. Tsunami's scales couldn't change color, but she bet she could still be pretty distracting.

She flared her wings open and closed, open and closed, as fast as she could, stirring up the water around them. She felt her attacker pause as if confused. On her third flare open, Tsunami suddenly lit up all the stripes all over her body in what she hoped was a blinding flash.

Her attacker's talons slipped, and Tsunami struck out with her claws again. Again she flared her stripes, as bright as she could make them, so she could even see the light through her hood. She reached to shove her attacker away, and suddenly whoever it was . . . was gone.

Tsunami flailed in the water for a moment, fending off the attacks she expected from every side, before she realized there was no one around her anymore. She reached up and yanked off the hood, then felt the movement of somebody coming up the tunnel from the outside.

She whirled around, ready to fight, and Riptide leaped back, waving his talons. Tsunami whipped her head back and forth, but there was no sign of anyone else.

All right? Riptide signaled.

Who? she signaled back with the stripes on her snout. *Who?* She didn't have any of the other words she needed.

He spread his webbed claws. *I don't know.* Then he pointed at her. *All right?* He lit up all his stripes, and she guessed he'd seen the light from outside.

She nodded impatiently. She didn't have any way to explain that she was grateful he'd come, but she needed to chase down her attacker now.

All right, she signaled back. Then she spun away, swimming fast down the tunnel toward the palace.

Tsunami burst out of the water into a scene of eerie calm. Dragons were lounging peacefully on beaches and cliff edges, or playing underwater and darting through the waterfalls. She searched the water and the pavilion with her gaze, looking for anyone who might have just been in a fight. Surely she had left some kind of mark on her attacker.

No one was acting suspicious. Tsunami glanced up and saw her mother's tail poking off a level of the pavilion near the top — the library level. She beat her wings, rose out of the water, and flew up to her.

"Hello, dear," Queen Coral said as Tsunami landed. She was surrounded by scrolls, several of them half unrolled. Anemone was curled on a curved white boulder beside her, looking bored out of her mind. "I've been reading out loud to your sister. It's her favorite part of the day. We've just finished the story of how I chose Gill to be my husband." She sighed gustily. "He adored my writing, too."

"Mother —" Tsunami started.

"He was a perfect candidate for king," Coral said. "He came from a very noble family. Nothing to worry about in *his* ancestry. A lot like Whirlpool in his intelligence, too." Coral sighed again.

"Mother —" Tsunami said again.

"Luckily you've arrived just in time for my epic poem, *On the Differences Between Oysters and Clams*. It's an elegantly well-crafted metaphor about class differences and genetic superiority, as Whirlpool always says."

"Mother," Tsunami interrupted firmly. "Someone just tried to kill me."

Queen Coral sat up, scattering drops of ink from her claws. "What? Who *dared*?"

"I don't know, but they must be here now," Tsunami said. "Somewhere in the palace. We should gather everyone and —"

"The eggs!" Queen Coral yelped. "The eggs must be in danger!" She started flinging scrolls back into cauldrons.

"What?" Tsunami said, bewildered. "What eggs?"

"Two eggs with female dragonets," Anemone explained to Tsunami. "They're in the Royal Hatchery, in the Deep Palace. They're due to hatch in a couple of days."

"And if someone attacked you, they'll probably go after the eggs, too!" Queen Coral cried. She dashed to the edge of the pavilion. "Moray! Whirlpool! Hurry!"

"But my attacker is here," Tsunami said. "I'm sure of it. Not at the Deep Palace."

"So we have to get there first," Queen Coral insisted.

"But we could catch them *here*." Tsunami didn't understand why her mother couldn't see the obvious thing to do.

"Mother, what about Tortoise?" Anemone asked. "She's supposed to guard them, isn't she? That's Mother's Council chief of dragonet care," she explained to Tsunami. "This week anyway."

"The others have all failed me," Queen Coral said with a grimace. "Tortoise probably will as well. She didn't even want the job. Nobody wants it! The most important duty in the Kingdom of the Sea, and all my cowardly subjects hide from it. MORAY!" she bellowed.

"Yes, Your Majesty." Moray slithered up from the level below. Tsunami eyed her as she climbed onto the library floor. Did she look like she'd just been in a fight? Tsunami couldn't tell. Moray wouldn't look at her, but that wasn't new.

"Moray, we must get to the Deep Palace at once," Queen Coral said. "I feel that my eggs are in danger. My scales tell me so."

"What about whoever attacked me?" Tsunami demanded. "We have to catch them and punish them!"

"It's more important to stop them from hurting my eggs," Queen Coral said grimly. "Someone has been killing my daughters for years. These are the last two Gill left me, and I won't let anything happen to them." She turned to Moray, who was sitting close beside her and gazing worshipfully at the queen. "I wish you would guard them, dear. You never fail me."

"But everything I do for your scrolls is so terribly important," Moray said. "They're like your other children, really. I couldn't abandon them."

"That's true," Queen Coral said. She patted her pearls and flicked her wings open. Behind her back, Tsunami caught Moray shooting a look full of hatred at Anemone. *Wow,* she thought. *I wonder what that's for.*

Do you hate all of Queen Coral's daughters?

Enough to try to kill me?

"I sent Shark on ahead this morning after breakfast, but he never worries enough," Queen Coral said, clicking her claws together. "He doesn't even believe there's an assassin. He thinks it's all bad luck." She shook herself with a hiss. "He even told me once that perhaps I wasn't meant to have daughters. He's lucky he's my brother — and your father, Moray — so I let him live. WHIRLPOOL! WHERE ARE YOU?"

Anemone winced and put her talons over her ears.

"Stay very close to me in the Deep Palace," the queen ordered Tsunami. "We really have to put a rush order on a harness for you. They've been working on two for the new dragonets, but clearly yours is an emergency."

"I can take care of myself," Tsunami said, ruffled. "Obviously. I'm still alive, so whoever attacked me failed." She gave Moray a hard look, but the Council dragon only shifted her wings as if she didn't care.

Pitter-patter, pitter-patter.

All the dragons glanced up at the canopy far overhead. Raindrops were spattering across the green leaves.

"Ah, the precipitation I predicted," said Whirlpool, landing beside Coral. "My apologies for not appearing instantly, Your Majesty; I was distributing scrolls to the kitchen staff." He didn't look as if he'd been in a fight — and Tsunami didn't really think the ridiculous dragon could have overpowered her for a moment.

"We're going to the Deep Palace — now, as fast as we can." Queen Coral dove over the edge so suddenly that Anemone was yanked off her talons after her. Tsunami followed and found herself in a swarm of dragons midair as all the Council members hurried after Queen Coral as well.

They crowded into the tunnel, tails smacking into snouts and wings tangling. Tsunami got pushed into the middle and found herself swimming beside Whirlpool.

Too late, she remembered she had meant to check on her friends. *Why can't I be a better dragon?* she berated herself.

She tried to turn and go back, but Council dragons were there shoving her forward. After nearly getting clawed in the face a few times, she gave up.

Surely they're all right. Especially if Shark is in the Deep Palace already. I'll come right back and see them after we check on the eggs.

Out in the sea, Queen Coral immediately found a current and swept off. One by one, each of the dragons followed her.

Tsunami glanced around, scanning the coral reefs and underwater boulders. Her heart jumped a little as she caught a glimpse of sky-blue scales. Riptide was still out there, watching for her. She waited a moment until she saw him dart from one rock to another. He was following them — following *her* — to the Deep Palace.

Pleased, although she felt a bit silly about it, she swam into the current and let it carry her after the others. She was starting to get the trick of how to angle her wings so it could sweep her along as fast as possible. It was a bit like flying, but with a lot more to dodge. Then again, fish managed to get out of the way pretty fast when they saw the dragons coming.

Above them, rain pattered down harder and harder on the water's surface. The light faded, and Tsunami imagined the dark clouds rolling in. She hoped her friends would be all right in the Summer Palace. Surely there were storms there all the time. At least they were in a cave, so they wouldn't get wet.

Two giant sea turtles swam by, going in the other direction. They eyed the dragons warily, but nobody stopped to eat them. Explosions of tiny pink fish popped in and out of the waving anemones along the coral reefs. Something large and yellow was lying flat against the sand; it opened its eyes, stared at Tsunami, and closed them again.

After a while, an island loomed in front of them, with immense coral reefs clustered all around it. Orange branches twined around purple star-shaped clusters. Lacy fans the color of rust sprouted from pale pink umbrella shapes. Blue-and-silver fish darted in and out of the holes.

The SeaWings swam out of the current and around the bend of the reef, and then the lead dragons ducked into a canyon in the ocean floor.

Tsunami followed them down. As her eyes adjusted to the growing darkness, she saw a vast expanse of white-and-green coral reef spreading along the sides and floor of the canyon. It curled into caves and towers and underwater gardens full of glowing colors. In the center of the canyon, the coral spiraled up into an enormous palace, swarming with SeaWings.

SeaWings were everywhere — swimming in and out of the windows and doors of the palace, shooting up to the surface and diving to the bottom of the canyon, tending the gardens, gently cleaning the coral, lugging large fish in from the hunt, or sitting in small circles with groups of dragonets, reading from thin stone tablets.

The only signs of the war were a few troops drilling in formation around the palace, and a group of soldiers gathered in one of the gardens, each with terrible bandaged wounds. Tsunami saw two with missing feet, one with scorched holes where his eyes should have been, and several with black scars twisting their wings or tail. Several couldn't swim anymore, but had to be helped through the water by nurse dragons.

As Queen Coral swam past, dragons snapped to attention, saluting or waving. She waved to each of them with a wide smile. Tsunami noticed that most of them waved to Anemone, too, and the little dragonet smiled and waved back.

Surrounded by Council members, for once Tsunami was able to sweep by without a whole lot of staring and pointing. For a little while, at least, nobody knew who she was.

They swam through the wide front entrance into a coral cavern sparkling with emeralds and sapphires. A statue of Queen Coral loomed in the center, her talons outstretched benevolently.

SeaWing servants hurried in from all directions, their luminescent stripes flashing at the queen. Coral swept past them all and charged down a tunnel at the back of the hall. Some of the Council broke away to swim to other parts of the palace, but Moray and Whirlpool stayed with the queen, and so did Tsunami.

The tunnel curved down and around in a spiral, getting warmer and warmer as they descended. Tsunami felt warm jets of water bubbling up through the coral under her talons. At the bottom was a stone door, and in front of the door a skinny seaweed-green dragon crouched, gobbling something hungrily in her claws.

Her eyes went wide when she saw the queen, and she dropped her octopus with a shriek. The remains floated up to the ceiling as she flapped her talons in a panic, flashing her stripes so fast she looked like a lightning storm gone mad.

Queen Coral roared and threw the door open, smacking the green dragon back against the wall. The queen shot inside, towing Anemone behind her.

This is where I should have hatched, Tsunami thought with a rush of confused excitement. She swam through the doorway and gazed around. *The Royal Hatchery.*

The warm jets bubbled along every wall, heating the room, which was shaped like the inside of a large, pale egg. A SeaWing dragon carved from dark green marble stood in the center of the room; garlands of blue and purple underwater plants were woven through her horns and along her wings. The base of the statue said ORCA. She looked tough and beautiful at the same time. Tsunami wondered if Queen Coral's first daughter had carved her own self-portrait, and if she'd known it would be a memorial one day.

She glanced around and caught the hateful look Moray shot at the statue. *Maybe all her fawning over the queen is for real,* Tsunami realized. *Maybe she actually means it when she goes on and on about how wonderful Queen Coral is.*

Maybe she would even do anything to protect Coral from her daughters.

Nests made of seaweed were tucked into niches in the floor, with wide pathways stretching between them. Dragon eggs took a year to hatch, so there should have been clutches at different stages, from newly laid to nearly hatched. But there were no new eggs to be seen. *Because Gill has been gone,* Tsunami thought with a stab of guilt. *And he's not coming back.*

One clutch of three eggs was tucked against a wall, and in the nest farthest from the door, there were two eggs . . .

Queen Coral hurried to the far nest and roared again, a howl of fury and despair that reverberated through the water. She sank down beside the nest and picked up a piece of broken eggshell.

Oh, no. Tsunami started forward, but Moray pushed past her and knelt beside the queen, leaning against her side. Anemone glanced back at Tsunami, looking sick.

One of the eggs was still intact, but the other was smashed. The little blue dragonet inside had been strangled to death. Her neck was twisted in a horrible way, and her head flopped sadly as Queen Coral gently picked her up.

Tsunami stared at the body in shock. It — *she* — was so tiny. Who would do this to a baby dragonet? How could anyone?

TO MY SISTER.

She felt Anemone's cold talons slip into hers, and she squeezed them tightly. Whoever it was wanted to do this to Anemone as well. This was why the queen insisted on the harness and protected her daughter in such an extreme way. Seeing the broken body of the hatchling, Tsunami felt nearly crazy enough to do the same.

No one would ever, ever hurt Anemone, not while Tsunami was around. And whatever she had to do to protect that other egg, she would.

CHAPTER 14

Queen Coral rose to her feet, knocking Moray aside. She shot back across the cave to the door, but the skinny green dragon was gone. Anemone yelped a stream of bubbles as the queen blasted up the tunnel with her in tow.

Tsunami started after them, then turned and looked down at the last egg. Moray had already followed Coral. Whirlpool was hovering uselessly in the doorway. If Tsunami went after Coral as well, who would be left to guard the egg?

But no one can get in except through that door, she thought, staring around. *That door from that tunnel. So how did someone get past Tortoise?*

She turned in a circle, staring at the smooth walls. *Come to think of it . . . how did Webs get in here to steal my egg?* Surely there had been guards back then, too. Surely the queen had tried to protect her eggs, even six years ago. Webs couldn't have fought past them alone. So how did he get in?

Tsunami narrowed her eyes at the nests and the stone dragon. *A secret entrance. There must be.*

Well, one thing was for sure. She wasn't leaving this egg alone in here.

She crouched beside the nest and gently lifted up the last intact egg. It was surprisingly heavy — or perhaps not that surprising, considering a baby dragonet was supposed to pop out of it in a day or two. Cradling the egg to her chest, Tsunami swam out the door of the cave.

Whirlpool flashed a whole lot of stripes at her, waving his talons indignantly and pointing at the egg.

Tsunami gave him a wide-eyed, puzzled expression. *Maybe you should have taught me some real Aquatic, sea slug. Then you could yell at me all you want,* she thought.

He lit up his scales again. With a friendly smile, Tsunami lit up the same patterns back at him, then added *squid-brain* with her tail stripes, like Riptide had taught her. She swam away up the tunnel, leaving him gaping in surprise behind her.

As she swam up and around, she started to hear shrieks of pain echoing through the water. She hesitated, then beat her wings faster.

In the main entrance hall, Queen Coral had Tortoise pinned under her talons. A crowd of SeaWings had gathered, watching in silence.

The skinny green dragon was shrieking in one long, high-pitched scream. Tsunami stopped and pressed herself back against the wall, horrified. Queen Coral had already yanked out each of Tortoise's teeth one by one. They rose through the water, tiny and white, toward the roof. Now Coral had her claws stabbed into Tortoise's exposed underbelly. Clouds of blood filled the water, nearly hiding the queen and Tortoise in a red haze.

Would I have to do that, if I were queen?

Could I ever, ever do that?

Anemone had rolled herself into a ball, floating in the water above her mother with her eyes tightly shut and her talons over her ears.

Queen Coral's scales lit up in a slow, menacing way. Tsunami didn't understand most of it, but she guessed Tortoise was hearing about how she'd failed the queen.

Tortoise's stripes flashed weakly.

The queen snarled and twisted her claws harder into Tortoise's underbelly. Tortoise gurgled up a bubble of blood. Her stripes flashed again, and then, as her head began to loll sideways, she spotted someone in the crowd around them. She clutched at the queen's talons and pointed, her stripes flashing frantically.

She was pointing straight at Shark.

He stared back, unblinking as always.

Queen Coral leaned down, pressing Tortoise into the floor. One more message flared through her scales, and then she seized Tortoise's head in her talons and smashed it against the rough coral floor.

Tsunami turned away just in time, huddling around the egg with her eyes closed. She didn't care if she looked like a one-year-old dragonet, hiding her face. She did not want that image in her head for the rest of her life.

What was Tortoise saying about Shark?

Whatever it was hadn't convinced Queen Coral, anyhow.

Tsunami kept her eyes closed until she felt the eddies from other dragons swimming away. She peeked around and saw Moray busily cleaning up the blood and bone fragments that were floating around the main hall.

GROOOOOOOSS, Tsunami thought. *Moray must really adore Coral to be willing to do that.*

Tortoise's body was hooked on an outcropping of coral by the front door, like a used-up deer carcass waiting to be taken to the trash heap after dinner. Queen Coral loomed over Shark, clutching Anemone to her chest and exchanging a heated luminescent conversation with her brother. All the other SeaWings had scattered to faraway parts of the palace.

Tsunami started toward her mother, but stopped as a strange shape flashed by one of the windows. *What the — that wasn't a dragon.* She swam a bit closer and peered out.

Sharks — actual, dead-eyed sharks with enormous jagged teeth — were swarming around the front entrance, sniffing at the blood that still leaked from Tortoise's body. They were bigger than Tsunami had expected — big enough to eat a dragonet the size of Anemone, she guessed — but even as she watched, two SeaWing guards darted down and killed five of them with a few blows of their tails.

She turned back and saw Whirlpool swimming up to Queen Coral. He interrupted her conversation, waving his talons furiously and pointing at Tsunami.

Uh-oh. Tsunami took a deep breath and held the eggshell closer. *Well, I'm not giving this up.*

Queen Coral swam over with a half frown on her face. She pointed to the egg and gestured commandingly for Tsunami to give it to her.

Tsunami flashed her stripes in one of the few patterns she knew. *I will protect.* She wasn't sure how to say *it*. She pointed at the egg. *I will protect.*

The queen blinked. She lit up a few of her stripes, including one pattern on her snout that Tsunami recognized as *how*.

Tsunami shook her head. She didn't have enough Aquatic to answer that. *I will protect,* she said again.

She spotted the eyes of several SeaWings peering around doorways at her. Most of them looked shocked and disbelieving. She saw her sister glance from Tsunami to the crumpled remains of Tortoise, then back again. Anemone's face was pale and anxious.

Oh.

Tsunami realized what they were seeing. She was putting herself in Tortoise's place. She was taking the job nobody wanted. She hadn't even thought of it that way.

Which meant, if she failed . . . she might be punished the same way, too.

CHAPTER 15

Queen Coral tried flashing some more questions at Tsunami, but finally she flapped her wings and pointed to the surface. Tsunami pressed the egg to her chest and followed her mother, up and up and up through winding tunnels and cavernous palace rooms, through emerald-studded coral and pearl-laced curtains of golden sea grass. They swam to the top of the palace, where a guard stood watch over a view for miles underwater.

He saluted to the queen, and she swam up past him toward the gray light overhead, where raindrops pelted the surface of the water. Anemone paddled in her wake, glowing like a pale blue pearl in the dark sea.

They emerged into a storm so fierce, it almost felt like they hadn't left the water at all. Tsunami faltered in the air as wind and rain tried to sweep her back into the ocean. The egg was slippery in her talons. *Don't you dare drop it,* she hissed to herself.

"This way," shouted the queen, banking toward the nearest island. A large cave yawned open onto the beach. Rough, dirty, and muddy, it was still the driest spot they could see. The three of them huddled into its shelter.

"What do you think you're doing?" the queen demanded as soon as Tsunami's claws touched the ground.

"Someone has to protect this egg," Tsunami said. "It's not safe in the hatchery."

"It'll be safe in the hatchery if I put all my guards on it," Queen Coral fumed.

Tsunami shook her head. "Haven't you tried that before? Has it ever worked?" She paused and glanced at her sister. "What did you do for Anemone?"

The queen shook out her wings. "I slept by the egg myself, for the entire year," she said.

"You *did*?" Anemone said. Rain dripped off her tiny pale wings into puddles around her feet.

"I barely left the hatchery. I let Gill run the war for me, but — that's how I lost him." Coral's voice caught and she frowned. "I can't neglect my duties as queen, now that he's gone."

"So let me do this," Tsunami said. "Let me protect this egg."

"But you have to stay in the hatchery," the queen insisted. "It must be kept warm, especially right before hatching."

Tsunami glanced down at the egg. She didn't trust the hatchery. Anyone could sneak in to attack both Tsunami and the egg, especially if there was a secret entrance. Besides, she couldn't stay in the Deep Palace; she had to go back and check on her friends. "I have a better idea," she said. "Trust me. I'll take it back to the Summer Palace."

"The Summer Palace!" The queen flared her wings. "No, you don't want to do that in this weather. It gets terribly flooded there during a storm. Better to wait out the rain here at the Deep Palace, where you'll hardly notice it's happening."

"Flooded?" Tsunami echoed. "Do you mean — the caves? And the beaches? *Where my friends are?*"

"Oh." Queen Coral waved her claws dismissively. "I'm sure they'll be all right. Can't they swim?"

"Not like we can," Tsunami said. "I'm going back to check on them."

"With my egg?" Coral growled.

"You've tried trusting everyone else," Tsunami said, taking a step back toward the pounding rain outside. "Now trust me. I promise this dragonet will hatch safely."

Her heart beat like the thunder in the clouds. Was this, finally, the right thing to do? Was she doing it for the right reasons? Or was she being impulsive again — trying to prove something instead of thinking it through?

I'm doing this for my father. I'm doing this to make up for all my mistakes.

And I'm doing this to save my little sister. How can that be wrong?

"If anything happens to that egg," Queen Coral hissed, "I'll lose two daughters that day."

So much for being a special princess. "I need a harness for it," Tsunami said, looking her mother in the eye. *See. I'm not afraid of you. Maybe you should think about how your next queen will come to power before you start threatening me.*

"The harnesses they were making for the dragonets," Anemone piped up. "One of those should work."

"How will you get back to the Summer Palace?" Coral demanded. "You don't know the way, and my court is staying here with me."

"I'll find it," Tsunami said, but a nervous shiver went through her wings. She did not want to be wandering the ocean alone during a storm — especially when her friends needed her.

If Riptide is still out there . . . Please let Riptide still be out there.

"Wait," she said as the queen started for the entrance. "I have a question. Tortoise pointed at Shark while she was dying. Was she saying he attacked the egg?"

Coral flared her wings, looking shocked. "Certainly not!" she said. "My own brother! He wouldn't dare!"

"She wasn't saying he killed the egg," Anemone agreed. "She said he'd given her permission to leave her post. He brought her an octopus to eat."

"The fool." Coral gnashed her teeth. "I've told Shark a million times that vigilance is the only way to protect the eggs. If that means going days without eating, then that is what my trusted councillor must do. He's too soft with them."

Right, Tsunami thought. "Soft" *is definitely how I'd describe Shark.*

"Well, Tortoise didn't think anything could happen," Anemone said. "Not while she was right outside the door and only away from the egg for a few moments."

"Why didn't she stay with the egg to eat?" Tsunami asked.

"*Nobody* eats inside the Royal Hatchery," Anemone said primly. "It's a pristine hatching place designed for royal dragonets. And if you get blood in the water, sharks will try to find their way in. Regular sharks who eat dragonets and eggs, that is. Hatcheries other than the Royal Hatchery get attacked by them all the time."

Tsunami shook her head. She couldn't help feeling like following all these rules was only helping the assassin. And it was pretty convenient that Shark had set Tortoise up like that — not to mention giving himself a chance to sneak in and kill the dragonet.

She shook out her wings. "Take me to the harness," she said.

Queen Coral reached toward the egg, then stopped herself. She gave Tsunami another hard look and led the way out into the storm.

This time they swam down through the murky, churning water and around to the back entrance to the palace. The queen burst into a room that seemed to be a workshop where small SeaWings crouched over sea grass weavings and marble carvings. Tsunami paused as her mother thundered to the far end of the room. She lifted one of the weavings in her claws and realized it was made of the same material as the harness — rubbery, stretchy, and waterproof — only these were woven in colors, not clear like the harness.

Queen Coral flared her stripes angrily at a dragon who had frozen over a marble carving. He hurried into a back room and returned with a tiny harness flopping in his talons. Coral pointed at Tsunami, and he took it over to her.

This dragon was old, she noticed, and shaking with fear as he tried to fit straps around Tsunami's neck and shoulders. They flapped loosely; it was meant for Coral and was too big for her. And of course the smaller harness was supposed to fit a little dragonet with limbs and a tail, not a smooth round egg.

The old dragon gestured helplessly at the harness, and Queen Coral poked it, growling a stream of bubbles. The queen yanked Anemone closer and pointed at the harness, flashing some of the royal stripes in her wings.

Anemone hesitated, then reached out unhappily and touched the harness. To Tsunami's astonishment, the straps around her shoulders suddenly shrank until they fit perfectly. The other webs snaked and wove closer until the egg was securely bound to her chest.

She grabbed Anemone's talon. Her sister felt cold and weirdly hard to the touch, and her eyes were out of focus.

Tsunami shook her, and Anemone blinked until she was looking at Tsunami.

What? Tsunami flashed the stripes on her snout.

Anemone shook her head and made the circular gesture: *Not right now, we'll finish later.*

Tsunami wanted to know more, but the gesture reminded her of Shark and her friends. She had to get back to them. Protecting this egg was important, but watching out for the other four dragonets had been her first duty her whole life.

She bowed politely at the queen and the old harness-maker, then swam out of the palace and back through the gardens she'd seen on their way in. She wasn't going unnoticed now. Everywhere she passed, SeaWings stopped to stare, then lit up their wings in hurried conversations after she went by. She could sense them pointing at the egg. She wasn't sure if they knew she was the missing princess, or if they only knew she'd volunteered for the suicide mission of saving the queen's last female dragonet.

She remembered swimming into the canyon, so she climbed out and swam around the bend in the coral reef. The Deep Palace disappeared behind her, and the wide dark ocean yawned in front of her.

All right, you asked for this.

Now what?

— CHAPTER 16 —

Tsunami twisted around, hoping to see something familiar.

To be honest, hoping to see Riptide.

But the ocean was dark and wild, and it seemed like everything alive had gone into hiding until the storm passed.

So I figure it out myself. Tsunami set her jaw. She patted the egg through the harness. *Don't worry. I can do this.*

They'd ridden a current most of the way here. Did she have to fight it all the way back? She swam slowly forward until she felt the water try to shove her away. Maybe she could just keep a wing tip in the current and follow it that way.

Several wingbeats later, she pulled away from the current to rest, exhausted and confused. Why was this so hard?

Riptide, where are you?

Perhaps she could find her way back in the air instead. She just had to look for the island shaped like a dragon skeleton — how hard could that be?

Tsunami lashed her tail to power to the surface. She burst out into a pounding cacophony of thunder and roaring waves. Rain crashed down on her scales like hailstones. The wind immediately tried to grab her and carry her off.

She fought to stay balanced and fly straight, but she was already lost. She could see an island to her left, but she didn't know if that was the one close to the Deep Palace, or if she'd been swept to another, and whether it was on the way back to the Summer Palace or not.

A dark shape on the surface of the water caught her eye. She rubbed her snout, shaking off the raindrops.

Riptide?

She flew lower.

It wasn't a dragon. It was some kind of odd vessel, like a large bowl, floating on the water. And huddled inside of it were two scavengers, scrawny and soaking wet.

That doesn't help me at all, Tsunami thought. *I'm not even hungry right now.*

She beat her wings to soar upward again, and one of the scavengers looked up. Its eyes were as green as Glory's, in a smooth face the same brown color as Clay's scales. Tangled dark hair snarled around its shoulders.

Tsunami had seen a few scavengers up close before — one in the mountains and two in the SkyWing arena. It struck her again how dragonlike their eyes were. It was sort of unsettling, really.

She wondered if they could breathe underwater or swim, because these two were about to get swamped and end up at the bottom of the ocean.

Unless I help them.

As if I have time for that!

She hesitated. Maybe all scavengers looked that way all the time, but if she had to guess, she'd say their expressions were terrified.

On the other hand, I might as well help somebody. *Maybe it'll give me luck.*

Tsunami swooped down and snatched up the vessel in her talons. It was heavier than it looked, and she immediately dropped it. The two scavengers let out their long, piercing bird shrieks as the vessel smacked back into the water.

Oh, calm down, Tsunami thought. She flew around in a circle, fighting the gusts of wind, and wrapped a front talon around each scavenger. They both shrieked some more and banged uselessly against her claws.

How do scavengers accomplish anything? Tsunami wondered, flapping toward the island. *They don't seem to have any useful dragon qualities. And yet they manage to steal treasure and occasionally kill a queen and start a war.*

That's right, she remembered, giving the scavengers a little shake. *I'm mad at your kind. It's your fault all of this is happening.*

They screamed in a satisfyingly terrified way.

On the other hand, it's pretty unlikely that it was these exact scavengers who killed Queen Oasis and set off the SandWing war of succession.

So I suppose I'll let them live.

She dropped them on the island beach. They staggered to their feet and fled up toward the trees and the caves without a backward glance.

Pathetic little creatures.

Tsunami's wings ached from fighting the storm. She had to try going back underwater.

She dove in with a splash and spun, searching the dark water again for Riptide. Had he given up on her? Was he hiding from the storm, like a smart dragon would, figuring she'd be safe in the Deep Palace?

Well, there was one thing that had gotten his attention before. She opened her wings and lit up all her stripes, like she had done in the tunnel. The glow blazed through the water, and then she shut them down again and waited.

Nothing.

She tried again. It gave her a bit of a headache, lighting up all her stripes like that, and left her dazzled blind for a few moments afterward. She'd done it sometimes for the other dragonets when the caves got too depressingly dark or Kestrel tried to punish them by taking away all the torches. Glory hated that the most. She couldn't stand the dark.

Tsunami thought about the Summer Palace, where there was no fire allowed except in one cave, and all the light came through the canopy up above. Not much light could be filtering down from the sky in the middle of the storm. Her friends were probably sitting in the dark right now, listening to the water climb up the beach toward them.

I have to get back to them, Tsunami thought, blazing all her stripes on again.

Right in front of her, Riptide flung up his wings to shield his eyes.

Tsunami grabbed his claws and turned down her stripes. She jabbed her talon in the direction she thought the Summer Palace was. *Oh, why don't I know how to say anything useful?*

He rubbed his eyes and squinted at the egg attached to her. His expression said, "Something you forgot to mention?"

She whacked his tail with hers and pointed again. She remembered the pattern for *urgent* and lit it up.

Riptide nodded and began paddling toward the surface.

We don't have time to chat, Tsunami thought, frustrated, but she followed him because she had no choice.

But before he reached the air, Riptide swung around and slid into another current. As far as Tsunami could tell, it went in the direction of the Summer Palace. He beckoned her after him, and Tsunami ducked into the current as well.

All right. I suppose I could have looked for one of those.

Maybe traveling the sea wasn't about being strong and fighting with it all the time. Maybe it was about trusting the currents and knowing where they were. Maybe it would just take time before she figured them out.

She lashed her tail to keep up with Riptide as they swung around islands and dodged billowing clouds of translucent jellyfish. The current sped them along, but the journey still felt endless, and Tsunami couldn't stop thinking about her friends.

She should have fought harder to make her mother accept them. How could anyone not trust Clay? Every thought he had was written all over his big, sweet, goofy face. And Sunny — those two were the most trustworthy of the bunch. Tsunami didn't think Sunny had ever had a negative thought in her life. She did what she was told, and happily. She believed the best of everyone, even Kestrel and Dune.

Which didn't say much for Sunny's judgment or intelligence, but the point was, the littlest dragonet would never hurt or betray anyone — not even a bunch of SeaWings she barely knew.

Starflight was the opposite of Sunny: very smart, totally unreliable, terrified of the world. He tried so hard to know everything, just so he could be useful in some way. He wasn't brave. He wasn't a good fighter. He didn't even have any useful NightWing powers yet. Most of the time, Tsunami felt sorry for him . . . at least, when he wasn't trying to steal her position as leader of the group.

But if Queen Coral would give him a chance, she might see that his intelligence could be really useful, especially in fighting the other tribes. He probably knew more about the war and the different tribes than any other dragon in Pyrrhia.

Glory . . . well, Coral didn't know it, but Glory was probably the least trustworthy and most dangerous of all of them. Her secret venom proved that. Tsunami curled her talons in. In the SkyWing palace, why had Glory waited so long to save her friends? If she'd used the venom on Queen Scarlet earlier, Tsunami wouldn't have had to kill her father.

Plus she always talked like she didn't care about the prophecy, then got mad when other dragons pointed out that she wasn't in it. It was hard to figure out what she really wanted.

And Tsunami could definitely live without her sarcastic comments.

But Glory *had* saved them all, in the end, in the Sky Kingdom. She'd killed to protect her friends.

And I notice nobody seems all mad at her about that, Tsunami thought bitterly. *Instead I'm the crazy impulsive one. Like that's fair.*

Still, if Glory would do that for them, then Queen Coral should learn to trust her, too.

When Mother gets back to the Summer Palace, Tsunami thought, *I'll talk to her. I'll make sure she treats them like my friends, not prisoners.*

No matter how mad they made her, Tsunami didn't want anything bad to happen to any of them. And after two days of SeaWings, she had to admit she kind of missed them . . . even Starflight and Glory.

The spiral horn rocks loomed out of the dark ahead of her, with the golden sea grass curtain behind them. Riptide paused at the rocks, swimming backward as if he was going to leave her there.

Tsunami wound her tail around his and faced him. *Come,* she said, wishing she knew the patterns for "please" and "I might need your help" and "the queen is far away and won't return until the storm is over." But all she could say was *come.*

Apparently that was all she needed to say. Riptide nodded and gestured to the curtain, letting her lead the way. She unwound her tail and ducked through into the tunnel.

The current in the tunnel felt faster and heavier than before. She splashed out into the Summer Palace cavern and turned toward the beach.

The white pebbles had been swallowed by the rising water, and the cave mouth was already partly underwater. There were no SeaWing guards, and no sign of her friends outside the cave. Tsunami looked up, wondering if they'd been moved to a higher cave. But all she saw was a few curious SeaWing faces peering down.

Most of the dragons had taken refuge out of the way of the dripping canopy. Being all wet was wonderful, but having your head splatted one annoying drop at a time was not as much fun.

Tsunami paddled over to the beach and felt the pebbles scrape under her claws as she climbed up to the cave. The water was only up to her underbelly, but she could tell it was rising quickly. It lapped around the egg, chilly and unwelcoming, and Tsunami remembered that she was supposed to keep it warm. *Hang in there, little sister,* she thought. *Not much longer.*

"Hello?" she called into the cave. Her eyes adjusted to the darkness, and she saw one giant lump of shadows piled near the back.

Her heart lurched.

No.

Were those her friends' bodies?

Had she come too late?

CHAPTER 17

A small head lifted up from the top of the lump. "Tsunami?" squeaked Sunny's voice.

"Are you all right?" Tsunami blurted. She waded over and realized the bottom of the lump was Clay, stretched out in the water, half-submerged. Lying on top of him was Glory, and on top of her was Starflight, and at the top of the pile sat Sunny, well out of reach of the water.

"This is a terrible strategy," Tsunami pointed out as her friends opened their eyes, one by one. She covered her relief that they were alive by scolding them. "Seriously, whose idea was this — Starflight's? Look, once the cave fills with water, you'll be stuck in here, and even if it only covers Clay, he can't hold his breath for the entire storm. Why haven't you moved to another cave?"

"Oh," Glory said icily. "The SeaWing princess has time for us all of a sudden."

"It's only been a day," Tsunami said uncomfortably. "Mother's kept me busy."

"Well, we feel so blessed that you found time to visit. Please do impart some more incredibly brilliant wisdom on us." Glory wriggled and twisted her neck to glare up at Starflight. "Get your honking great claws off my wings before I bite you."

"We can't go anywhere, Tsunami," Sunny said as Starflight hurriedly adjusted his position. "We couldn't leave Clay." She pointed down at Clay's talons.

Clay lifted his front talons with an apologetic expression. Silver chains ran around each ankle and were bolted to rings in the floor. He had them around his back talons as well.

Shock stabbed through Tsunami, followed by fury. Had her mother ordered this? If so, she must have known Clay could drown in the storm, and she didn't care. She'd *lied* to Tsunami that her friends would be all right.

But maybe she didn't know. Maybe this was Shark's doing.

If that's the case, I'll rip him apart.

"I knew you'd come for us, though," Sunny said. "I mean, I thought you'd come yesterday. Or this morning. Or when the storm started. But I knew you would come. Eventually. Well, I was pretty sure."

"I was sure you wouldn't," Glory said. "Don't you have a feast or a coronation or a beheading to attend?" She squinted at Tsunami. "Is that an *egg*? Wow, they work fast in the Kingdom of the Sea. Who's the lucky father?"

"Glory, stop sniping at me for TWO SECONDS, please," Tsunami said. She slung the harness off and carefully passed it up to Sunny. "Sunny, I need you to take care of this. It has to stay warm, and you're the only one who can keep it that way." She hoped the natural warmth from a SandWing's scales would be similar to what the egg would have in the nursery.

"Me?" Sunny's voice was filled with delight. "You want *me* to do something important?"

"Really important," Tsunami said. "That's the very last female dragonet Queen Coral may ever have. Somebody wants it dead, and we're going to make sure that doesn't happen."

Sunny wrapped the harness around herself twice and nestled the egg into her warm scales. When Tsunami glanced up, she thought she saw a pulse of dark blue moving inside the egg. "So keep it warm and safe, and for goodness' sake don't break it, and don't let Clay anywhere near it in case he accidentally sits on it."

"I would never!" Clay protested. His stomach growled loudly.

"Haven't they at least *fed* you?" Tsunami asked.

"We got some breakfast leftovers this morning," Clay said with a sigh. "Very extremely tiny small crabs."

"I am going to claw someone," Tsunami snarled. So was Lagoon lying to Queen Coral? Or was she neglecting the dragonets on the queen's orders?

Tsunami crouched to study the chains. "Did you try melting them?" she asked Sunny and Starflight. "Like you did when you freed me, under the mountain?"

Starflight leaned over and pointed at a few blackened sections of the chain. "We tried," he said. His voice sounded more deflated than usual. "It didn't work. This metal must be like the SkyWing wires, reinforced in some way."

Tsunami heard splashing behind her and whirled around, but it was only Riptide.

"How do we get these off?" she demanded.

He rubbed his snout nervously. "You'll need the key from the guards," he said. "But they'll never give it to you."

"We'll see about that," Tsunami growled. "Hide if you need to," she said to Riptide. "I might have to bring a guard back with me. By force, with my claws through his ears," she muttered as she stomped out of the cave.

SeaWing faces disappeared all over the palace when they saw her glaring around. But she remembered the lower pavilion level where she'd seen guards resting and drinking from cauldrons. She could see a few huddled shapes there now. Perhaps they assumed they could watch the cave from over there, out of the rain.

Tsunami flapped over to the pavilion and landed next to a large cauldron that bubbled and smelled like green tea. Four guards were clustered around a low table, playing a game that involved rolling fish bones. They all froze when they heard her talons thud down. Slowly they turned toward her, and she guessed by their guilty faces that they weren't supposed to leave the cave.

She couldn't tell if they felt guilty about leaving her friends to drown, too, or if they were only worried about how the queen would react when she found out Tsunami had sauntered right into the dragonets' cave.

"Give me the key," she growled.

"Uh," mumbled one of the guards. "What key?"

"Don't make me bite you!" Tsunami shouted. "The key! Right now!" She stepped forward, lashing her tail threateningly.

Although all four of the guards were larger than her, they quailed backward. She wondered how many of them she could hurt, if she attacked quickly.

"We can't!" protested a second guard. "We have orders!"

"Orders from whom?" Tsunami demanded.

"Our — our commander," said the first guard.

"Shark?"

They all nodded fervently, as if they were hoping she'd now go away and yell at him instead of them.

"Too bad for him," Tsunami said. "Key." She held out her talon.

"But we *can't*," said the second guard again.

Tsunami studied his scales, looking for weak spots. She knew she was fast and strong, and she was pretty sure she could knock two guards over the side with her tail while she clawed a third in the face with her talons. Perhaps she could use her teeth on the fourth —

She remembered the feeling of SeaWing scales sliding under her claws and shuddered. She'd looked at Gill this way, too, in the arena, sizing him up so she could defeat him. What was she about to do? Hurt more dragons, just for being in her way?

Dragons she didn't even know — dragons who could be her brothers, her cousins — dragons who had families, who were more than nameless guards to somebody.

Maybe her friends were right about her.

The guards looked terrified, as if they were waiting for her to attack them. But they also knew what Coral was capable of, and surely Shark as well. Tsunami couldn't think of anything scarier than what her mother had done to Tortoise. She didn't really want to try.

So if she couldn't be more scary than her mother . . . maybe there was another way. Maybe she could convince the guards, instead of fighting them.

She remembered the dragons in the SkyWing prison, singing the song about the dragonets coming to save the day. Maybe these guards were like those dragons — believing in the prophecy, wanting it to come true. Maybe she could use that instead of just hitting them with her tail like she was tempted to.

"Listen," she said fiercely. "Don't you know about the prophecy?"

The guards exchanged glances. She guessed that the prophecy had been talked about plenty since the dragonets arrived.

"Great. So do you remember anything in the prophecy about a group of octopus heads letting the MudWing drown before he could save the world? Did I miss that part?" She lashed her tail. "Do *you* want to be the ones who ruined Pyrrhia's only chance of stopping the war?"

"No," blurted the third guard. "The war *has* to end." He ducked his head. "You saved my brother today when you sent him to have his wounds tended. She would have kept him standing there for the rest of the Council meeting."

Tsunami was shocked into silence for a moment. Was that true? Did Queen Coral let soldiers die like that? For no reason?

"Which one was your brother?" she asked.

He indicated his throat — the one with the gash and the blood coming from his gills.

"Oh," Tsunami said. "What happened to his friend?"

All the guards shook their heads. "Too late," said the first guard. She crushed the fish bones between her front claws and looked away.

"We want to help you," said the third guard. "But if we support a new queen before the challenge is even made . . . it could go really badly for us."

So somebody does *see me as a potential queen,* Tsunami thought, pleased.

"I told you, she can't be our new queen," said the first guard. "The dragonets in the prophecy have to be *outside* the war to stop it."

"Besides, Anemone is supposed to be our next queen," growled the fourth guard.

"You don't know what the prophecy means," argued the third guard. "Maybe they're all supposed to rule their tribes and stop the war that way."

"That's not possible," insisted the second guard. "Two of them are male."

Tsunami got the feeling they'd been having this argument for a while.

The third guard turned to her suddenly. "You tell us," he said. "What's your plan? If you really are the dragonets of the prophecy, how are you going to make it come true?"

Tsunami shifted her weight on her talons. That was the question she couldn't answer. The Talons of Peace hadn't taught them what to do. Nobody seemed to know. As much as she liked to talk about how the dragonets would choose the next SandWing queen, she couldn't imagine how that would work. Who would listen to them? Even if they went around the whole continent saying "How about Blister, we like her. Let's have Blister win," what good would that do? It wouldn't stop Burn and Blaze from fighting.

But some dragons believed in the prophecy — soldiers exactly like these four. She couldn't let them see that she had no idea what she was doing.

"Listen," she said. "I don't know if I'm supposed to be the next SeaWing queen or not. Sometimes I think Queen Coral is doing everything right, and then sometimes —" She stopped, remembering Tortoise. Would Anemone be a better queen, one day when she was old enough? Would Tsunami?

"But I do know this," she went on. "We *can't* fulfill the prophecy without Clay. He's the heart of our group. Without him, the rest of us will fall apart, and we won't be worthy of any destiny at all."

She stepped toward the first guard, whose expression was wavering between belief and worry. "I know you don't trust MudWings. I know you obey Shark in everything. But we're talking about the end of the war. You thought nothing you ever did could bring peace or save the dragons you care about, but right now you can make all the difference." She took another step closer. "Just give me the key."

The guard twisted her talons together and looked at the others. Two of them nodded; the fourth looked away, her tail twitching, as if she wanted to be left out of the blame.

"I'll do everything I can to protect you," Tsunami promised.

The first guard reached into a niche in the table and pulled out a pair of heavy silver keys. She placed them carefully in Tsunami's talons.

"Thank you," Tsunami said. "What are your names?"

"Snail," said the first guard. She pointed at the others. "Flounder, Herring, and Kelp. Please." She paused. "If you do become queen, please remember us. Whatever she does to punish us, please take care of our families."

"And stop the war," Herring said fiercely. "Whatever you have to do."

Tsunami stepped back, curling her claws around the keys, and saluted to the guards. She took off from the pavilion and flew back down to the cave.

The water was nearly up to her wings by now. Clay was standing, watching the rising water unhappily, with Sunny still perched on his back. Glory and Starflight were in the water with Riptide. They both looked tremendously irritated at how wet they were.

"Hooray!" Sunny yelped when Tsunami held up the keys.

"Wow," Glory said. Swirling waves of bright yellow shifted through her scales. "I did not think that was going to work."

Tsunami plunged her head under the water and lifted the shackles around Clay's ankles. She found the lock for the front talons quickly, inserted one of the keys, and freed him. The other key unlocked the chains on his back talons. Clay kicked them away and shook out his wings as Tsunami stood up again.

"All better," he said, grinning at her. His stomach roared in disagreement. "Well, almost all better," he amended.

"Let's find somewhere dry, and I'll see about food," Tsunami said. She herded them out of the cave ahead of her. Riptide paused, still in the shadows, and she turned to him.

"Thank you," she whispered. "You saved my friends."

"I didn't do much," he whispered back. "I could never boss anybody into doing what I want. You're really good at it."

"Well," Tsunami said. "Sometimes bossing doesn't work, and you have to try something else. It'd be much easier if everyone just did as I told them."

He laughed. "I should get out of here before someone sees me."

She nodded and wound her tail around his. "I'll look for you again tomorrow, if I can. There's a lot of Aquatic I still have to learn."

He smiled and slipped out of the cave into the water. She waded onto the beach and watched his sky-blue scales vanish into the underwater tunnel. She was glad she'd found at least one dragon she could trust in the Kingdom of the Sea.

"OOOOOOOOOOOOOOOOOO," Glory started.

"Don't you dare," Tsunami said, shoving her into the lake.

The RainWing squawked indignantly and flapped up into the air, showering them all with cold droplets. Rain was still dripping down through the canopy, and small waves scudded across the surface of the bay.

"Let's try that cave," Tsunami said, pointing to one far up the cliff. "If there's anyone in it, I'll clear them out."

Glory snorted.

But the cave turned out to be empty and dry, and once they all huddled into it, it felt warm as well. Sunny immediately curled around the egg, stroking it and murmuring to it.

Starflight blew a small spurt of flame into the air to heat them up.

"The dragonet can't hear you," Tsunami pointed out to Sunny.

"We don't know that," Sunny said. "She might be scared. I'm just telling her it's all right, and we'll take care of her."

Tsunami hid a smile. She was glad Sunny had agreed to take the egg — she'd been a little worried that the little SandWing might still be too mad at Tsunami to want to help. But maybe she'd forgotten about Tsunami attacking the SkyWing soldier. Or maybe Sunny was always willing to help. She didn't fight about everything just to be difficult, like Glory did.

Clay nudged Tsunami with his snout. "We're happy to see you," he said. "Tell us about the tribe. Does everyone adore you? Are they good fighters? What do they eat?" he finished wistfully.

"Let me find you some food first," Tsunami said, turning toward the cave entrance. She was surprised at how warm and happy she felt to be back with her friends again.

This was how she'd expected to feel among the SeaWings — like she was coming home.

So why don't I?

CHAPTER 18

Tsunami dropped three cauldrons on the cave floor — one packed with fish, one with clear water, and one with a seaweed-mushroom salad. She'd found them on the kitchen level, unguarded, so she thought they might as well go to the dragonets.

Sunny seized the salad cauldron and shoved her nose into it. Starflight peered at the fish, and then, without even asking the others if they'd mind, he shot a burst of fire into the cauldron, which left all the fish blackened and smoky tasting.

"Hey," Tsunami protested. "I like them raw."

"Overruled," Glory said. "Raw fish is gross."

"Raw fish is awesome," Tsunami insisted.

"You have unreliable taste," said Glory. "You think your terrifying mother is awesome."

"She is *not* terrifying!" Tsunami said. "She's a wonderful queen!"

"That is what all the scrolls say," Starflight pointed out through a mouthful of charred fish.

Tsunami looked up at the cave ceiling and shifted from talon to talon. "Er," she said. "Well. Apparently she . . . wrote a lot of those herself."

"*Really?*" Starflight blinked in astonishment. "She's a writer? I had no idea. That's so — I mean, I wish I — do you think she'd read something I —" He stammered to a stop and fidgeted for a moment with the cauldron. "It's cool, is all," he mumbled, shoving a fish in his mouth.

"Anyway, it's not just the scrolls. Her subjects think she's a great queen, too," Tsunami said loyally. *Most of them. I think.*

"Compelling," said Glory. "Except for the part where she's killing off all her daughters."

Tsunami stared at Glory, too shocked to respond.

"Well, wait," Clay said. "That's just a theory."

"A good theory," Starflight observed. "With her daughters dead, and no sisters either, no one will ever be able to challenge her for the throne. She could be queen for a hundred years and die peacefully in her sleep instead of in combat."

Sunny pulled the egg closer to her and patted it reassuringly.

"No!" Tsunami blurted. "You're so wrong! She would *never* — you haven't seen how protective she is. I mean, look at how she takes care of Anemone."

"Like a crazy dragon," Glory interjected, waving a smoky fish at Tsunami.

"It's a good way to make herself look innocent," Starflight offered. "Besides, think about when the murders started." He waited, with an "isn't it obvious?" look on his face.

"Oh dear," Clay said, rubbing his head. "Did we really study this?"

"I don't know either," Sunny whispered to him.

"Starflight," Tsunami growled. "Just tell us."

"Very well," he said. "It was right after the only challenge Queen Coral has ever faced. Her first clutch of eggs had one female in it —"

"Orca," Tsunami guessed.

Starflight nodded with a pleased expression. "You do remember! She challenged the queen almost the moment she was full grown. I'm sure Coral was more shocked than anyone. Especially when Orca almost killed her. Queen Coral only won by accident, impaling Orca on that narwhal horn she has on the end of her tail."

"So?" Tsunami said. "Why would that make her murder all her future daughters?"

"Seriously?" Glory scoffed. "She saw how close she could come to death. She realized if she let any of her female children grow up, she might be dead within seven years. Much easier to kill them all in their eggs, or as little dragonets, before they become a threat."

"Stop it!" Tsunami clutched her head. It *couldn't* be true. "She's not like that. She loves her daughters. When she found the other egg broken —" Tsunami paused, realizing how much they didn't know. She backed up to tell them all about the Council, her mother's scrolls, the mysterious dragon who'd tried to kill her in the tunnel, and the way Queen Coral had reacted when Tortoise failed her.

"So you see," she finished, "it can't be her killing off the female dragonets. She wants them alive more than anyone."

"Someone tried to kill you?" Clay said. "Are you all right?"

"I'd like to know what would have happened to *us* if they'd succeeded," Glory said angrily.

"Are you saying Sunny's in danger now?" Starflight demanded at the same time. "Because of that egg? Why would you do that to her?"

"I don't mind," Sunny said, cuddling the egg to her chest. But she looked paler than usual.

"No, *listen*," Tsunami said. She took a step back toward the cave entrance. "Don't you see? We're doing a good thing by keeping this egg alive. And now Queen Coral has to take care of all of us, because we're protecting her daughter. She can't chain you up and not feed you anymore — if that was even her idea in the first place."

Glory and Starflight exchanged "yeah, right" glances. Tsunami frowned at them.

"And if we find the real assassin," she hurried on, "then we'll be heroes."

"Not if it's your mom," Glory said firmly. "Which it is."

Tsunami wanted to kick her. "It can't be my mother," she said again. "The dragon who attacked me in the tunnel didn't have a dragonet attached. Where are you suggesting she stashed Anemone while she came after me? And how could she have broken one of her eggs when Anemone is with her at all times?"

"She could have sent someone else," Starflight said. "Or the attack on you could be unrelated to the princess murders. Perhaps there's another reason someone wants you dead."

"Ooo, I have a few guesses," Glory said.

"*I* think it's Shark," Tsunami said, ignoring her. "Tortoise pointed at him before she died. He was at the Deep Palace before the rest of the Council. If I'm right and there's a secret entrance to the hatchery, he could have snuck in to kill the dragonets without anyone knowing. And he could have attacked me in the tunnel, too. Queen Coral thought she'd sent him on ahead already, so nobody knew where he was exactly."

"Tsunami," Clay said, nosing her with his snout. His forehead crinkled worriedly. "It doesn't sound like you're safe here. Maybe we should go."

"Or at least *we* should go," Glory suggested. "You can stay here if you really want to. We could leave now, while no one is guarding us."

Tsunami hesitated. It was so much harder to fit in with the SeaWings than she'd expected. And she didn't like seeing sides of her mother that scared her. She preferred the image in her head that she'd dreamed about her whole life — the loving queen from *The Missing Princess*.

She fingered the pearls around her neck, thinking of how Coral had given them to her the moment she saw her, and how happy she had been.

"No," Sunny said unexpectedly. "I'm not leaving this egg until it hatches." She rested her talons on it protectively. "And we can't split up. We have to fulfill the prophecy *together*."

"I agree with Sunny," said Starflight. "I don't love it here either, but we have to stay until we meet Blister. That was the whole point of coming here."

Not for me, Tsunami thought. She'd forgotten that Blister would be coming to meet the dragonets. She was not at all sure that was something to look forward to.

"Then I think you should stay with us," Clay said, taking Tsunami's talons in his again. "So we can keep one another safe."

That was what Tsunami had planned to do anyway, but hearing it from Clay, and seeing Sunny nodding vigorously behind him, made her feel much better. They couldn't hate her too much if they wanted her to stay with them.

"All right," she said as if he'd convinced her. "Then I can help you protect the egg as well."

"You'd better," Starflight muttered, glancing at Sunny with a worried look.

They curled up together to sleep, sheltering the egg in the middle of their pile. Tsunami rested her head on Clay's shoulder and listened to the rain pattering on the canopy far above them. Last night she'd slept underwater on seaweed, and it had been the most comfortable sleep she'd ever had. But even though she was back in a cave, something about the rise and fall of Clay's deep breathing under her snout was more calming than any seaweed bed or pearl-studded underwater palace.

It wasn't until she was almost asleep that she remembered she'd forgotten to tell the others about Kestrel.

—— CHAPTER 19 ——

"WHERE ARE THEY?!"

Tsunami bolted awake out of a nightmare about the last egg slipping through her claws and smashing on a coral reef. She blinked and checked under her wing. Sunny was still curled neatly around the egg, keeping it warm. The little SandWing lifted her head as if something had woken her up as well. What was it?

"WHERE ARE THE DRAGONETS? WHERE IS MY DAUGHTER? WHERE IS MY EGG?"

"Up here," called an unfamiliar voice with a weird hiss to it.

Tsunami leaped to her feet. A shape was coiled in the cave entrance, watching them. Glittering black eyes met Tsunami's. A poisonous tail barb flicked up and down. White-gold scales marked with black diamond patterns caught the glint of sunlight now trickling through the canopy.

The storm had passed.

And there was a SandWing watching them sleep.

Tsunami didn't have to remember the illustrations in

their scrolls to guess who it was. She poked her friends with her claws.

"Wake up, you lazy snoring manatees," she hissed.

"*You're* a lazy snoring manatee," Glory mumbled with her wings over her head. "And you smell like one, too."

"You're going to feel very silly in a minute," Tsunami whispered crossly.

"Oh, if you insist," Clay muttered, mostly asleep. "I suppose I could eat one more hippo."

"Clay!" Tsunami yanked on his ears, and he sat up with a bewildered look, shaking his head.

"Aww," he said, his wings drooping. "What happened to the hippos?"

"Look," Tsunami whispered, pointing toward the cave entrance.

Her friends all went silent as they saw the SandWing in the shadows.

"Well, hello," said the stranger with a sly smile. Tsunami shivered without quite knowing why. "So nice to meet you. I'm Queen Blister. They're up here," she called again. "Staying dry out of the storm, I presume," she went on conversationally. "Very wise. I would have done the same thing."

A flurry of wingbeats announced Queen Coral's arrival on the ledge behind her, followed by Anemone and three SeaWing guards. The queen poked her head into the cave and saw Tsunami.

"Where is my egg?" she demanded, eyeing the other four dragonets.

"Safe. And warm, like I promised." Tsunami stepped aside and let her see Sunny coiled around the egg.

Queen Coral hissed and lashed her tail. "You never said anything about a SandWing touching my egg."

"Oh, but think about it, Coral," Blister interjected. "These are not ordinary dragons. These are the dragonets of destiny. If they can't be trusted with our future, who can?" She smiled again, but Tsunami couldn't shake a weird feeling of uneasiness.

Queen Coral took a deep breath, then turned to Blister with outstretched arms and wings spread wide. "Queen Blister, my friend," she said. "You got my message! I'm so glad you came. I knew you'd want to hear right away that we found the dragonets." She waved her tail at Tsunami and her friends.

Tsunami squashed a flare of irritation.

Blister clasped Coral's front talons in hers and quickly let go. "I was thrilled to hear it," she said. "And one of them was your beautiful missing daughter, as we always suspected."

"I *knew* the Talons of Peace must have sent Webs to steal her," Queen Coral said. "Tsunami, say hello to my ally, Queen Blister."

"We've met," said Tsunami. She felt her friends behind her: Starflight frozen in fear; Sunny craning her neck for a better view; Glory studying her claws as if she wasn't that interested; Clay curious but mostly trying to keep his stomach from growling too loudly.

"Then introduce your friends," Coral ordered, smiling at Blister again.

"Clay, Sunny, Starflight, Glory," Tsunami said, flicking a claw at each of them as she said their names. Queen Coral frowned at her.

"Marvelous," said Blister smoothly. "All so brave and clever-looking. I heard you weren't a SkyWing, Glory, but that doesn't bother me. SkyWings are overrated, don't you agree?"

Glory's wings twitched, and a ripple of dark pink shifted across her stone-gray scales.

"You 'heard'?" Tsunami demanded. "How? Nobody knew that except our three guardians. They didn't even tell the other Talons of Peace."

Anemone gazed at her from behind Coral's wing, her blue eyes wide. The SeaWing guards shuffled on their feet nervously.

"Hmmm," said Blister. Her eyes flicked to Tsunami and away. "Let's just say I have friends. NightWing friends." She slithered up to Starflight and brushed one claw slowly down his neck. "So I've heard a lot about *you*."

The NightWing dragonet really looked as if he might turn to stone and never move again. Tsunami would have kicked him if she'd been closer. *Don't be so impressed by her.*

We're the ones with the power. According to the prophecy, we choose the next SandWing queen, and she knows it!

Blister glanced down at Sunny, who was frowning. "Sweet," she said, chucking Sunny under the chin. "And you must be the burly one," she said to Clay. She reached out and squeezed one of the muscles in his forearm.

"I guess," Clay stammered.

"I'm sure you've heard things about me, too," Blister said, returning to Queen Coral's side. Her tail slid across the cave floor like a snake, the poisonous tip rattling on the stone. "But you can't always trust rumors and propaganda, especially when it comes to a big responsibility like the prophecy. So ask me anything you like. I'd be delighted to help you make your decision — although of course I hope you'll choose me." Her glittering eyes swept over all of them again and back to Coral. "So, Coral, what's for breakfast?"

"Let me guess," Glory muttered. "Fish."

Clay blinked at the queen hopefully.

"Yes, what a good idea. Let's go eat," said Queen Coral. "And then you can tell me the latest updates from the war. We hear something odd is going on with the SkyWings. Anemone, Tsunami, come."

Tsunami's gills flared. She was not a baby dragonet to be ordered around. And she had no intention of leaving her friends alone again.

"Let the others come, too," Blister said before Tsunami could speak up. "I'd love to get to know them better."

Coral wrinkled her snout at the dragonets. "All right," she said doubtfully.

"You can leave that here," Blister said, nodding at the egg.

"No!" Coral and Sunny said at the same time. The SeaWing queen gave the little dragonet a surprised look.

Sunny hugged the egg closer. "No way," she said. "It stays with me."

Blister shrugged, and Tsunami suddenly wondered how she felt about new dragonets who might threaten her ally's life. Maybe it was in Blister's best interests to make sure no one survived to challenge Coral. She certainly seemed sinister enough to be the assassin.

But Blister couldn't breathe underwater, so she couldn't get to the Royal Hatchery. She might be involved, but she couldn't actually be committing the murders. It had to be a fellow SeaWing.

The feasting hall was two levels above the kitchens, so the smells of pickled fish and roasting seagulls ("in honor of our SandWing guests," Queen Coral explained) surrounded them as they arranged themselves around the long, low oval table. Queen Coral's seat was higher than everyone else's, but Blister's, right beside her, was not much lower.

Starflight was seated to Blister's right, with Tsunami next to Anemone on her mother's left. On Tsunami's other side was Whirlpool, who played with his hoop earring, slurped loudly as he ate, and droned on about Coral's latest book even when nobody seemed to be listening.

SeaWing guards were arranged around the perimeter of the floor, interspersed with SandWing soldiers who had arrived with Blister. The SeaWings stamped their talons and swished their tails, casting dark looks at the SandWings.

Tsunami spotted Snail and Herring among the guards. Their eyes darted anxiously from side to side, as if they were wondering how they were still alive.

Because Mother wants to make a spectacle of them, Tsunami guessed. Coral was probably waiting for the right moment to punish them in public, the way she'd punished Tortoise.

Well, two can play the spectacle game, Your Majesty.

"MOTHER!" Tsunami declared dramatically as the wait-staff set bowls of soup in front of each dragon. Beside her, Whirlpool jumped and nearly tipped his bowl onto himself. Even Queen Coral looked startled.

"I have something DREADFULLY SHOCKING to tell you!" Tsunami announced. She wanted this to be loud, so every dragon could witness it.

"Oh?" said Coral. "Could we discuss it after breakfast? In a civilized fashion?"

"NO," Tsunami said, louder than before. "This is TOO SHOCKING."

Even SeaWings not invited to the feast were starting to peer out of their caves and poke their heads out of the lake to hear what was going on.

"Well, perhaps —" Coral started.

"WOULD YOU BELIEVE," Tsunami said, "that my friends — the DRAGONETS OF DESTINY, remember — were CHAINED UP? And STARVED? In YOUR CAVES? By YOUR DRAGONS?"

"What?" Coral said, flapping her wings. She looked thoroughly alarmed, but Tsunami couldn't tell whether that was because the news actually surprised her or because she was being confronted openly with what she'd done.

"I *KNOW*!" Tsunami practically bellowed. "It's UNBE-LIEVABLE. I'm sure *you* didn't know anything about it, of course."

"Of course," Coral said in a hurry. "I would never treat any dragonets that way! Especially my dearest daughter's dearest friends. Who are part of the prophecy and everything."

"And I'm sure you'll want to punish the dragons who *disobeyed* you by treating my friends so terribly," Tsunami said. "Right? Like, for instance, the one who lied to you about keeping them well fed?" She shot a glare at Lagoon, who froze with a sea snail halfway to her mouth, suddenly realizing what was going on.

"Absolutely," said the queen. "Guards! Throw Lagoon in one of the underwater dungeons!"

"But —" Lagoon said. "But I was only —"

"Next time you'll obey my orders," said the queen. A stripe quickly flashed under her wings, but Tsunami spotted it, and it was one Riptide had taught her.

Silence.

Oh, Mother, Tsunami thought sadly.

"Can't I even —" Lagoon said, reaching wistfully for her cauldron of soup as the guards pulled her away.

"No breakfast for you," the queen ordered. "Think about how that feels as you sit in my dungeon."

Tsunami was fairly sure Lagoon wouldn't actually suffer very much. Queen Coral would have her back at Council meetings before long. But Tsunami wasn't done.

"And GUESS WHO ordered your guards to chain up Clay?" Tsunami demanded. She flung an accusing talon toward Shark. "COMMANDER SHARK! Of all the dragons who should obey you in everything! Is that not UTTERLY SHOCKING?"

"It is," Coral said. Tsunami thought she might be grinding her teeth, but she hid it well. "I find it *quite* hard to believe."

"Imagine the distress the poor guards felt," Tsunami said, "when I explained to them that *you* would never have ordered those chains on Clay. To have to choose between their commander and their queen! Naturally they chose you, of course. That's why they gave me the key to Clay's chains. Because they understood that's what *you* would have wanted them to do. Right?"

Queen Coral gave Tsunami an appraising glance. Beside her, Blister was eating her soup with an amused expression.

"Very good," Coral said slowly. "It sounds like those guards are practically heroes."

"And Shark —" Tsunami prodded her.

"To the dungeon with him as well," the queen said with a wave.

Shark didn't protest like Lagoon had. He snarled at the guards who approached him, shot Tsunami a look full of hatred, and headed off to the dungeon without another word.

Splendid, Tsunami thought to herself. It didn't guarantee that Snail and the other guards would be safe, but surely that had to make it more difficult for Queen Coral to punish them for last night.

Not only that, but with Shark in the dungeon, even for only a day or two, Tsunami felt like she and her friends and the egg would all be a lot safer.

"Such excitement," Blister said. "If we're quite finished with our morning theatrics, I would love to ask you brilliant little dragonets about the prophecy."

"Starflight can recite it for you," Tsunami said. "He's really good at memorizing things. And then repeating those things over and over, especially when no one cares to hear them." She shot a grin at Starflight, wishing he would relax. He looked too petrified to eat.

"How splendid! How impressive!" Whirlpool said from beside her, in a voice of sincere admiration. Tsunami wrinkled her snout at him. He probably *would* get along well with Starflight, now that she thought about it. But Starflight was not even remotely as awful or annoying as Whirlpool.

"I assume you have a plan about how to fulfill this prophecy," Blister said. "I mean, you must, right?"

A tense hush fell over the feasting table. Ears were pricked all over the palace. Every dragon in Pyrrhia wanted to hear the answer to this.

Tsunami felt like bees were crawling under her scales. Of course they didn't have a plan. They'd only recently escaped from under the mountain and then the SkyWing palace. They'd barely had time to stop and think, or even a safe place to do that. And nothing they'd ever been taught had prepared them for what they had to do. *Thanks for that, too, Talons of Peace,* she thought bitterly.

But they couldn't admit that to all these dragons . . . especially the ones who were counting on them.

"We're working on it," she said. "Obviously we can't say too much."

"This is the information-gathering phase," Glory offered unexpectedly.

Blister gave Starflight a significant look.

"Um," he blurted. "But. We think *you*, of course — I mean, obviously *you* — er — you'd make a great, uh, queen. Of the SandWings. That is. The other two — hardly any competition — really, it's, um, a clear, so to speak, sort of, um, choice."

"Starflight," Tsunami said sharply. "What are you doing? You don't speak for all of us."

"Oh?" said Blister. She narrowed her eyes at Starflight. "Then who does?"

"We each speak for ourselves," Glory said before Tsunami could answer.

"Yeah," Sunny piped up.

"And we haven't decided anything," Tsunami said firmly. She wished she were close enough to kick Starflight and make him shut up.

"I'mjustsayingshe'dbeallright," he mumbled, subsiding. Blister looked mildly disgusted.

"You're quite right, NightWing," Coral said, patting Blister's talon. "She's an excellent queen."

Blister smiled, but Tsunami noticed that she moved her talon away as soon as she could. She also noticed that Blister called her mother simply "Coral," while the queen of the SeaWings kept referring to her ally as "Queen Blister." Tsunami wasn't sure she liked the way they acted around each other.

Tsunami wanted to trust her mother's choices. She *wanted* to like Blister. It would be uncomplicated to choose Blister as the SandWing queen. Then the dragonets could stay safely in the Kingdom of the Sea and support the SeaWing side of the war.

So why didn't she want to do that?

What was it about Blister that felt so . . . wrong?

"Oh," Queen Coral said. "Queen Blister, I meant to tell you, the strangest thing happened. We found a dead SkyWing in our territory the other day."

Oops. Tsunami still hadn't told the others about Kestrel. Something new for them to be mad at her about. She sighed.

"Really," Blister said. "That sounds like good news to me."

Coral laughed. "You're right, that's true. But what's really strange is she'd been poison-stabbed by a SandWing. Why would a SandWing and a SkyWing be fighting all the way out here?"

Tsunami hadn't known about the SandWing poison. She only remembered the blood pouring from Kestrel's neck.

Her tail uncoiled as she realized — *I don't have to worry, then. Mother will know it wasn't us who killed her. None of us could do that, not with Sunny's useless tail.*

At the same time, questions began pounding in her head. What SandWing would want to kill Kestrel? She scratched her gills, puzzled. Had Burn found her and punished her for what happened to Queen Scarlet? But why would either of them be in SeaWing territory?

Blister shrugged, resettling her wings. "That *is* very peculiar," she said.

"I wonder who she was," said Queen Coral. "She had these odd burn scars on her palms —"

Tsunami reached over Whirlpool and grabbed for Sunny's forearm, but it was too late to stop her gasp of horror.

"Oh, no!" Sunny cried. "That sounds like Kestrel! Tsunami, what if it was Kestrel?" She pressed her claws to her snout, her eyes welling with tears.

A heavy silence fell over the table. Every SeaWing in the entire palace seemed to be staring at Sunny and

Tsunami. Queen Coral was giving Tsunami a particularly intent look.

Across the table, Glory and Starflight both had their mouths open in shock.

"Tsunami?" Coral said slowly. "Is there something you want to tell us?"

"All right," Tsunami said, squirming. "Yes. I'm sorry. I saw her. It was Kestrel."

Sunny let out a sob and buried her head in her talons. Clay patted her on the back awkwardly.

"Your SandWing seems surprisingly distressed about this SkyWing," Blister observed.

"Kestrel was one of the guardians who raised us," Tsunami said. "Although she wasn't very nice, Sunny. She doesn't deserve your grief."

Sunny's wings trembled, and she didn't look up.

"So," Coral said, leaning toward Tsunami. "Explain this to me. You recognized this SkyWing — a SkyWing I have now been wondering about for *days* — and you chose not to tell us who she was. Why is that?"

"I didn't think knowing who she was would explain anything," Tsunami said. "I knew her, but I have no idea why she was out here or who killed her." She glanced at Glory and Starflight and Clay apologetically. "And I wanted to tell my friends first. Kestrel wasn't a good parent, but she was one of the only parents we ever knew. I thought they should know — and I just haven't had a chance to tell them."

"I understand perfectly," Blister purred. She stroked Coral's talon with one claw. "Forgive her, Coral. It can be very shocking, seeing the dead body of a dragon you know. Especially when you've probably wanted to slash her throat yourself once or twice in your lifetime — right, Tsunami? I know I felt that way about my mother most of the time."

Tsunami looked up slowly, her green eyes meeting Blister's cold black gaze.

How did she know?

Queen Coral had only said that Kestrel was stabbed by a SandWing. Tsunami clenched her talons under the table.

So how did Blister know that Kestrel's throat was slashed?

CHAPTER 20

Tsunami didn't know what to do. Should she accuse Blister of lying — of murder — in front of all these dragons? How would Queen Coral react?

Stop yourself, she thought. *Think. Don't lash out immediately, the way you want to.* She shot a glance at Starflight. He was smart enough to have noticed Blister's mistake, and sure enough, there was a puzzled expression on his face.

He met her eyes and shook his head a tiny bit.

Tsunami took a deep breath and let it out slowly. Perhaps he was right. She might put her friends at risk if she picked a fight with Blister right now. Better to wait and watch. And hope that Starflight could use that giant brain to figure out why in the world Blister would have killed Kestrel.

Blister's dark tongue flickered in and out of her mouth. She leaned toward Coral, smiled at Anemone, and said, "How is our secret weapon coming along?"

Anemone dropped her head and stared unhappily at the table.

"Wonderfully!" Coral said. She patted Anemone's head,

beaming with pride. "Why don't we show you? Whirlpool, come along."

Whirlpool puffed out his chest and stood up. Curious, Tsunami got to her feet at the same time, but Queen Coral shook her head, her pearls dancing in the green light. "You can skip this, dear. I'm sure it won't interest you."

"I'd like her to come," Anemone piped up. "Please?"

Coral and Blister exchanged a significant look. *They don't trust me,* Tsunami guessed. *They don't want me to know about any "secret weapon" until they're sure I'm on Blister's side.*

Well, too bad.

"I'm sure it'll be *very* interesting," Tsunami said with earnest enthusiasm. "Everything you do is interesting, Mother." She blinked her large green eyes at Queen Coral. Across the table, Glory snorted and then tried to hide it with a bout of coughing.

"Please?" Anemone said again.

"All right," Coral said with a sigh. "But not the others." Her gaze flicked suspiciously to Clay.

Tsunami followed Coral, Blister, Anemone, and Whirlpool to a high level of the pavilion she hadn't visited before. It was shaped like a bowl, with low walls and a slight slope down to the center. Weapons were lined up along one side: white twisting horn spears like the one attached to Coral's tail; battle armor of chain link or scales hammered over more scales; gleaming metal claws like the ones scavengers carried in all the scrolls. None of the weapons looked particularly special or secret.

But — Tsunami looked sharply at the wall of weapons again. That battle armor . . . surely that was what her attacker had been wearing in the tunnel. That was why she hadn't been able to claw him (or her). She remembered her claws scraping uselessly against metal. And one of the vests definitely had a nick in it. So who had access to this level?

Probably everyone, she thought ruefully.

"May I?" Whirlpool said officiously, gesturing to one of the strands of pearls on Coral's wings. She dipped her wing so he could remove it. He strutted to the center of the bowl and carefully laid the rope of pearls on the floor in front of him.

"All right," he said, rubbing his talons together. "See if you can make it crawl over to the wall."

Tsunami looked around. Who on earth was he talking to? Where was the secret weapon?

Anemone sat down next to Tsunami and sighed. "Do I have to?" she said. "It seems like a waste." Tsunami stared at her.

"Practicing is never time wasted," Whirlpool said, wagging a claw in a way that made Tsunami want to snap it off.

"But I don't want to end up like Albatross," Anemone said. She flicked her wings and edged a little closer to Tsunami.

"He made an entire pavilion grow from stone before he went mad and tried to kill everyone," Whirlpool said patronizingly. "You have a way to go before that happens. Now. The necklace, please."

Anemone sighed again. She held out her front talons and, to Tsunami's amazement, the necklace began to slowly wind toward the wall, moving in curves like a snake.

"Oh my gosh," Tsunami blurted. Suddenly everything made sense — the "magic" in Whirlpool's title, the self-adjusting harness in the Deep Palace. "Anemone! You're an animus!"

Anemone dropped her talons, and the necklace stopped moving. "I know," she said with an expression like she would rather be descended from sea cucumbers.

"We've had a few animus dragons in the royal family," Coral said proudly. "But not in several generations. Anemone was hatched just in time to help us win this war."

"Careful," Blister said with a hiss.

"She doesn't have to know our whole plan to guess that an animus dragon would be very useful in battle," Coral said. "There are lots of marvelous things we can do with this power."

"Yes, watch this," Whirlpool said. He picked up a metal armor breastplate and flung it up in the air, over the edge. "Catch it with a spear!" he called to Anemone.

None of the spears moved. The breastplate plummeted toward the lake.

"Sorry," Anemone said, not looking very sorry. "You didn't give me enough warning."

"Ow!" someone yelled from below.

"Anemone," Whirlpool said with a sigh. "Battle is all about quick thinking."

"How would *you* know that?" she said.

He frowned at her.

"Try it again," Queen Coral said, clapping her front talons together. "And this time do as you're told, Anemone."

Whirlpool flung another flat piece of metal armor into the air. Instantly one of the narwhal spears shot after it and pierced it through.

Blister and Coral applauded, but Tsunami thought it was more interesting that the spear then carefully brought the armor back to rest safely on the floor.

"Impressive," Blister said. "But not much more impressive than what I saw last time. What about progress? What about bigger objects? How much longer must this training go on?"

"I'm sure she's nearly ready," said Queen Coral.

"Years. Lots more years," Anemone said at the same time.

Blister's forked black tongue slipped through her teeth, and she narrowed her eyes at Anemone. "Coral," she said, tilting her head.

"Stay here," Coral ordered. She slid as far away as the harness would reach and crouched with her wings spread, whispering to Blister.

Whirlpool strutted over to Tsunami and Anemone. Anemone gave him a glare, and suddenly the pearl necklace he'd left on the floor whirled around, whipped under his belly, and soared off the ledge. With a yelp, the green dragon raced after it, diving over the edge.

"This is what you have to save me from," Anemone whispered quickly.

"Boring lessons with Whirlpool?" Tsunami answered. "Sure, I'll get right on that."

"No, not just that," Anemone said, wrinkling her snout. "Although he is awful. All he ever asks me to do is make things move. I can enchant any inanimate object to do my bidding, and he's like, 'Make this spear dance! Now make that chair walk from here to here!' It's insulting, really."

"What else could you do?" Tsunami asked. She glanced at Coral and Blister, but they both had their backs turned and were sharing their own secrets.

"According to Blister, I should be able to enchant the Sky Kingdom's palace to cave in on all the SkyWings," Anemone said softly, looking up at Tsunami. "She also wants me to curse a spear so it will search for Burn's heart and not stop until it kills her."

Tsunami coiled her tail closer, trying not to look as shaken as she felt. If Anemone could do either of those things, she really was a secret weapon. Power like that could end this war in a week.

"I don't know for sure if I can do any of that," Anemone said. "I'm scared to try. I don't *want* to try. Every time an animus dragon uses her power, she loses a bit of herself." Tsunami's sister held out her talons as if they might not really be hers. "Albatross was a prince and a hero at first, but they didn't know about the price of animus magic then. Building the pavilion turned him evil." She slipped one talon into Tsunami's grasp. It felt colder than ice and hard as stone. "I don't want that to happen to me."

How can I possibly save you? Tsunami wondered. Even she was tempted by the kind of power that could bring peace so quickly. But she couldn't ignore the fear in Anemone's eyes.

"First I'll catch the dragon who's trying to kill us," she said, curling one wing around Anemone. "Maybe then Mother will let you off the harness and start to trust you more. Maybe she'll listen when you tell her you don't want to use your power."

"Ha," Anemone muttered.

Tsunami didn't know what else to say. She had no words of advice ready for dealing with strange magical problems. But she did have a lot of other questions for Anemone, and this might be her only time to ask them.

"Can I ask you a question?" she said. "If none of Coral's daughters survived, who would be queen after her?"

Anemone flicked her tail around and studied the end of it. "Who knows? I don't think a queen has ever died and passed on the throne peacefully, at least not in our kingdom. And who else would challenge her? I heard Uncle Shark say once that maybe a son should inherit. But I guess it would probably be our cousin Moray. Except she doesn't want the job — she wants Coral to be queen forever. At least that's what she says."

"You don't believe her?" Tsunami asked.

"There's just something weird about her," Anemone said. "Isn't there? It's like she must be faking, because nobody could really act like that all the time and mean it."

"Maybe," Tsunami said. "But I think the assassin is Shark. I bet he wants Moray to be queen, and if none of Coral's daughters survive, it'll have to be her."

Anemone snorted. "Moray would rather die than challenge the queen."

Tsunami saw Queen Coral's wings flutter closed. "In the meanwhile," she whispered quickly, "keep acting like you need more training. Make mistakes sometimes if you have to. Make them think you aren't ready for as long as possible."

"Mistakes," Anemone said with a sigh. "Why didn't I think of that?"

Queen Coral slid back to them, twisting her snout from side to side. "Where's Whirlpool?" she asked.

"I think he lost something," Anemone said innocently.

"Queen Blister wants you to try —" Coral started, but stopped as the SandWing's head suddenly went up. Blister stared around the cavern, poised in her eerie stillness, nothing but her eyes moving. Tsunami felt hypnotized by her; Anemone and Coral were equally silent, waiting.

Blister's gaze slowly lifted to the canopy of leaves and vines overhead.

Then Tsunami heard it, too.

Something was moving around up there.

Something big.

CHAPTER 21

Queen Coral hissed softly. "I'll call my guards," she said.

"Wait." Blister lifted one claw. Her voice barely stirred the air. "We want to catch whoever it is, not scare them away." She flicked her tail. "Come." Quietly she slid over the side of the pavilion and flew to the cliff wall.

Coral and Anemone went after her, and Tsunami followed close behind. She wasn't sure she'd been invited, but she didn't care.

Blister landed on a ledge beside the tallest waterfall. The water spilled out of a hole high above, nearly at the level of the canopy. It rushed in torrents down the cliff wall, dividing around boulders and sending out small clouds of spray.

And it was loud, loud enough to hide the sound of their wingbeats as the four of them flew higher, staying close to the falls.

She is clever, Tsunami thought, glancing at Blister. *Why does that make me more nervous about her instead of less?*

At the top of the waterfall, the SandWing hovered for a moment, studying the canopy with her glittering dark eyes. From this high, the dragons far below looked like lizards, scurrying around the pavilion and swimming in the lake. Tsunami spotted Whirlpool, paddling frantically in circles with his talons outstretched. He was still trying to catch the pearl necklace as it twisted away from him.

The canopy was thick and green, with vines twisted together over centuries and leaves the size of dragon talons. Up close, Tsunami could also see small blue flowers shaped like broken eggshells shining in the small sunlit gaps.

Something stirred the leaves. Something was crawling through the vines not far from the edge of the cliff. Something the size of a dragon.

"A spy," Queen Coral hissed under her breath.

Suddenly Blister darted up into the leaves, quick as a cobra striking. She sank her talons into the hidden dragon and ripped it out of the canopy. In the same movement, she whirled and threw the dragon at Tsunami.

Startled, Tsunami reached to catch him and found herself face-to-face with Webs.

Webs, one of the guardians from the Talons of Peace. The traitor who had stolen her egg from the Royal Hatchery, who had never taught her the underwater language.

She barely had time to register the terror on his face before he slammed into her, and they both crashed into the cliff wall. He flapped his wings, pulling back, and she caught her breath as she righted herself.

"Oh," Blister said, sounding disappointed. "It's just a SeaWing."

"Not just a SeaWing." Queen Coral seized Webs by his neck and shook him. Her green eyes were sparks of rage and triumph. "This is Webs, our tribe's biggest traitor. I've been looking for him for years."

"Your Majesty," Webs croaked. He scrabbled at his throat. "Please. I've come to beg for mercy."

"Mercy," Coral hissed. "After what you did." She shook him again, harder. "Mercy denied." She flung him into the air and slammed her tail into the side of his head with a horrible-sounding *CRACK*. Webs went limp, his eyes closed, and he plummeted toward the lake below.

"Webs!" Tsunami yelled. She knew she should hate him, too, considering the life he'd forced on her. But she found herself diving after him.

All over the Summer Palace, SeaWings stopped to look up, gaping at the sight of a dragon falling from the sky. None of them moved to help him. Tsunami beat her wings desperately, trying to catch up. Would he die if he hit the water from such a height?

"Clay!" she shouted. "Clay! Help!"

Clay immediately burst out of their cave, blinking and befuddled but ready.

"Catch him!" Tsunami shouted, pointing. Clay shot away

from the cliff, banking around to intercept Webs's body as he fell. The two dragons collided in midair, and Clay tumbled, trying to hang on to the heavier, larger dragon.

But he slowed him down enough for Tsunami to catch up. She lifted Webs from the other side until his front half rested on Clay's back and his back half lay across her shoulders. Carefully she and Clay struggled over to the pavilion, collapsing on the first level they could reach — the library, as it turned out.

Webs sprawled across the black and blue talon prints, his head lolling to the side. Blood trickled out of one ear.

"Wake up," Tsunami said, shaking him. "Come on, you can't die. Not before I get a chance to yell at you."

"Where did he come from?" Clay asked.

Thump, thump, thump. The other three dragonets landed around them. Glory looked down her nose at Webs, dark green zigzagging through her wings. Sunny crouched beside his head. The egg was cradled underneath her, making it hard for her to get too close, but she reached out and touched his snout with one front talon.

"Webs?" she said softly. "What are you *doing* here?"

"Search the area." Tsunami heard Queen Coral's voice barking orders. "Make sure there are no more Talons of Peace lurking around." She spat out the words *Talons of Peace* as if they tasted like rotten fish.

Tsunami glanced up uneasily at the canopy overhead, where a dragon-sized gap now yawned in the green leaves. A bolt of sunlight shone through, and she couldn't help but worry what else might find its way through the protective cover. Had Blister thought about that at all before she struck? Surely she wouldn't deliberately endanger her allies . . . but maybe she didn't care about them enough to treat their defenses cautiously.

Queen Coral swooped into the library, her face majestic with fury. She loomed over Webs as Blister, Anemone, and Moray all arrived behind her.

"Why would you save his life?" the queen hissed at Tsunami. "After everything he did to you?"

I don't know, Tsunami thought. Why didn't she want Webs dead? It had been instinct that sent her flying after him. *Maybe I want to give Riptide a chance to meet his father, like I never really got to. Or maybe I'm not ready to lose our last guardian yet.* For most of her life, she'd only known seven dragons, and two of them had died in the last ten days. That seemed like more than enough to her.

"I thought he might have information we need," she lied. "Maybe about the Talons —"

"Or," Blister interjected smoothly, "perhaps now we can find out how he snuck into the Royal Hatchery to steal the egg. Clever dragonet. Tsunami must get her brains from you."

Queen Coral hissed and glared down at Webs. "I suppose interrogating him would be useful," she said. "Moray, wake him up."

Moray dove over the edge and returned with a large clam-shell full of seawater. She threw this in Webs's face with no particular gentleness. Sunny let out a little yelp and jumped away from the splash.

Webs coughed and sputtered and snorted water back out his nostrils. He sat up slowly, holding his head and gingerly wiping his snout dry.

His gaze landed first on the dragonets, and Tsunami was surprised to see his whole face light up with joy. He stared from Clay to Glory to Starflight as if he couldn't believe they were all alive. He held out his front talons, and Sunny clutched the one closest to her, smiling back at him.

"But the SkyWings," he said. "I thought you were dead! How did you — ?"

"We escaped," Glory said coldly.

"No thanks to the Talons of Peace," Tsunami added. "Or stupid unhelpful Morrowseer."

"It was amazing," Sunny said. "You should have seen us! We —"

"We'll tell you about it some other time," Clay interrupted. Sunny looked up at him, then over at the SeaWings, and snapped her mouth shut.

Webs saw Queen Coral and the thunderous look on her face, and Blister coiled menacingly behind her. He shuddered, then winced as if that had made his head hurt even more.

"Welcome back," Coral snarled at him. "I thought you were too cowardly to ever return here."

"I know I am not worthy of your mercy, Your Majesty," Webs said, staggering to his feet so he could kneel in front of her. "But I heard — I hoped . . ."

"Why did you steal one of *my* eggs?" Queen Coral demanded. "You could have stolen from any other dragon in the Kingdom of the Sea."

Tsunami's wings twitched. *And that would have been all right? Are you only angry because he stole from you? Not because a dragonet's life was ruined?*

"It had to be an egg due to hatch on the brightest night," Webs said in a wavering voice. "And it had to fit the prophecy — *the SeaWing egg of deepest blue.* I'd seen your eggs when I was guarding them, before I . . . before I left."

"You mean ran away," Coral snarled. "In the middle of a battle."

Looking at Webs, Tsunami couldn't believe he was Riptide's father. Riptide was so much stronger and braver than this shivering old dragon.

"I remembered her egg," Webs pressed on, his wings drooping. "It was so blue — it had to be the right one. I'm so sorry, Your Majesty," he said in a rush. "But the prophecy is so important. I would never have betrayed you for anything else, but for peace . . . How could I not do as the Talons asked?"

"So how did you get into the hatchery?" Coral's tail lashed threateningly. "I had guards posted at that door every moment until the eggs hatched."

Tsunami leaned toward him. If he knew of a secret way in, surely that would point them to the dragonet killer.

Webs hung his head. "I drugged the guards," he said. "I — I knew someone who helped me slip a sleeping potion into their evening meal. They were asleep when I crawled in and out again with the egg. It wasn't their fault."

"Well," Coral said dismissively, "I killed them anyway. As for the *someone* who helped you — your wife, I assume?"

Webs flinched.

"I wondered about that," Coral said. Her expression was mildly pleased, as if she was finally putting the pieces of an old puzzle into place. "Stupid of her not to run away with you. Of course, that's why she was reassigned from the kitchens to active duty in the war soon after. Too bad that first battle was such a bloodbath."

Webs looked as if all the light had been scraped out of his scales. Sunny made a woeful, sympathetic noise and edged closer, twining her tail around his. Even Glory looked a little sorry for him.

Tsunami had never thought about Webs leaving behind a family until she met Riptide. Even then, she hadn't pictured him abandoning a wife and baby dragonet. Maybe he really did care about the prophecy more than anything, if he was willing to give up so much for it. She would not have made the same choice, herself.

"Now I know the dragonets are safe," Webs said quietly. "So you can do whatever you like to me."

"I will," Coral rumbled. "We can start with you telling me where to find the Talons of Peace."

"Why?" Tsunami asked as Webs shook his head. "Why would you want to find them?"

Coral showed all her sharp white teeth. "Revenge, dear. They stole from me, and no one has ever gotten away with that. Now I must hunt them down and exterminate them."

"Don't you have more important things to do?" Tsunami demanded. "I think they're awful dragons, yes, with a really misguided sense of how to raise dragonets to fulfill a prophecy. But all they want to do is end the war. Isn't that what everyone wants?"

"We're not trying to *end* the war," Blister said in her slithering voice. "We're trying to *win* it. I hope you can see the difference."

"But killing the Talons of Peace won't help with that. They haven't hurt anyone but us five," Tsunami said, waving her talons at the other dragonets.

"In fact," Starflight said out of the blue, "they almost certainly saved Tsunami's life."

The NightWing froze as everyone turned to stare at him. Queen Coral hissed menacingly. Even Webs looked confused.

"What?" Coral growled.

"Well," Starflight stammered, "the — the — the other female dragonets in her hatching — all died. The same way every one of your potential heirs has died. Whoever is killing them, Webs took her egg away before the assassin could get to it. If her egg had stayed in the hatchery, she'd be dead. By stealing her, he — and the Talons of Peace — actually saved her life. Uh. Right?"

Tsunami felt like she was shape-shifting, all of her bones being shoved from one skin into another. *No. The Talons of Peace ruined my life. I've always known that. It's the truest thing I know. They didn't* save *me.*

But she knew in her scales that Starflight was right. They did save her. By accident, but they did. Webs did.

She remembered all her dreams of how her life should have been if she'd hatched here and been raised by her own mother. None of them would have happened. She'd have been dead within the first week, her neck snapped like the sad little dragonet in the eggshell.

"Your Majesty!" The small messenger dragon from before — Urchin, Tsunami remembered — tumbled out of the air and skidded to a stop at Queen Coral's claws. He bowed as low as he could, covering his head. "We found a suspicious dragon lurking outside. He must be working with Webs."

"Bring him to me," Queen Coral growled in a voice that rang off the cavern walls.

Urchin pointed down at the tunnel, and they all leaned over to see Piranha and a troop of SeaWing soldiers dragging someone into the Summer Palace. They heaved him out of the water to fly him up to the queen. His webbed talons flopped to the side, his eyes were closed, and a claw mark slashed along his sky-blue scales was bleeding heavily.

Tsunami's stomach flipped inside out like a jellyfish.

It was Riptide.

CHAPTER 22

Webs's green scales paled nearly to gray as Riptide was tossed onto the floor between him and Queen Coral.

"No!" he cried. "He had nothing to do with this! He's never had any contact with me."

Moray tossed another clamshell of water over Riptide, and he groaned, shielding his eyes.

"It's true," Tsunami said desperately. "Riptide wasn't here with Webs. He's — he's been helping me. Um, with my Aquatic." It was true, but it sounded like a lie, even to her own ears.

"Whirlpool is supposed to teach you that, not this miserable creature," Queen Coral said with narrowed eyes.

"*Whirlpool* is a *horrible* teacher," Tsunami flared. "I'd be better off taking lessons from a barnacle."

Riptide pushed himself slowly up to sitting. He glanced around at all the faces staring at him. His gaze stopped on Webs, and the two dragons looked at each other for a long moment.

"Admit your treachery," said the queen. "Betrayal runs in your family, after all." She swiped at Riptide's snout, but he stepped out of reach. Piranha hissed and poked him in the side with a narwhal spear.

"Don't hurt him," Tsunami said. "Please. He's not working for the Talons of Peace, I promise." She was surprised to see Riptide wince. He looked down at his claws, avoiding her eyes.

Was there something he hadn't told her?

"Throw them both in the new prison," Coral said with deep disgust. "We'll find out what we need to know about the Talons later, when I'm feeling a little more violent."

"Don't you have one more question for them?" Blister interjected. She'd been quiet for so long, it made Tsunami jump to hear her voice.

Coral swung her head to look at the SandWing.

"Why they killed all of your heirs," Blister purred. "I mean, *obviously* it was them, right?"

"Obviously!" Coral burst out. She glared at Webs and Riptide.

"Working together," Blister murmured. "It's the perfect climax to the story."

"It *is*," Coral agreed.

"No!" Tsunami said. "That makes no sense!"

"Just like one of your brilliant mysteries," Blister went on, ignoring Tsunami. "*The Claws of Murder*, for instance. Or *A Tail of Blood*. That one was genius."

"It *was*," Coral agreed even more fervently. "They're the perfect murderers! It all fits!"

"No, it doesn't!" Tsunami shouted. "Why would they do that? There's no motive!"

"Of course there is," Coral snarled. "Blister, explain it to her."

"So that Tsunami could return as the only living heir, of course," Blister said smoothly. "If they killed off all the other possible heirs, she would become more and more valuable. A bargaining chip if they ever needed it. A powerful tool when they wanted to use her."

"Nobody uses me," Tsunami spat.

"Wait, Webs can't be the murderer," Clay said. His large brown head tilted to the side. "He hates killing other dragons. That's why he ran away from you in the first place."

"Nonsense," Queen Coral said, waving a talon. "He ran away to protect his own scales."

"Even so, I'm not sure that theory works," Starflight said, gazing vaguely into the air as if he was trying to solve a math equation. "The princess murders started two years before they stole Tsunami's egg, so the Talons, and especially Webs, wouldn't have known they were going to steal a royal egg at that point — Webs didn't even know he was going to *be* a Talon at that point. And Webs has been underground with us for the last six years. He couldn't have flown here and back every time he wanted to murder a dragonet."

Starflight shook his head. "No, I'm afraid it doesn't —" His eyes met Blister's, and he abruptly slammed his mouth shut.

"What he said," Tsunami said desperately. "Exactly."

"So his allies in the Talons of Peace did his dirty work," Blister said, unperturbed. "You know it makes sense, Coral. The Talons have been your enemies for so long. Of course it would turn out that they're the ones behind the murders. It's the ending that wraps everything together."

Coral nodded. Her talons twitched toward the nearest scroll, as if she couldn't wait to write all this down.

"Why are you doing this?" Tsunami demanded, stepping closer to Blister. "Why pin the murders on Webs and Riptide, unless you're covering your own tracks?"

Blister gave a hoot of laughter. "It doesn't matter to me what happens to SeaWing princesses," she said. "Except that I feel my poor ally's pain, of course. I'm merely pointing out the obvious to her. These two should be executed for their crimes as soon as possible."

You want Webs dead, Tsunami thought. *And you killed Kestrel, I'm sure of it. But why?*

"Brilliant, just brilliant," Coral said, clapping her talons together. "Take them away, and we'll plan their execution later." Piranha and her guards closed around Webs and Riptide. Tsunami didn't have a chance to say anything more to them before they were dragged off, and Riptide still wouldn't meet her eyes. She clenched her talons in frustration.

"You know what this means?" Coral went on, delighted. "We can return the egg to the Royal Hatchery. It's safe now."

"It isn't!" Sunny cried. She wrapped her talons around the egg.

"It certainly is," said the queen. "With Webs locked up, the egg can hatch in the Royal Hatchery, just like it's supposed to."

"You're wrong," Tsunami said. "I'm not risking a dragonet's life because you've fallen for this crazy story Blister has invented."

Blister's obsidian-black eyes glittered malevolently at Tsunami.

"It will be perfectly safe," Coral said, waving her claws. "Besides, every queen in SeaWing history has hatched in the Royal Hatchery."

Silence prickled between them. Tsunami was thinking, *I didn't,* and surely Coral was, too. *You'll eat those words when I'm queen,* Tsunami thought, but she wasn't sure she meant it anymore. Did she even *want* to be queen here? Especially if it meant allying herself with Blister — or breaking away from her and then dealing with the consequences?

Only one dragon could change Coral's mind about the egg. Tsunami glanced at Blister and realized at least one thing was true: Blister couldn't care less what happened to the SeaWing heirs. She was studying her claws, looking slightly bored.

"Fine," Tsunami said, squaring her shoulders. "But I'm staying with it until it hatches."

Queen Coral tilted her head. "In the Royal Hatchery?" she said. "All night?"

"I'll make sure she hatches safely," Tsunami said. She glanced at the egg, glowing blue and green below the white shell. The dragonet was close to hatching, pressed against the thinning walls. Every once in a while the egg rocked in Sunny's arms.

"But when I catch the real murderer," Tsunami went on, "I want you to promise that you'll let Riptide and Webs go free."

"Ha," Coral snorted. "Webs will never be free again."

"Even if I save your last heir?" Tsunami demanded.

Coral scraped her claws across the rock. "You won't have to," she said. "We have the assassins now."

"So it should be an easy bargain to make," Tsunami said. Blister stared at her coldly.

"All right," Coral said, waving one talon. "I'll promise you Riptide. But Webs has too much to answer for." Tsunami noticed Blister settling back. So it was definitely Webs she wanted dead, not Riptide.

That was the best she could do for now. She'd have to think of another way to save Webs.

"But Tsunami, we said we should stay together," Clay protested. "We can't protect you down there."

"And whoever's coming after the eggs will be just as happy to kill you, too," Glory pointed out.

Tsunami shook her head and flexed her claws. "Not if I catch him first."

Ice Kingdom
Sky Kingdo
Under the Mountai
Burn's Stronghold
Kingdom of Sand
Scorpion Den
Jade Mountain

PART THREE

OUT OF THE EGG

CHAPTER 23

It was pitch-dark in the Royal Hatchery. Dark and horribly quiet.

Tsunami could see in the dark, of course, but everything was gray and a little blurry. The only flashes of color came from the eggs when the dragonets inside moved. Across the cave, she could see the three male eggs peacefully leaning against one another. *They* had nothing to worry about.

Guards were stationed outside the door, but Tsunami was the only one in the hatchery. As soon as the door closed behind her, she prowled around all the walls, poking everything that stuck out and hoping a hole would suddenly yawn open in the floor. She circled the statue of Orca several times, shoving at its talons and tail and pedestal. But nothing happened. There was no sign of a secret entrance anywhere.

Finally she curled up beside the egg and stared fiercely around the room.

All right, assassin, she thought. *I'm ready for you.* She had a narwhal spear lying on the floor beside her, although she had no idea how to use it. But she wouldn't be taken by surprise again.

The warm jets of water billowed silently up through tiny holes in the coral, surrounding the eggs in a bath of heat and small bubbles. It was a little *too* hot for Tsunami, but she didn't want to move away from the egg. She poked her nose underneath it, checking again for a secret trapdoor, but the floor was smooth and polished like the egg itself.

A flutter moved in the eggshell, like a heartbeat, as the dragonet inside tried to stretch her wings. Tsunami rested her front talons on it for a moment. She wondered if Sunny was right that the dragonet could hear them. She pressed her snout up to the egg and whispered through the water.

"Don't worry. I'm here to protect you."

The tiny wings fluttered again. Tsunami leaned closer, wishing for some noise, some light, in the hot, silent, dark room.

Scrrrrrraaaaaaaaaape.

Tsunami's head shot up.

Stillness. Darkness.

And yet . . . she had a creeping feeling that *someone* was suddenly in the room with her.

Scrrrrrrraaaaaaaaaape.

Her scales tingled between her wings, as if squirrels were scuttling down her back.

She stood up and flexed her claws. The one door to the hatchery was closed. The eggs were still. The only movement in the room was the blip of small bubbles rising from the floor.

But wait . . .

The statue.

Hadn't it been facing the door before?

She stared at it until her eyes hurt.

Had it turned its head? Was it *looking at her*?

Tsunami's whole body was shaking. She blinked through the darkness at the statue of Orca.

The statue stared back. Its eyes were sapphires, she remembered, but in the shades of gray here they gleamed as obsidian-dark and vicious as Blister's. She was sure the statue had been facing the door when she came in. But now its head was turned toward her and the egg, watching them darkly.

Impossible, she started to think, and then —

Scrrape. Scrrape. Scrrrrape.

Stone claws curled around the top of the pedestal.

A stone tongue flicked between jagged sharklike teeth.

Nobody's sneaking in, Tsunami had a moment to think. *The assassin's already here. She's been here all along.*

And then the statue hurtled off the pedestal, talons reaching to snatch the egg.

Tsunami flung herself between the statue and her unhatched sister. Green marble claws raked Tsunami's neck, heavier and thicker than a real dragon's, like shards of rock stabbing between her scales. One caught in her gills and ripped a wider hole. Blood bubbled out as Tsunami shoved the statue away.

Sorry, broke the rules, blood in the hatchery, Tsunami thought dizzily. She staggered back, pressing one talon to her neck.

How could she fight a statue? How could anyone beat a dragon of solid stone?

It attacked again, relentless as the tide. The statue plowed into Tsunami and knocked her backward. Its weight bore down on her, crushing her against the floor. She struggled, clawing at its snout, but her claws scraped uselessly against marble and sang with pain.

The statue was trying to walk over her, willing to trample her on its way to the egg. One foot came down heavily on Tsunami's chest, and she felt tiny *crack crack crack*s stabbing through her ribs.

You are not *getting to that egg.*

Tsunami reached up and wrapped her front talons around the dragon's snout. She yanked it down toward her, dug her claws into the eye sockets, and popped the two sapphires free. They tumbled into her palms, gleaming and heavy.

The stone dragon didn't roar in pain or collapse or any of the things Tsunami had been hoping for. It stopped, swung its head from side to side for a moment, and sat back on its haunches, lifting its weight just long enough for her to wriggle free.

She took a deep breath, thick with gurgling blood, and yelled, "HELP!" as loud as she could. Even muffled by the water, surely a scream would be heard by the guards outside. "HELP! HELP!"

If there were still guards outside.

Queen Coral, convinced of her own theory, might have promised them to Tsunami and then sent them away, certain they wouldn't be needed.

Whether they couldn't hear her or weren't there at all, nobody came.

The statue felt its empty eye sockets curiously, then patted the floor around it as if it thought its eyes might have accidentally slipped out. Tsunami took a step back and dropped the sapphires through two of the water jet holes. She needed all the advantages she could get.

Carefully she reached over the egg and picked up the narwhal spear. Would this do anything against stone?

The statue flicked its tongue in and out, tasting the water. Slowly it turned its sightless face toward Tsunami. She knew an animus dragon must have cursed the statue, but she didn't know how these enchantments worked. Would blinding it stop it, or was it set to keep trying, to kill no matter what, until all the royal heirs in the hatchery were dead?

She guessed it was enchanted to kill only when it was sure no guards were around — no queen, no one to witness its crimes and stop it from striking again.

But Tsunami was an heir. She wasn't a witness. She was a target.

It stepped toward her. The floor trembled a little at the weight of each talon coming down.

Tsunami wanted to lead it away from the egg. If she could open the door, would that be enough to turn it into a frozen statue again? Or if there was no one there, would it chase her into the palace?

But she was afraid to leave the egg, even for a moment. The statue was fast. It could crush the egg with one foot and keep chasing her without missing a beat.

And if she tried to carry the egg with her, the statue could crash down on both of them, shattering it easily. It was safest in the nest, as long as Tsunami stood in front of it.

She hefted the spear and pointed it at the dragon. Normal fight rules didn't apply here. She could try piercing the eye socket, but there was no brain in there to skewer. No heart to find through the scales, not even the vulnerable spot on the tail all dragons had.

The statue's snout lifted, its empty eyeholes as dark as deep sea canyons.

Was it smelling her? Tasting her in the water? Or could it hear her?

Whatever it was doing, it seemed to know exactly where she was, eyes or no eyes.

The statue leaped straight at her. She braced the spear against the floor, and the statue's chest slammed into it.

Jarring shock thrummed through Tsunami's talons, as if she'd been stabbed in both palms. The statue ricocheted back, and Tsunami saw bits of dark green stone crumble away into the water. *So maybe it can be smashed into little pieces.*

The statue came on again, fast, but this time reaching out in front of it. Tsunami tried to move the spear out of its reach, but it caught the narwhal horn in its front talons and yanked it sharply out of her grasp. It swung the spear around in an arc, and Tsunami had to duck and roll away to avoid being skewered.

The only sound the statue made was the scraping of stone against stone. It didn't roar, or growl, or grunt like a regular dragon in battle. It was as horribly silent as the rest of the hatchery.

Tsunami wondered if it *could* talk, or hear, or communicate in any way.

"Can you hear me?" she shouted at it, throwing caution to the currents. "Who enchanted you?"

Instead of answering, it tossed the spear aside and leaped at her once more. Tsunami dove underneath it, grabbed the spear, and whirled to put herself in front of the egg again.

She couldn't smash the statue while it was moving. It was too fast and too strong. But if she could trap it somehow . . .

The statue spun and crashed its tail into her side. Tsunami was knocked off her feet, flying through the water into the wall. *Crack* went something in her chest and *stab* went another bolt of pain through her whole body. Breathless, she forced herself back to the egg, jabbing at the statue with the spear to push it away.

It reached for the spear again. This time she tilted the spear up and stabbed it violently into the statue's open mouth.

The spear lodged in the stone and stuck. The statue's claws scrabbled along the shaft of the horn and tried to yank it out, but it was wedged in tightly. Tsunami shook the spear from side to side, and the statue's head wobbled along with it.

She leaped to an empty nest and jammed the blunt end of the spear into one of the crevices. Now the statue was pinned like a sheep in a dragon's claws. It whipped its tail and beat the floor with its talons, trying to push itself free. Its wings thrashed the water into wild currents so Tsunami could barely stay upright.

Tsunami fought her way back to the egg and picked it up. Just as she did —

Tap tap tap.

The egg cracked down the middle and a small green head poked out. Dark green eyes blinked at Tsunami.

Tsunami smiled and flashed a few tiny stripes along her snout to say hello.

The statue was writhing and smashing the floor now. Tsunami was afraid it would knock itself free in a minute. She clutched the dragonet and swam for the door as fast as she could. When she kicked it open she found that, indeed, there were no guards outside.

But as the door opened, the statue went still.

Tsunami turned in the open doorway to look at it.

The enchantment only worked in secret. It dropped away when the door was open. Whoever had set the curse didn't want anyone to look in and catch the statue at its deadly work. Tsunami guessed that the spell also alerted the statue when someone was coming down the passageway, so it normally had time to return to its pedestal. And the statue would remain still as long as anyone else was around — like the queen or her guards. This statue was meant to keep murdering dragonets for as long as it could.

Well, not anymore, Tsunami thought fiercely.

Even Queen Coral would have to believe the truth once she saw the statue as it was now. Marble Orca, once serene and regal on her pedestal, was trapped by the spear in battle position. Her claws reached out hungrily and a snarl transfigured her face. Coral would know for certain that this was the killer who had been hiding in her hatchery all these years.

Now the question was . . . who had enchanted it? An animus dragon, of course. But it couldn't be Anemone, who hadn't hatched yet when the princess murders began.

Tsunami had a new theory. *Animus power runs in the royal family.*

But if Shark or Moray had this kind of power, they would

be using it for so much more. They would use it to fight battles, to win the queen's favor, to be the secret weapon she wanted so badly. If Shark's goal was the throne for his daughter, he'd have used his magic to get rid of Coral herself instead of knocking off her dragonets.

And if the animus was Moray, she'd have offered her power to the queen long ago, for Coral to use however she wanted.

No, it was another royal dragon. Tsunami was sure of it.

She stepped back into the room, leaving the door open. She remembered Coral's words. *My first daughter was a very talented sculptor.*

Tsunami settled the newly hatched dragonet around her neck, wincing at the pain from her gills.

Orca may have died years ago, but she left a deadly gift behind.

Carefully she stepped over the nests and stared into the statue's face.

Empty. Lifeless. Just a statue now.

A statue that she and Coral would be happy to smash and smash and smash until it became a million of the smallest pieces of rock in the ocean.

Orca's weapon would never assassinate another dragonet or crush another egg. Its killing days were over.

CHAPTER 24

Bright morning light filtered through the canopy, casting puddles of green sunshine all across the Summer Palace. Tsunami opened and closed her wings, grateful that she didn't have to be at the Council meeting with Blister that was going on overhead. After last night's battle in the hatchery, Tsunami just wanted a break from scheming dragon queens and war plans for a little while.

The little emerald-green dragonet romped on the beach, kicking up sand and stopping in surprise when it drifted into her nose. She sneezed hard enough to knock herself backward, then sat up and gave Tsunami an indignant look.

"Well, stop putting sand in your nose, then," Tsunami suggested.

Her little sister shook herself, spotted a tiny crab digging in the sand, and pounced. The crab vanished into its hole, and the dragonet looked at her empty talons in confusion.

"What's her name?" Sunny asked. She leaned into Tsunami's side for a moment, and Tsunami felt a fizz of relief in her chest. Sunny had forgiven her, or forgotten she was mad in the first place. Either one was fine with Tsunami.

"I'm trying to think of the perfect name," Tsunami said. "Mother said it was up to me."

The dragonet glanced up from her digging. Sand covered her snout like a mustache.

"Maybe you should call her Walrus," Glory offered, dissolving in giggles.

"She's not a Walrus!" Tsunami said. "She's much more dignified than that!"

The dragonet jumped at an insect in the air, lost her balance, and landed with her head in the sand and her tail sticking straight up. She flailed her wings furiously until Sunny gently lifted her free.

"Very," Glory said. "Very dignified."

"She's awfully cute," Clay said. "I think she has your snout, Tsunami."

Tsunami flicked her tail, pleased. She looked around proudly and noticed that Starflight was sitting a short way from the rest of them. He was staring up at the pavilion with an anxious expression, running sand through his claws.

Glory followed her gaze. She leaned over and poked the NightWing sharply in the ribs.

"What's going on with you?" Glory demanded. "Why are you crawling around licking Blister's talons?"

"I'm not!" he protested.

"You really are," Tsunami said. Starflight wouldn't meet their eyes.

"I just think she'd be a good queen," he mumbled.

"No, you don't," Glory said. "Back under the mountain, you specifically said she was kind of evil and probably had sinister plans for all of Pyrrhia."

"Oh, you did say that," Clay agreed. He poked a hole in the sand for the dragonet to climb into. "I remember that."

Starflight flashed him an annoyed look. "*That* you remember?"

"So why do you suddenly *looooove* her so much?" Tsunami asked. Her little sister rolled into the hole and then jumped back out, flapping her wings to shake off the sand.

"Blister's smart," Starflight stammered. "She's — uh — she's better than Burn or Blaze."

"I don't like her," Sunny said, to Tsunami's surprise.

"Really?" Starflight said, his wings drooping.

Sunny shook her head. "She called me 'sweet' like that's all anyone needs to know about me."

"But you are sweet," Clay said, patting her head.

"It kind of does sum you up," Tsunami agreed. Sunny scowled at both of them in a way Tsunami thought was pretty cute. "But I agree that I don't like her either. More than that, I don't trust her. I think we need to meet Blaze. Maybe all the stories about her brainlessness have been exaggerated."

"Doubtful," said Starflight glumly.

"So we can go?" Glory asked Tsunami. "And look for Blaze? You mean we're done here?"

Even the baby dragon stopped digging for a moment to look at Tsunami. She felt a stab of guilt at the hopeful expressions on her friends' faces. She hadn't realized they wanted to leave the Kingdom of the Sea so badly.

Wingbeats sounded in the air above them, and they all looked up to see Coral, Anemone, Blister, and Moray circling down from the Summer Palace pavilion.

The green dragonet scampered up to Anemone as soon as she landed and tackled one of her talons. Anemone laughed and flipped her over. Their little sister yelped, struggled upright again, and started clawing her way up Anemone's leg.

"Have you picked a name?" Anemone asked Tsunami.

"What do you think of Auklet?" Tsunami said.

"That's a kind of seabird," Starflight said in his know-it-all voice to Clay.

"Oh," Clay said. "Cool. I mean, I knew that."

Tsunami liked the look on her mother's face, watching the two sisters. She looked proud, protective, happy for them. Tsunami was right about her: Queen Coral wouldn't kill her own daughters, even though one of them would one day grow up to take her place. She cared about them, perhaps a little too much, but Tsunami thought that was better than not caring at all.

She wondered if Blister or Burn had any dragonets. Starflight would know; it must be in the scrolls somewhere. Tsunami had a feeling Blister would happily kill off her own dragonets if she thought it was necessary. Those glittering black eyes hid more secrets and plans than Tsunami wanted to know about.

"Orca's statue has been destroyed," Queen Coral said with a sigh. "It was so beautiful, too. She was so talented. I can't believe she hid her animus powers from me. *She* could have trained with Whirlpool, too."

"Wow. She really missed out," Tsunami said, winking at Anemone.

"We'll have to examine all the things she carved," Coral mused. "Just to make sure there aren't any other enchantments lurking around."

"We're sure it was Orca, right?" Tsunami asked. "No one else in the palace could be an animus?" She wasn't able to stop herself from glancing at Moray, who glared back.

Coral shook her head. "Before we destroyed it, Anemone reanimated the statue and made it reveal who had enchanted it. It said Orca, plain as day." She sighed again. "Orca carved that statue and dedicated it to the hatchery shortly before she challenged me. I gather she expected to win, so she was setting up a way to get rid of her possible heirs and challengers."

"That explains her last words to you," Moray hissed.

"Yes," said Coral sadly. "She said, 'I did this all wrong. You're going to rule forever, aren't you, Mother? You should thank me. No one can stop you now.'" The queen looked down at Anemone and Auklet, playing in the sand. She stroked Anemone's head with a wistful expression.

"But . . ." Clay said hesitantly. "But if Orca was the assassin, then who attacked Tsunami in the tunnel?"

Queen Coral shrugged. "We'll catch them eventually," she said. "That's how stories work."

Anemone gave Tsunami a frustrated look.

Tsunami still thought that her attacker might have been Shark. He was already out of prison, patrolling the Summer Palace with a bad-tempered expression on his snout. And he certainly hadn't been pleased or supportive when she staggered out of the hatchery with the dragonet, blood pouring from her gills. She reached up and touched the seaweed bandage on her neck. Her ribs ached whenever she moved, too, but the healers said she just had to rest and let the fractures fix themselves.

Rest! The dragonets of destiny have no time for rest! she thought ruefully.

"Now that we know the real assassin," Tsunami reminded Coral, "you promised to set Riptide free."

"I know I did," said the queen. "But I'm not sure quite what to do with him. Clearly he can't stay in my kingdom. He'll have to crawl back to those Talons of Peace and see if they'll take him."

"Maybe he can come with us," Tsunami said, then snapped her mouth shut. But it was too late. Coral and Blister were both staring at her in a very uncomfortable way.

"With you?" Coral said slowly. "Are you going somewhere?"

"We — I — yes — I think we should," Tsunami said. She felt her friends shifting closer together behind her. "I don't belong here, Mother. I wanted to, but — I'm only causing trouble, and I'm not doing what I was hatched to do. I don't speak the underwater language. I don't understand the Council. You have two daughters now who could be great queens one day." She nodded at Anemone. "But my destiny is somewhere else. I have to go stop the war. With my friends."

"And how do you plan to do that?" Blister said softly.

"I don't know," Tsunami said. "We'll figure it out."

"We were thinking we should go meet Blaze," Clay suggested. "Just to be fair."

Ack, Clay, shut up, Tsunami thought with a wince.

"But it won't change how we — I mean that we think you're —" Starflight said hurriedly to Blister, then trailed off under Tsunami's baleful look.

"No," said Blister. The diamond patterns on her back writhed as she stepped closer. "No one is leaving."

"You can't tell us what to do," Tsunami said.

"*I* am your choice," Blister hissed. "The Ni — the Talons of Peace want *me*."

"Oh?" Glory said. "Do they know that?"

"It's not their decision anyway!" Tsunami said.

"Your lives could be very easy from here on," said Blister. "All you have to do is tell everyone the dragonets of destiny have chosen me as the next SandWing queen. And you can do that from here, where I can keep an eye on you."

"Where you can keep us prisoner, you mean," Tsunami said angrily. "We've had quite enough of that, thank you. Mother, tell her you wouldn't do that to me."

Queen Coral gave Blister an anxious look. "My dear, I'm sure they will still choose you after meeting Blaze. No one would choose *her* in a million years."

"Perhaps, but first they have to survive that long," Blister said smoothly. "You know better than anyone how dangerous it is out there, Coral. Remember what happened to Gill. We'll really be protecting the dragonets by keeping them here."

"Oh, that makes sense," Coral said, sounding relieved. "She's right, Tsunami. Just stay here and we'll take good care of all of you."

Tsunami looked back at her friends. Starflight looked miserable, but the others — they looked hopeful, as if they trusted Tsunami to get them out.

"This isn't the right place for my friends either," Tsunami said. "Glory wants to go home — right, Glory? And Sunny should find her parents. It's not fair that I get to do those things and they don't. We just —" She squared her wings. "We have to go, and if you try to keep us, you'll be no better than the Talons or Queen Scarlet."

Blister glared at Starflight. "Don't you have something to say about this, NightWing?"

He stared miserably at his talons and didn't respond.

She hissed. "Useless. There *is* something wrong with all of you, isn't there? But you're the dragonets I have, and I'm not letting you go." Blister turned to Coral. "Throw them in your prison."

"She wouldn't do that," Tsunami said. "Mother? Right? You wouldn't do that?"

"It might help your decision," Blister hissed, "if you knew exactly *who* killed your husband in the SkyWing arena."

Tsunami felt her scales turn to ice. This was it. The moment her secrets came out and she got what she deserved.

Coral's gills flared and her eyes widened. "What are you saying?"

"You know he died in the arena," Blister said. "But do you know who his opponent was? The dragon who ripped the life out of him?"

"Maybe you should also know," Starflight said suddenly, "that Blister killed Kestrel and is lying to you about it. And that she wants Webs dead for her own reasons and doesn't care about your daughters at all."

Blister arched her neck like a cobra and hissed at him.

Starflight threw his wings over his head as if he expected her tail to come stabbing down. But all she said was, "You'll be sorry for that, useless NightWing."

Coral wrapped her wings around Anemone and Auklet and took a step back toward the water. She looked from Blister to Tsunami like she wasn't sure who to trust anymore.

"Don't listen to them, Coral," Blister said. "They're only dragonets. And dragonets never know what's best for them."

"I think we can be pretty sure *prison* isn't at the top of the list, though," Tsunami snapped. "And from now on, Blister, you show some respect and address my mother as Queen Coral."

Smoke curled from Blister's snout. Tsunami wondered what Coral would do if the SandWing attacked the dragonets of destiny right in front of her.

"I don't know what's going on," Coral said, signaling with her tail. A platoon of SeaWing guards appeared from one of the caves. "But for your own safety, Tsunami, you're staying here for now."

"Mother!" Tsunami yelled. She smacked a guard in the snout with her tail and bared her teeth at another. "Think for yourself for once! Let us go!"

But Queen Coral turned away, avoiding Blister's gaze as well. She curled Auklet into one of her talons and flew back to the pavilion with her daughters.

Tsunami fought the guards, but there were too many of them, and her ribs were still screaming with pain from the night before. One by one, each of the dragonets was over-powered and dragged off to the same prison cave where Riptide and Webs had disappeared the day before.

SeaWings watched from all over the pavilion. Tsunami had never been so humiliated. Some dragonets of destiny they were, tossed around like lumps of treasure to be hoarded.

They'd come to the Kingdom of the Sea looking for safety, and instead they were prisoners once again.

── CHAPTER 25 ──

The prison cave was high on the cliff wall, not far from the canopy, overlooking the pavilion below. Tsunami hadn't paid much attention to it before, except to notice that Riptide and Webs had been taken there. But as the guards flew them up to the cave, she realized that it glowed with a weird blue light, and she could hear strange crackling sounds coming from inside.

Sharp spears prodded her into the cave entrance, and she felt damp stone under her claws. As her eyes adjusted to the dim light, she saw a path winding into the huge cavern ahead of them.

This wasn't the underwater prison Lagoon and Shark had been sent to. This was where Queen Coral kept the real threats. Including, Tsunami realized as she was shoved along the stone floor, several prisoners of war. She saw at least three SkyWings, hissing short blasts of flame at their captors. An IceWing lay with his wings spread out, gasping faintly from the heat he wasn't used to. Two SandWings were caged together, one of them curled in a ball with his eyes pressed shut, the other pacing and snarling.

There was even a giant MudWing with chains around her ankles like the ones that had been on Clay. She tilted her head curiously at Clay as he went by.

But the strangest thing about the prison wasn't the dragon prisoners, or even the staggeringly large size of the cavern.

It was the cages.

There were no bars, no doors. Instead, a channel of water as wide as two dragons encircled each prisoner, trapping them on islands of stone — some large enough for multiple dragons, some with barely room for one. More water poured from grooves in the ceiling down to the channels, creating cascading walls around the islands.

And all the water walls and all the moats glowed the same bright blue and gave off the same fizzing, crackling sound. The imprisoned dragons flinched away from any stray droplets that splashed toward them, and they kept their tails carefully tucked up on dry land.

The path wound around and between the islands like a long bridge. The ceiling above was covered in glowworms, casting an eerie light over all the strange prison cells.

Tsunami twisted to peer into the moats. What were the prisoners so afraid of?

Iridescent purple jellyfish pulsed here and there, adding their light to the glowworms up above. Tsunami knew that their tentacles could sting, but surely not badly enough to keep the prisoners in. If it were her (*and soon it will be,* she thought), she'd leap right through the water wall, splash through the moat, and fight her way out, no matter how many jellyfish were in her way.

Suddenly she caught sight of a dark green shape swimming in one of the channels. It was as long as a scavenger and as thick around as a dragon tail, with no legs or arms or wings. As she squinted at it, another one surfaced not far away, and she caught a glimpse of a flat head with sunken, dead eyes. Nostrils flared at the end of its snout, and then it sank into the water again. Bubbles fizzed and snapped for a long moment where it had been.

Sunny pressed close against Clay, her gray-green eyes enormous and terrified. Tsunami glanced around at Starflight and saw him studying the cages as well. Maybe he would understand what was going on.

She didn't spot Webs or Riptide, but the dragonets were pushed along so fast, and the water blurred the features of the prisoners so it was hard to distinguish between the few imprisoned SeaWings she could see.

The guards finally stopped at one of the largest prison islands. There was the same moat around it, but no water came from the ceiling here. Tsunami couldn't see anything swimming in the moat either.

"Hop over," growled one of the guards. "All of you."

"What if we don't?" Tsunami asked.

"Then you'll be dragged off to separate cages, instead of getting to share one," he answered.

Clay jumped over the moat immediately. His talons scraped against the hard rock floor as he landed with a heavy thud. He turned and reached out to catch Sunny as she leaped after him. Starflight followed, and then Glory, and finally, reluctantly, Tsunami flapped her wings to lift herself over the chasm and land beside her friends.

Another guard pulled on a chain that hung along the wall. Something clanked and groaned from within the stone as she drew the links through her claws. Tsunami leaned forward and saw a small door opening in the underwater wall of the moat. Three of the thick green creatures wriggled through it, their dead eyes staring creepily up at her.

A whoosh sounded from above, and talons yanked her back from the edge just as water came sluicing down. Tsunami looked up at the cave roof, then around to see that it was Starflight who had pulled her back. He let her go and twisted to watch the waterfall that now surrounded them. His claws tapped nervously against one another.

"What are those creepy things in the water?" Tsunami asked him.

"I think — I think they're electric eels," he said.

"Oh, brrrr," Glory said, shaking out her wings as if they were covered in bugs. "The scrolls about them gave me nightmares for months."

Sunny twined her tail around one of Clay's forelegs as if she was trying to get even closer to him. "What's an electric eel?" she asked.

"They give off a kind of shock," Starflight explained. Behind him, a blue fizzing light sparked up the waterfall and vanished again, making them all jump.

"It would feel like getting hit by lightning," Glory added.

"And it can be strong enough to kill a dragon," said Starflight. "Especially in salt water, and when the eels are as big as the ones down there."

"So all this water around us —" Tsunami started.

"Could be charged with deadly force at any time," Starflight said. "Not all the time — it's not a constant current. But if they're mad or hungry, they're probably giving off shocks pretty frequently, and then just touching the water could transfer that to you. Even if it only stunned you, it would hurt a lot."

Tsunami frowned at the cascade. Through it she could see the blurry outline of the guards slithering away. Evidently they trusted their nasty prison setup to keep the dragonets in.

"I can't believe we're prisoners again," Clay said with a sigh. "Why does this keep happening to us?"

"I *know*!" Sunny agreed. "Doesn't anyone trust the prophecy? If they believe in it, can't they have faith that we'll do the right thing?"

"Everyone is trying to make sure the prophecy turns out the way *they* want it to," Tsunami said. She turned in a circle, but there wasn't enough room to pace without brushing her wings or tail into the water. She sat back down with a growl. "It would be *helpful* if the stupid *prophecy* had been a little more *clear* about what was supposed to *happen*."

"Why didn't you use your venom when they grabbed us?" Starflight asked Glory.

"Believe me, I will," the RainWing said fiercely. "I'm waiting for the right moment."

"I think that's smart," Tsunami said. "Even with Glory's magical death spit, we probably couldn't have fought off the whole palace, and it would have given away our best secret weapon."

Glory looked surprised. "Well, thank you," she said. "Although I'm going to vote against calling it 'magical death spit,' please."

"Maybe tonight," Tsunami said, lowering her voice. "When most of the palace is sleeping. Maybe we can fight our way out then."

"Past the water with the shocks that might kill us?" Sunny asked. "What good is magical death spit against lightning eels?"

"Electric eels," Starflight corrected her.

"We are NOT CALLING IT MAGICAL DEATH SPIT," Glory said.

"Or —" Tsunami remembered the guards who had given her the key. "Maybe we can convince someone to let us go."

"I like that plan," Clay said, bobbing his head.

"I like the one where we melt everyone's eyeballs on our way out the door," Glory said.

"With magical death spit," Sunny said, then buried her head in Clay's wings to hide her giggles as Glory glared at her.

"Three *moons*, Glory," said Tsunami. "That's *horrible*."

"Who are you?" Glory asked. "What happened to the SeaWing who'd fight her way out of anything?"

"I'll still fight," Tsunami said. An image of Gill flashed in her mind and she shivered. "I'm just saying, there are a lot of these guards who are really on our side. I bet we can find someone to help us."

Sunny lifted her snout. "Did you hear something?"

"Like what?" Starflight asked.

The little SandWing hesitated. "It's hard to be sure over the water sounds."

"Probably nothing," Tsunami said. "Nothing helpful anyway." Sunny frowned at her.

"Someone's coming," Glory observed. They could see a pale shape flitting along the path toward them, although it was blurred by the waterfall.

"Is that what you heard?" Starflight asked Sunny.

She shook her head, looking perplexed.

As the dragon came closer, Tsunami thought she recognized her coloring. But surely it couldn't be —

"Anemone?" she called.

"There you are!" Anemone hurried over to their cage. She stood as close as she could get to the moat and the crackling water. Tsunami wished she could reach over and wrap her wings around her little sister.

"You're unharnessed!" she cried.

"I know, isn't it wonderful?" Anemone stretched her wings wide and beamed. "It's only for a little while." She tugged at the web that was still fitted closely around her chest. "I'll be snapped in again later. But Queen Coral said I could go fly around while she has Auklet fitted for *her* harness, as long as I don't leave the Summer Palace. This would be the happiest day of my life if I weren't so worried about you."

"Can you set us free?" Clay asked hopefully.

"And then come with us," Tsunami suggested. "We'll never make you use your powers, I promise."

Anemone shook her head. "I wish I could. But Coral and Blister will be furious enough about losing the dragonets of destiny. Think about it — if their secret weapon disappears, too, they'll hunt you down like sharks after prey."

"That's a good point," Starflight agreed in his let's-all-be-sensible voice.

"I don't care," Tsunami said. "I don't care if every dragon in Pyrrhia is searching for us. We'll keep you safe, a lot safer than you are here."

Anemone shifted her wings. Even through the water, Tsunami could see the mournful expression on her snout.

"I just — I just don't think I'm ready to live my life like Webs did, never able to return home," she said. "I'd miss Auklet. And I think the SeaWings need me here. I think Mother needs me, so she's hearing another voice besides Blister's."

Tsunami knew that was all very logical, but it still made her scales itch to think she'd have to abandon her sister when she'd only just met her.

"All right," Clay said. "You could still set us free, though, right?"

"They'd know it was her," Glory pointed out.

"That's true," Tsunami agreed. "It's too dangerous."

"But there's something else I wanted to do for you," Anemone said. She lifted something in her front talons, and Tsunami realized she was holding a pure white narwhal spear.

"Spear," Anemone said solemnly, "find the dragon who attacked Tsunami in the entrance tunnel and bring him or her to us." She let go, and the spear flew up the path out of the cave.

The other dragonets stared at her in awe.

"Is that really possible?" Clay asked. "That'll actually work?"

"We'll see," Anemone said, pressing her claws together.

"You didn't have to do that," Tsunami said, worried. "Do you feel all right?"

"Just a little cold," Anemone answered. She rubbed her tail between her talons with a rough scraping sound.

They waited. And waited.

And finally they saw someone stumbling down the path toward them. The spear seemed to glow in the dark as it jabbed the dragon in the back and wings and tail, driving it along.

"Ow!" a voice echoed through the cavern. "What is the meaning of — why am I — ow! what — ow! Stop! Ow! I will report you to the — OW!"

"Well, that's not Coral," said Glory.

"And it's not Shark," said Tsunami. She scratched her horns, confused. She'd been so sure it had to be Shark.

"Not Moray either." Anemone stood up as he approached.

The spear prodded the dragon into place beside Anemone, on the edge of the electric moat.

It was Whirlpool.

— CHAPTER 26 —

"Whirlpool?" Tsunami said, thoroughly astonished. "Why would *you* want to kill me?" She'd rather thought he was too boring to be a suspect.

"Rubbish," said the green dragon with a haughty air. "I would never —" The spear poked him again, a little harder this time. "*Ow.* My goodness. Anemone, I had no idea you were capable of such powerful magic. I must be a brilliant teacher. Of course, I'd be more impressed if it weren't *stabbing me* — OW.*"

Anemone shifted on her talons uncomfortably. "I didn't think it would be you," she said.

"We should tell Queen Blister how accomplished you are," Whirlpool said in his oozy voice. "She'll be so terribly pleased."

"Don't you dare," Tsunami snapped.

"Do you really think I'll find you threatening from in there?" he asked.

"If you do, I'll tell Mother you tried to kill me," she said. "How do you think she'll feel about that?"

He shrugged and reached up to play with the gold hoop earring in his ear. "She may find it quite admirable, actually. After all, I was merely trying to ensure that Anemone dear would be queen."

"Me?" Anemone's wings fluttered open and closed. "You don't even like me that much. Why do anything for me?"

"Well," Whirlpool said, "frankly, I don't want to marry her." He pointed at Tsunami.

"Wow," Glory said cheerfully. "That was totally on my list of reasons why someone might want to kill you."

"Don't worry," Tsunami snapped. "I'd rather be torn apart by tiger sharks than ever marry you."

"But I do want to be king," Whirlpool said. He held out his talons as if imagining more gold rings looping around his claws. "So I thought if I got rid of you, I'd improve my chances of marrying a more agreeable daughter."

"I don't ever want to marry you either!" Anemone cried.

"It's not really up to you," Whirlpool said, taking a step back up the path to the cave entrance. "Once I tell Queen Coral and Queen Blister about what you can do, they'll be so grateful, they'll let me have anything I want. But of course, then you'll be very busy using your powers to win the war. And you probably won't survive that. So I should really ask for Auklet instead." He tapped his snout thoughtfully, as if he was musing to himself.

"You can't tell them!" Tsunami shouted. She was supposed to protect Anemone from being used like this. It was the one thing her sister had asked of her — and instead now it would be her fault if Anemone became Blister's pawn.

She lunged toward the waterfall, but Clay jumped forward at the same time and held her back. Blue light crackled in front of them, and down below, the eels clustered menacingly like a sinister clump of seaweed.

But at the same time, on the other side of the waterfall, Anemone was moving, too. She seized the spear from the air, spun it around, and smacked the side of it into Whirlpool's head.

He staggered forward, then crumpled without a sound. His wings tipped sideways, overbalancing him, and in one sudden movement, his body slipped over the edge into the electric eel moat.

Anemone yelped with fear and dropped her weapon. She reached her talons toward the water . . . but it was too late.

A blinding flash of blue sizzled up the cascading waterfall. Tsunami jumped back, and all five dragonets huddled close in the center of the island. The water in the moat churned and seethed around the spot where Whirlpool had disappeared. Thick green tails thrashed through the bubbles and sparks flew as if several bolts of lightning were striking at once.

Sunny covered her eyes, and Clay put his wing around her. Tsunami wished she could do the same for Anemone — on the far side of the moat, her little sister looked petrified in place.

Slowly the flashes calmed down until only an occasional zap appeared in the wall.

And then they all stopped. The waterfall was quiet, and so was the moat.

Tsunami could see the eels, still clustered around a large, dark shape at the bottom of the pool. But their frenzy had subsided, and she guessed she was lucky she couldn't see any details of what they were doing now.

"Anemone!" she called. "Are you all right?"

Anemone didn't answer. Her blurred outline was motionless, as if she were one of Orca's statues.

"I'm not sure I should tell you this," Starflight said, "but you might be able to go through the water right now."

Tsunami whipped around toward him. "Really? Why?"

He pointed to the eels. "After a burst like that, they'll need a while to recharge. I *think*. So they might not be able to let off any shocks for at least a minute or two. Wait —" he added as Tsunami flared her wings. "But I'm not sure. I didn't read those scrolls as often as the ones about dragons. I'm sorry." Starflight's black head drooped. "It's probably not worth the risk. I wouldn't listen to me."

"But Starflight, you know everything," Sunny said. "I'm sure you're right."

"I could go through and turn off the waterfall," Tsunami said. "Then it would only be me risking it."

Starflight looked miserable. "But it was my idea," he said. "And if I might be wrong, shouldn't I —"

Poor Starflight. Tsunami twined her tail around his. She knew he wanted to be brave and helpful. But this was the kind of thing she did, not him.

"Don't be silly," she said. "This is my kingdom. I'm responsible for doing the crazy things here."

"Do you remember what the scrolls said about electric eels?" Clay asked Glory.

The RainWing lifted her wings slightly. "I don't think it was specific," she said. "They can run out of charge for short periods of time, but I don't know if this is definitely one of them, or how long it might last."

Think it through. Be more like Starflight. Don't be impulsive, Tsunami thought. But then . . . *what if this is our only chance to escape?* She glanced over at Anemone. *And I have to help her.*

But if I die, what happens to the others?

She clenched her talons. An image of her mother's Council flashed through her head. "All right," she said. "Let's vote."

"Holy moons," Glory said. "Seriously, what have you done with the real Tsunami?"

"Quickly," Tsunami said, shooting a glance at the quiet waterfall.

"I believe Starflight," Sunny said. "I think you can make it through. Definitely."

"I don't," Starflight said glumly. "I vote that nobody tries, just to be safe."

"Well, *I* want to get out of here," Glory said. "And I'm

willing to risk Tsunami's bossy scales to do it." She shot Tsunami a toothy grin.

Clay shook his head slowly. "I don't know. You're too important to all of us, Tsunami. I don't think you should do it."

"Well, that doesn't help," Tsunami said with a snort. "Now I just have to decide for myself anyway. Some Council you guys are." But those were pretty much the votes she'd been expecting. And she'd listened to all of them, and she knew what she wanted to do.

She took a deep breath, spun around, and launched herself at the wall of water. It felt like leaping into a freezing hailstorm, icy drops pelting her snout and closed eyes, slicing into her gills through the seaweed bandage, hammering the fractures in her ribs. She braced herself for lightning-sharp pain, but a moment later, her talons thumped onto solid rock.

Tsunami opened her eyes as she skidded to a stop. She'd made it to the other side of the moat, and her scales were still intact.

She grabbed Anemone's shoulders and shook her until the pale little dragon looked up to meet her eyes.

"You have to get out of here," Tsunami said. "We're going to escape, and I don't want it to look like you were involved. Go find Mother and hang around where she can see you so you have an alibi. All right? Are you listening?"

"But look what I did," Anemone whispered, pointing to the pool.

"You didn't mean to do that," Tsunami said. She knew way too clearly how Anemone felt right now. "Anemone, it was an accident — you didn't push him into the moat! And if it hadn't happened, think how many dragons you might have had to kill with your powers. Now you can tell Mother that with no trainer, your powers seem to be getting weaker. Mess up all the time. Make sure she thinks you aren't ready and won't be for a long time."

"But one day —" Anemone started.

"One day very soon, this war will be over. We're going to end it. Trust me." Tsunami squeezed Anemone's front talons in hers. "Now get out of here."

"Good luck," Anemone whispered.

Tsunami wrapped her wings around her sister. "Good luck to you, too."

Anemone fled up the cave path. Her pale wings fluttered like moths as she disappeared around the bend.

Tsunami hurried to the chain on the wall. The guard had yanked it down — could she pull it back up? She tried hauling the chain in the opposite direction and felt it slide jerkily through her claws. Clanking noises rattled from the ceiling, and she stopped for a moment, glancing up the path where the guards had gone. Were there guards at the entrance? What if they heard her?

"Hey, kid," a raspy voice croaked. Tsunami jumped and looked around.

A scrawny SandWing was watching her from his prison island. Even through the waterfall, Tsunami could see the dark glitter of his eyes. "You could do the same thing for me," he hissed. "Set me free!"

Tsunami turned back to the chain and kept pulling. She didn't know what was in store for Coral's prisoners, but she also didn't know why they were here, or whether they deserved it.

Except for two of them.

Somewhere in this cavern, Riptide and Webs were trapped, possibly awaiting execution. She had to find them, too.

What sounded like an enormous metallic groan echoed overhead, and then suddenly, the cascading water around her friends shut off. There was a beat of silence as they all stared up at the ceiling.

Sunny leaped off first, flapping her wings to clear the moat, and the others followed her quickly. Tsunami pushed past them to lead the way up the path.

"What about me?" yelled the imprisoned SandWing.

"I have to find Riptide and Webs," Tsunami said to her friends. "Did anyone see them on the way in?"

"I did," Clay said. "They're on one island together, not far from the entrance."

The five of them hurried along the path. Tsunami kept her wings curled in and tried not to look at the fizzing blue water walls or the lurking eels.

They rounded the last corner and saw the greenish light of the Summer Palace up ahead. Tsunami spotted the guards first, and pushed her friends back into the shadows.

Only three, she thought. Three guards stood on the ledge outside the prison, chatting and tossing their spears from talon to talon. They didn't look very threatening. And perhaps they were secretly on the dragonets' side, if they had allowed Anemone through to see Tsunami.

She didn't want to fight them if she could avoid it. She didn't want to shed any more SeaWing blood ever again.

"There," Clay whispered in her ear. He pointed over her shoulder. "That island, just inside the entrance."

Tsunami spotted the two blue shapes moving beyond the wall of water. She also saw a chain running along the stone beside their island. If she could get to it without the guards noticing, and then move the mechanism without the guards hearing it, Riptide and Webs would be free to escape with the dragonets.

"There it is again," Sunny whispered. "Don't you all hear that?"

"Hear what?" Clay whispered back.

"I don't know," Sunny said. "I keep hearing — I think I'm hearing wingbeats."

"There are SeaWings flying all over the palace," Glory pointed out.

"I know," Sunny said. "This is bigger, higher — I'm not sure."

"Don't worry so much," Tsunami said. "I'm sure you're imagining things."

Sunny stamped one of her feet and craned her neck toward the outside. "No, I'm definitely sure," she said firmly. "I hear wingbeats above the canopy. Lots and lots of them."

"Sunny —" Tsunami started, but then Clay's head shot up, and so did Starflight's.

"I think she's right," Clay said.

Tsunami inhaled sharply, realizing what that meant. "You don't think —"

Starflight lashed his tail. "I smell fire, too."

Tsunami didn't have time to think or come up with a safe, logical solution. She burst out of their hiding spot and ran toward the guards.

"Look out!" she yelled. "Warn the palace!"

All three guards jumped and two of them accidentally dropped their spears over the ledge. They stared at Tsunami as if her horns were blazing columns of fire.

"Move!" she shouted. Tsunami shoved them aside, stood on the ledge, and yelled, "SeaWings! Mother! Look out! We're under attack!"

And then the first firebomb crashed through the canopy.

CHAPTER 27

Panic.

Screaming.

For a palace surrounded by water, it was surprising how much caught on fire so quickly.

Large sections of the canopy collapsed, carrying flaming branches and leaves and debris down onto the Summer Palace. Tsunami saw dragons spiraling toward the lake, their wings alight with flames, shrieking with pain.

The firebombs were just logs set on fire, but they caused terrible damage as they crashed through the pavilion and knocked SeaWings out of the air.

"The SkyWings found us," said one of the guards, looking skyward in terror. As he said it, they all saw a wing of red and orange dragons soar overhead, dropping more bombs and breathing more fire down on the canopy.

"But how?" said the second guard.

Tsunami thought of the hole left in the canopy when Blister ripped Webs out of it. Would that have been enough to lead the SkyWings here? So quickly? What were the chances a scout had spotted the hole, reported back, and gathered the forces for an attack only a day later?

It had to be something else.

She looked down and saw the lake water churning as frantic dragons tried to shove their way into the exit tunnel. Only one way in meant only one way out, and it wasn't big enough for everyone at once. She felt sick at the thought of all those dragons crammed into the small space together.

There was one other way — but flying out through the canopy, into the claws of the SkyWings, could be suicide.

Tsunami searched the mass of dragons for her mother, but she couldn't see ropes of pearls or wings the exact shade of her own anywhere. At least Coral wasn't one of the shapes with charred wings floating limply in the water.

Blister was nowhere to be seen either.

Shark swooped past, yelling orders. Most of the dragons seemed too panic-stricken to listen to him, but a few rallied around and followed him up into the sky. Surely they would be outnumbered, Tsunami thought. Surely they didn't stand a chance.

She took a step toward the edge and felt someone grab her tail.

"Don't do it," Clay said, pulling her back. "I know you want to fight, but we can't lose you like that."

Tsunami stopped. Every muscle in her body wanted to be up there, clawing at SkyWing snouts and smashing them out of the sky with her tail. *The impulsive thing to do,* she thought.

Or she could listen to her friends.

She turned to the guards, who were all three trembling with fear, their eyes fixed on the fiery canopy up above. "Go," she said. "Defending the palace is more important than guarding the prisoners."

"But —" one of them started. "But we can't let you —"

"You have to save yourselves," Tsunami said. "And so do we. Trust me, fate wants the dragonets of destiny to survive this."

The guards didn't stick around to argue. They launched themselves off the ledge, and Tsunami saw one fly down to join the crush of dragons around the tunnel, but the other two flew up to fight alongside Commander Shark.

She spun and ran back to the prison island where Webs and Riptide were trapped. Clay was already there, fumbling with the chain on the wall. Tsunami showed him which way to pull it.

"Can you hear me?" she called to the prisoners. "We're getting you out of there. Get ready to fly."

"Tsunami?" Riptide's voice was lost in the creaking and clanking and rumbling of things moving in the ceiling. Abruptly the water stopped flowing, and Tsunami found herself standing across from the sky-blue SeaWing.

He smiled at her.

"Hey there," she said. "The dragonets of destiny specialize in dramatic rescues, you know. Are you impressed?"

"Very," he said, hopping over the moat to land beside her. Webs staggered after him, landing unevenly on the stone. It didn't seem like a good sign that a thin line of blood was still trickling from his ear.

Another pair of fiery logs crashed past outside, and more screams echoed from below. Riptide flared his wings, looking startled and horrified.

"The palace is under attack," Tsunami explained. "It'll make escape tricky, but —"

"Wait," Riptide said, catching one of her talons. "Tsunami. I have to tell you something. I — I do work for the Talons of Peace."

Tsunami stared at him. Her mother was *right* about Riptide? He was working with the dragons who'd ruined her life. She'd always hated the Talons of Peace. How could she have fallen for one of them?

"Please listen. I joined them because I wanted to find out more about my father, but they wouldn't tell me anything except that he was safe." He looked down. "I've been working with them for a few years now, passing them information about the SeaWings."

Sounds like betrayal to me, Tsunami thought, although she wasn't sure whether she felt more betrayed for her tribe or for herself.

"You have a very bad habit," she said, "of not telling me some critically important things."

"I know. I'm sorry. I was meeting with one of their agents right before I met you." Tsunami remembered the dragon with the black spirals on his scales. "He told me to keep an eye out in case the dragonets of destiny showed up in the Kingdom of the Sea."

Tsunami pulled her talon out of his grasp. Riptide had acted surprised to hear the Talons even existed. He'd pretended not to know anything about the dragonets of destiny.

Clearly he was a good actor, hiding a secret like this while living in the tribe all these years. So could she believe anything he'd said to her?

Blood trickled from the gash on his side as he moved. "I stayed close to make sure you and the other dragonets were safe." He spread his wings and held out his talons to Tsunami. "I'm sorry I couldn't tell you the truth. I didn't think you'd trust me if you knew."

He was right about that. But she didn't particularly trust him *now* either.

An enormous crash sounded outside as something smashed into the pavilion.

"We have to go," said Glory from behind Tsunami. For once, she didn't add anything snide, and Tsunami wondered if she'd overheard Riptide's confession.

"Um," Clay's voice said behind them. "Tsunami? Webs? Do we know this dragon?"

They all turned and saw a large MudWing looming in the mouth of the cave. Her brown wings were creased with soot and a horrible scar pulled down one corner of her mouth into a strange grimace.

Webs flicked his tail in surprise. "I do," he said. "She's with the Talons of Peace. She saved my life. Crocodile! What are you doing here?"

The MudWing chuckled. "Poor Webs. So wrong in so many ways." She stepped into the cavern and gave the dragonets an appraising look. "These are the brats the Talons are so obsessed with? Scrawny." She lashed her tail. "But the SkyWings want you back anyway. For the next queen to play with, I assume."

"Queen Scarlet is dead?" Glory blurted. "For sure?"

"You're not working with the SkyWings!" Webs cried at the same time.

"Of course I am," Crocodile said. "Who knew that infiltrating the Talons of Peace would be so *useful*? I never thought I'd get the chance to follow an idiot SeaWing back to the secret palace we've been searching for all this time."

Webs blanched and his wings drooped heavily, as if a whole new mountain of guilt had just landed on him.

"Plus, bonus dragonets of destiny," Crocodile said. "I am so getting a promotion."

"Is Queen Scarlet really dead?" Glory asked again.

"Nobody knows," Crocodile said with a shrug. "She seems to have vanished. Nobody can even tell the same story about what happened to her."

"Well, lucky you," said Glory, "you're about to find out." She snapped her mouth open and shot her black venom straight into Crocodile's eyes.

The MudWing bellowed in agony and fell back, scraping her wings against the cave walls. She clawed at her snout, but the acid was already eating into her scales. With another shrieking roar, she shot out of the cave and dove for the lake below.

"Let's go!" Tsunami shouted, spreading her wings.

The five dragonets, Riptide, and Webs burst out of the cave. Below them, dragons were still trying to shove their way into the tunnel, and the churning mass of wings and scales around the exit didn't look any smaller than it had before.

"We can't go that way," Starflight said.

"We'll have to go out through the canopy," Tsunami said. They all looked up and saw three red dragons shoot by, breathing fire.

"I don't really love that plan either," Starflight said in a smaller voice.

Tsunami spotted her mother at last. Queen Coral was standing on the library level, casting one last look at her scrolls. They weren't on fire yet, but they were the most flammable things in the palace. If they went up, the smoke would fill the palace and kill even more dragons.

Her littlest dragonet was wrapped tightly to the queen's chest. Anemone stood on the edge of the pavilion, unharnessed, waiting.

As they watched, Queen Coral began flinging her scrolls over the edge into the water. After a moment, Anemone joined her, and the queen paused to touch her daughter's head affectionately.

She can be a good mother, Tsunami thought sadly. *And a good queen.* She wondered if there was any version of Pyrrhia where they could have grown up as a family, she and Coral and Gill and Anemone and Auklet, normal and happy, with no one trying to kill anyone.

Too late now. She had this other family, not at all normal, and they needed her more than anyone.

She soared up toward the tattered remains of the canopy. Another flaming log came barreling down toward them, and Tsunami yanked Glory out of its path. It plummeted toward the lake, careening off the pavilion and setting another dragon on fire as it fell.

"Sunny," Tsunami called. "Starflight. Stay below Clay's wings." Clay stretched his fireproof wings out, and the two dragonets ducked underneath on either side of him.

Tsunami surged ahead to scout the sky outside. She flew out past the smoking leaves and nearly collided with a SkyWing. He held a log in his claws and was about to breathe his fire onto it before dropping it into the palace. But Tsunami sent him swerving out of the way, and when she saw what he held, she slammed her tail into his side. The log flew out of his claws into the ocean, and he tumbled after it.

Five more SkyWings were flying around in formation to make another pass. Off to her left, Tsunami spotted a wing of huge MudWings carrying extra logs. The SkyWings zipped up to them, took a log apiece, and flew back to the palace to set them alight.

She hissed with anger. This was a brutal, carefully planned attack on a palace full of dragonets and innocent civilians. There was nothing fair or honorable about this fight.

Shark and his SeaWings were fighting another set of SkyWings in the sky to her right. Fire blazed and talons clashed against scales. She wanted to join them. She itched to be over there, slashing and clawing and battling the intruders who'd dared attack her family's palace. That was the kind of fighting she wouldn't feel guilty about afterward.

But the other dragonets were flying up beside her now, and she couldn't leave them.

"That way," she said, jerking her head at the biggest swathe of clear sky. From the sun she guessed it was south — south, toward the continent, which was where they needed to go.

Glory shot past her immediately, and as she reached the sky her scales turned pale blue and white and gold, and she shimmered into nothingness. Tsunami couldn't even see a ripple in the air as the RainWing flew away.

Clay went next, spreading his wings to shield Sunny and Starflight. A SkyWing in the battle spotted them and swerved in their direction. Tsunami lunged at her, grabbed her snout, and kicked her underbelly as hard as she could. The SkyWing kicked her back, sending bright arcs of pain along Tsunami's fractured ribs. Tsunami lost her grip, and the SkyWing roared a blast of flame at Clay's departing back.

He shuddered as the heat licked along his scales but beat his wings and flew on, the other two dragonets safely protected. The SkyWing blinked with astonishment as Clay's wings faded back to brown instead of turning black or twisting into painful burns.

"Surprise," Tsunami said, and punched her in the snout.

The SkyWing crumpled and fell toward the ocean, landing with a splash and vanishing instantly below the waves.

Riptide soared up out of the canopy, twisting around to make sure Webs was safe behind him. Tsunami turned to fly south and heard Riptide call her name.

"I have to help them," he called, lashing his tail toward the fighting SeaWings.

"But they'll put you back in prison," Tsunami protested. "They'll punish you because we escaped."

"Maybe," he said. "Probably. But I have to help if I can. This is my home."

She knew exactly how he felt.

"Tsunami . . ." He paused. "I really am sorry. I hope next time . . . well, I hope there is a next time. When things are better for everyone."

She hoped so, too. She wasn't sure she'd forgiven him, but she wanted the chance to decide. She wanted him to survive the war, and she wanted to meet him again in a world with no Talons of Peace or destinies or secrets to worry about.

But there wasn't time to say all that. Tsunami flashed one of the patterns he'd taught her. *All right*. Then she added *squid-brain*, and Riptide smiled before turning to fly away into the heart of the battle.

Webs and Tsunami swerved south together, wings beating side by side.

But other wingbeats were close behind them. Tsunami twisted just in time to see Blister lunge out of the canopy and seize Webs by the tail. She yanked him back toward her and stabbed her poisonous barb toward his heart.

With a yell, Tsunami barreled into them, knocking the SandWing off of Webs. Blister fell back toward the palace, hissing.

Tsunami grabbed Webs by his front talons and towed him after her.

A few wingbeats later, Webs groaned softly.

"Did she get you?" Tsunami demanded.

"She missed my heart," he said, "but —" He lifted his wing to show an oozing graze near his tail. "It's still poisonous," he said.

"We'll find a way to fix it," Tsunami said. "Just keep flying until we get to land."

She looked back again and saw Blister hovering in the air, watching them go. Her cold, glittering black eyes seemed to follow Tsunami all the way to the edge of the sky.

CHAPTER 28

Tsunami was on a beach again.

This time it was dark, long after sunset, and small stars shone in the sky like the silver scales on the underside of Starflight's wings. Tsunami stared down at the waves lapping over her talons.

She wondered if she'd ever see Riptide again. Or Anemone, or Auklet, or her mother.

"I know it's dark," Starflight said uncomfortably behind her, "but —"

Tsunami sighed. "But we should stay under the trees." She stood up and followed him into the woods, shaking the sand off her talons. "I'm *trying* to be more like you, you know," she said to him. "I'm trying to stop and think and use my head and all that smart stuff, but it drives me a little crazy sometimes."

Starflight stumbled on a tree root and turned to stare at her. "Be more like me?" he echoed. "Why would you want to do that? I wish I were anything like you! Especially brave."

Tsunami brushed his wings with hers. "You're all right the way you are," she said. "Someone has to be the thoughtful, careful one. And you made Blister pretty mad — that took some courage. Besides, I don't think this group could handle two of me." In the moonlight, she caught a half smile flitting across his face.

Webs lay on a patch of moss, breathing in a nasty shallow way. Sunny was curled up beside him so her scales could give him a little warmth. Clay was peering at the scratch near his tail, which was still oozing and starting to turn black around the edges.

"We need help," Clay said. "I have no idea how to fix this." His expression was woeful.

"Who would know how to cure someone of SandWing venom?" Sunny asked. "SandWings, I guess," she answered herself. "But I don't know where we'd find one we could trust."

"The Talons of Peace?" Starflight suggested doubtfully.

"I can't go back there," Webs said. "And you shouldn't either."

Tsunami tilted her head at him curiously. After all these years of being a good Talon foot soldier, obeying their every command, suddenly he'd changed his mind?

"If Crocodile was an infiltrator," he said, catching her look, "there could be others. I don't know who's safe for you and who's not."

"Seriously. Even the 'good' dragons all seem to have plans for us," Tsunami said, thinking of her mother.

"*Gosh*, I hope Blaze is better than the other two," Sunny said fervently.

Starflight winced, but didn't argue with her. "We can probably find her with the IceWings," he said, "but we'll have to be very, very careful this time."

"Yeah," Clay agreed. "I vote for not getting locked up *ever again*."

"Maybe we should try a different approach," Glory suggested. "Maybe this time we could *not* barge in yelling, 'We're the dragonets of destiny! We're awesome and special! We'd make terrific prisoners!' Just an idea."

"Do you know what we're supposed to do?" Sunny asked Webs hopefully. "Did the Talons have any plans about how we could fulfill the prophecy?"

"If they did," Webs said, "they didn't share them with me."

"Awesome," Glory muttered. Tsunami glanced at her. The RainWing's scales were shades of black and dark green, blending in with the dark forest around them. An idea struck her.

"I know who might help Webs with the poison," Tsunami said.

"Who?" Clay asked.

"The RainWings," she said. Glory twisted around to give her a sharp look. "Think about it," Tsunami went on. "They have venom, too, obviously. They must know something about what to do when you poison the wrong dragon."

"True," Starflight said. "Even if it's a different kind of venom . . . that's still a good point."

"And then we can look for Glory's family," Tsunami said. "Which I think is only fair."

Glory's face was expressionless, but small puffs of rose pink were blooming in her scales. Tsunami guessed that meant she was happy, since it wasn't a color they saw very often on her.

"Are you — are you sure?" Glory said. "That's what we should do next?"

"Absolutely," Sunny said. "We should definitely go find your home, Glory."

"I bet it's beautiful," Clay said in his sweet, earnest way. "And your family will be so happy to see you."

Webs let out a small groan, but when they turned to look at him, he closed his eyes as if he'd fallen asleep. Tsunami was sure he was pretending, but what they did next wasn't up to him anyway.

"It's also closer to here than most of the other tribes," Starflight pointed out. "We have to cross the outskirts of MudWing territory, but the rainforest should be basically due southwest of here."

"I know that," Glory said crossly. "You're not the only one who can memorize maps, Starflight."

"Perfect," Tsunami said. "That's what we'll do."

"After we rest?" Sunny asked hopefully.

Tsunami thought she could keep flying, all night if she had to. She wanted to put as much distance between them and Blister as possible. She wanted to shove all the other dragonets ahead of her all the way to the rainforest without stopping.

But she looked at Sunny's tired eyes and Starflight's drooping wings, and she settled herself close to Webs's tail. "After we rest," she agreed.

Sunny lay down again with a relieved sigh. A few moments later, Tsunami saw her back rising and falling in deep sleep.

Clay flopped down next to Tsunami, his tail draped over hers. "I'm sorry about your mother," he said. "And the palace. And Blister. And Whirlpool. And Riptide. And —"

"All right, I get it, thanks," Tsunami said, cutting him off with a nudge.

"I hope they all make it through the attack," he said quietly.

"Me too," she said. "But they'll be safe in the Deep Palace. At least they have somewhere else to go." She thought for a moment. "And I think Anemone will be a good queen one day. She has Coral's good qualities, but she thinks for herself, and she's still young. She'll get stronger and more independent as she gets older."

"If she's anything like you, 'independent' will be an understatement," Glory said. She tucked herself along Clay's other side and he put one wing over her. Starflight had tentatively nosed in beside Sunny, and now his eyes were closed as well.

"The Kingdom of the Sea wasn't the right place for me anyway," Tsunami said, partly to convince herself.

"What about your great royal destiny?" Glory teased. "What about how you'd be the greatest queen of all time?"

"Well," Tsunami said with a shrug, "I guess I'll have to settle for being the boss of you guys."

"Ha!" Glory said, but not in her usual sarcastic way. Amused yellow bubbles floated through her wings, and she reached over to nose Tsunami's shoulder. "You can certainly keep trying."

I will, Tsunami thought, *but not because I think I'm the greatest and everyone should listen to me. I'll keep trying to lead you because it's the only way I know to keep you all safe. And maybe sometimes I'll have to listen, the way Mother listens to her Council, and sometimes I won't be able to do exactly what I want.*

But even when she was mad at her friends, she knew she could trust them. And she had to be the kind of dragon they could trust as well.

She glanced up at the moons, two of them glowing pale and ghostly beyond the trees.

There were more important things than becoming queen.

Stopping the war was one of them. If the five of them were the only ones who could — then maybe that was what they had to do, whether Tsunami believed in destiny or not.

She wriggled closer to her friends. All of them were sleeping soundly now.

So the Kingdom of the Sea wasn't home after all, she thought. *I wonder if anywhere ever will be.*

EPILOGUE

"Well," Morrowseer said. "So that didn't go as planned."

"You neglected to mention a few things," said Blister calmly. "Such as the fact that your five dragonets are remarkably annoying." She draped her barbed tail pointedly over her talons and folded her wings back.

"Yes," said the NightWing. "True. But you might have tried to be a little less sinister at them." He stared down at the charred ruins of the Summer Palace. Fires were still smoldering on a few floors of the pavilion. Three days after the battle, nothing remained but smoke and corpses.

"At least Webs is dead," he said.

"Should be by now," she answered, flipping her tail up and down.

"Queen Coral survived?" he asked.

"And both her brats as well," said Blister. "It wouldn't be convenient for me if she died." She bared her teeth and hissed softly. "Of course, now she's hiding in her Deep Palace where I can't get to her. And she insists that my secret weapon will be no use to me for years still. She's gotten all squeamish about animus powers since finding out about her first daughter — like she'd rather waste that little one's magic just to keep her from turning homicidal." Blister sighed a small burst of flame. "It's not been my favorite week of the war."

She batted away a piece of smoking foliage. "So, NightWing, I hope for your sake that you bring me news I want to hear."

"There is another option," Morrowseer said, "but I'm not sure you'll like it much better." He spread his wings and beckoned to a green shape circling in the sky overhead.

The SeaWing landed carefully on the cliffside, vines crumbling to ashes below his claws. He glanced down at the palace and shuddered. Morrowseer noticed that he stayed well away from Blister. Perhaps he'd heard — or guessed — what had happened to Kestrel.

"This is Nautilus," Morrowseer explained. "One of the leaders of the Talons of Peace. Nautilus, explain your backup plan to the queen."

"Possible future queen," Nautilus corrected, then jumped back nervously as Blister raised her poisonous tail. "Er," he said quickly, "we have a . . . a set of *alternatives*."

Blister's black eyes glittered with interest. "Alternatives?" she said. "Really. My, my. I had no idea the Talons of Peace could be so devious."

Nautilus frowned. "We prefer to think of it as planning for every contingency," he said. "We have to do whatever's necessary so the prophecy will come true."

"Or true-ish," Morrowseer interjected.

"Of course," Blister said. "Dragonets can be so unpredictable. You are very wise."

"Well," Nautilus said, pleased, "it *was* my idea."

"Of course it was," she said. "Very clever. We are talking about false dragonets, yes?"

"But," rumbled Morrowseer.

"Yes," Nautilus said. His tail twitched. "But. They're, ah — not quite perfect."

"Hmmm," said Blister. "Worse than the originals? Is that possible?"

"Well . . . different. Or else they'd be plan A," Nautilus said. "Obviously."

"All I want to know is whether they'll do as they're told," Blister said.

"Um." Nautilus wrinkled his snout and stared at the sky. "Maaaaybe?"

"This does sound promising," Blister said drily. "I can't wait to meet them."

"Perhaps we can take the best options from each group," Morrowseer said. "Kill the RainWing, obviously. We can probably work with the original MudWing."

"Your NightWing is useless," Blister said. "Worst traitor I've ever seen."

Morrowseer shook his head. "That is very disappointing. We don't often kill off our dragonets, but . . ." He sighed. "If we must."

"Uh," said Nautilus, "you might want to meet our other option first. I mean, not to interfere. Just a suggestion."

"And we'll definitely kill the SeaWing," Blister snarled.

Nautilus flapped his wings, backing away in a hurry.

"Not you," she said impatiently. "Well, not right now."

"I thought Tsunami had some potential," Morrowseer muttered.

"Potential to annoy my tail off," Blister growled. "No, she definitely has to go."

"We have dragons working on it as we speak," Morrowseer promised. "Recruiting assassins is surprisingly easy in the middle of a war."

"Good." Blister flicked her tail menacingly. "Those dragonets need to know they're not as valuable as they think they are. Anyone can be replaced." She smiled with all her teeth. "After all . . . there's more than one way to fulfill a prophecy."

The adventure continues in

WINGS OF FIRE

BOOK THREE:
THE HIDDEN KINGDOM

"Glory," Tsunami scolded. "Bright-yellow scales are the one thing they *might* see. Go back to camouflage."

Glory glanced down and saw the starbursts of gold that had appeared all across her scales. Those meant happiness or excitement — as far as she knew, since she'd seen them pretty rarely in her life. It drove her crazy when her scales changed color without her telling them to. They did that way too often. She had to squash every big emotion before it splashed all over her.

She concentrated on the steady *drip-drip* of the swamp around them, staring down at the thick brown mud oozing through her claws. She imagined the fog winding around her wings, slipping into the cracks in her scales, and spreading like gray clouds rolling across the sky.

"Aaaand she's gone," Tsunami said.

"She's still there," Sunny piped up. She edged closer to Glory and bumped into one of her wings. "See? Right there." She stretched out a talon to touch Glory, but Glory moved out of reach. Sunny felt around in the air for a moment and then gave up.

The little SandWing had been unusually quiet for the last few days. Glory guessed Sunny hated the rain, too — the desert dragons were designed for searing heat, blazing sun, and endless clear-sky days. Even an odd-looking SandWing like Sunny still had the instincts of her tribe.

Really, Clay was the only one happy about the weather. Only a MudWing could appreciate the squishing and squashing under their claws as they traveled through the swamp.

Starflight swiveled his head suddenly. "I think I smell someone coming," he whispered. He shuddered from horns to claws.

"Don't panic," Tsunami whispered back. "Clay, you hide me and Sunny. Starflight, find a shadow and do your invisible petrified NightWing thing. Glory, you can shield Webs."

"No, thanks," Glory said immediately. She wasn't going anywhere near Webs, and certainly not to save his life. "I'll take Sunny." She didn't like touching other dragons, but Sunny was better than Webs.

"But —" Tsunami started, stamping her foot.

Glory ignored her. She lifted one wing and tugged the little gold dragon in close to her side. When she lowered her wing again, Sunny was hidden by Glory's gray-brown camouflage.

"Yikes," Clay said. "That was so weird. Like Sunny just got eaten by the fog." His stomach grumbled woefully at the word "eaten," and Clay shuffled his big feet in embarrassment.

Starflight peered at the spot where Sunny had just been, twisting his claws in the mud.

"She's fine," Glory said. "Go follow orders like a good dragonet, or Tsunami might fling you to the eels."

Tsunami frowned in her direction, but Starflight slunk away and found a dark tree hollow where his black scales melted into the shadows.

Now Glory could hear it, too: the *tramp-squelch-tramp-squelch* of enormous claws marching toward them through the swamp. The heat from Sunny's scales was uncomfortably warm against her side.

Webs hadn't moved while they talked. He lay curled against the tree roots, snout resting on his tail, looking miserable.

Clay shepherded Tsunami up next to Webs and spread his mud-colored wings to hide them both. It wasn't a perfect solution — a blue tail stuck out on one side, the edges of blue-green wings on the other. But in this fog, they looked mostly like a blobby mound of mud, which should be good enough.

Tramp. Squelch. Tramp. Squelch.

"I don't like this patrol," a deep voice grumbled. Glory nearly jumped. It sounded like it was coming from two trees away. "Too close to that creepy rainforest, if you ask me."

"It's not really haunted," said a second voice. "You know the only things that live there are birds and lazy RainWings."

Years of learning self-control kept Glory from flinching. She'd heard "lazy RainWings" thrown around often enough by the guardians under the mountain. But it felt like an extra stab in the eye to hear it from a total stranger.

"If that were true," said the first voice, "then Her Majesty would let us hunt in there. But she knows it's not safe. And you've heard the noises at night. Are you telling me it's the RainWings screaming like that?"

Screaming? Sunny turned her head a little, as if she were trying to hear better.

"Not to mention the dead bodies," the first voice muttered.

"That's not some kind of rainforest monster," said the second guard, but there was a tilt in her tone that sounded unsure. "That's the war. Some kind of guerrilla attacks to scare us."

"All the way down here? Why would the SeaWings or the IceWings come all this way to kill one or two MudWings here and there? There are bigger battles going on everywhere else."

"Let's go a bit faster," said the second voice uneasily. "They should really let us patrol in threes or fours instead of in pairs."

"Tell me about it." *Tramp squelch tramp squelch.* "So, what do you think about the SkyWing situation? Are you for Ruby, or do you think . . ."

Glory strained her ears, but their voices faded into the mist as the two MudWing soldiers sploshed away. If only she could follow them — she badly wanted to know what "the SkyWing situation" was. Maybe her friends wouldn't notice if she slipped away for a moment.

"Be right back," she whispered to Sunny, lifting her wing and stepping away.

Sunny caught her tail, wide-eyed. "Don't go!" she whispered. "It's not safe! You heard what they said."

"About rainforest monsters?" Glory rolled her eyes. "Can't say I'm terribly worried about that. I won't go far." She shook Sunny off and slipped after the soldiers, carefully stepping only on the dry patches so her claws wouldn't splash in the mud.

It was weirdly quiet in the swamp, especially with the fog muffling most sounds. She tried to follow the distant rumble of voices and what she thought might be the sound of marching MudWing talons. But after a few moments, even those became impossible to hear.

She stopped, listening. The trees dripped. Rain drizzled moodily through the branches. Small gurgles burbled out of the mud here and there, as if the swamp were hiccupping.

And then a scream tore through the air.

Glory's ruff flared in fear and pale green stripes zigzagged through her scales. She fought back her terror, focusing her colors back to gray and brown.

"Glory!" Sunny yelled, behind her somewhere.

Shut up, Glory thought furiously. *Don't draw attention. Don't let anything know we're here.*

The other dragonets must have had the same thought and stopped her, because she didn't call out again.

Unless it was one of them who screamed. But it couldn't have been. The scream had come from somewhere up ahead.

Glory checked her scales again to make sure she was well hidden, and then sped up, hurrying through the trees toward the scream.

The fog was so dense, she nearly missed the two dark lumps that looked like fallen logs. But her claws came down on something that was decidedly a dragon tail, and she leaped back.

Two brown dragons were sprawled in the mud, surrounded by pools of blood that were already being washed away by the rain. Their throats had been ripped out so viciously that their heads were nearly severed from their bodies.

Glory stared into the rolling gray fog, but nothing moved out there except the rain.

The MudWing soldiers were dead, and there was no sign of what had killed them.